ENCOUNTER WITH TERROR

In front of him stood the room he had come to see. Somewhere, in the back of his mind, he had constructed a mock-up of what it would be like: dark and ominous, crowded with secrets.

What he saw was a bare room, with a fire throwing agonized shadows against the walls —and Julie, faint with terror, her gray eyes fixed with horror, her lips white as death . . .

Leslie Ford mysteries

Leslie Ford
BURN FOREVER

WILDSIDE PRESS

1

Marie Davidge, elegantly groomed from the top of her snowy perfectly coiffed head to the tip of her silver sandal, completely assured of her position and her charm, put her glass down on the ivory lace cloth and smiled at the heavyset baldheaded man with the red ribbon diagonally across his white shirt front.

"My son? How charming of you to remember him. Well, he's quite mad . . . like most of his father's people."

She smiled at her husband opposite her across the gleaming candle-lit sea of silver and flowers.

"He finished Harvard, spent a couple of years moping wretchedly in his father's office, and then went quietly out of his mind. Packed up, went to the Northwest and did something about trees for three years. Now he's a forester down in the Tennessee Valley, and he loves it. Quite mad!"

She laughed a soft golden laugh that showed how little she meant it, and raised the glass to her lips.

"We exposed him to every temptation. We even sent him to Paris. I think I should have died of mortification if he hadn't been so incredibly in demand every time a débutante or her mother laid eyes on him."

The bald man smiled.

"But he writes to you?"

"Never. Apparently they didn't teach him to write at St. Paul's. We do get a telegram, once in a while, and sometimes we look up from the bridge table and there he is, just putting his bag down and knocking out his pipe in the goldfish bowl."

"You are not worried?"

"Worried? My dear Baron, we adore it. Imagine anyone simply walking out on all the cocktail parties and assorted follies of the world."

Mrs. Davidge's delicate face with its luminous dark eyes clouded. She glanced across the table again.

"I think it's what his father would have liked to do. But *his* father kept him at it. I used to see something in his eyes that looked like the wide open spaces when we were first married. I think he's glad Ben went out to find them."

2

The harvest moon was a smooth yellow apricot rolling up behind the wooded Tennessee ridge, throwing the long shadow of the Curriers' great cedar across the Hollow like a sharp black brush stroke across a silver screen. It drenched the log cabin, vine-covered under its sloping moss-grown roof and long swayback ridgepole, with white unearthly light, thrusting it deep into the shadows at the foot of the hill rising obliquely behind it.

The dirt courtyard before the cabin was empty. The low stable on one side, against the hill, and the corn crib on the other, at the edge of the river branch, lay deep in the shadows. Soft smoke fingers wove like frail ghosts out of the broken-lipped chimney at the end of the cabin, a chicken flew cackling from under the porch and scrambled across the yard. A dog moved lazily out of the recesses of the porch and stood for a moment on the top steps, his huge gaunt head raised, sniffing the night.

The girl hidden behind the corn crib pressed her slim body closer into the deep shadows and closed her eyes.

"Oh, God, I'm afear'd," she whispered. She clung to the rough boards with trembling icy hands. The crib was nearly empty, there were only a few bushels in the bottom where the wire netting to keep out the rats caught in her stocking and scratched her leg. She could see through the spaces between the boards, and she waited, her heart bursting in her throat, waited for the dog sniffing at the air. She saw him wag his long straight tail and come stiffly down the steps, stretch himself, dragging his lean belly on the ground, coming towards her.

"They'll see him here. Then they'll find me."

The girl's throat ached with an agony of stark living terror.

The dog crossed the shadowy black path of the great cedar tree on the hill, and thrust his wet muzzle into her hand. His bony tail thwacked against the corner of the crib.

She crouched down, her rough copper-toed shoes scraping on the dry ground.

"Here, boy!" she whispered. She drew the dog into the shadow, pressing his hard starved body close to her side. "Peace, boy! Peace, Kilgore."

She laid her head against his long ears. The dog flicked her cheek with his wet tongue and growled uneasily. She could feel his body stiffen in her arms. Her fingers tightened convulsively in his loose hide as she raised her head. Her lips moved, breathing a pitiful little prayer.

"Oh, God, please don't let 'em catch me. Let me get away. I can't marry him, God. Amen."

The dog licked her aching throat above the homespun collar. Julie Currier pressed her forehead against the cool wood of the crib and peered through the wide cracks out to where the black shadow of the cedar fell like a burden across the porch steps. Her mind went back over the grim months since fear had crept into the Hollow, eating through their lives like a brown worm in an ear of ripe corn.

At first it was only a rumor that the mail carrier had brought over the ridge, about the great dam, and the water sixty-five feet deep where the rain barrel with the big C burned in it stood under the eaves at the corner of the cabin. They hadn't believed it, not until the roads got passable again in the spring and government agents began coming back into the hills, making strange marks on the trees and talking with her grandfather down by the gate. It was then that they began to follow her with their eyes, the three of them—Nathan Currier her grandfather, Old Doss his brother, and Young Doss, Old Doss's son—until she felt the cold terror of a snared bird. She knew what it meant when her grandfather came up from the workshop alone and sat on the porch whittling a stick, his head bent on his rough homespun shirt. They were trying to make him let young Doss marry her.

They had been trying since she was fourteen and Doss was twenty-five. Other girls married at fourteen, and Doss could have any girl he wanted, even the school teacher across the ridge. Any but Julie. Her grandfather had always stood, a gnarled gaunt figure, stern and unbending, between her and Old Doss and her cousin—always except when she was to go to school after her mother died, and they had held out against it until he gave in. But Julie hadn't minded as long as she didn't have to marry Doss. And after that they had quit talking about it, until the government agents came. Even then they had never said anything to her, but she knew what they were thinking. They had to leave the Hollow, and Nathan Currier was growing old, and there was no one to take care of her, no one to protect her, except Doss.

For weeks she had watched her grandfather, despair growing in her heart. She did not dare to speak to him. He would have thought there was someone else. She had to wait, hoping against hope that he would turn away from them. Then had come the afternoon when the truck full of boys from the CCC camp had waved at her, and one of them had come

7

up to the cabin steps to talk to her. Julie's face burned suddenly, Old Doss's scathing accusing taunts still in her ears, saying things she could not understand except to know they were wicked and cruelly wrong. It was because of that that they were in there now. She had known it at supper, when her grandfather did not raise his eyes from his food and Doss sat there with his dark face flushed, while Old Doss followed her from the table to the stove with faded colorless eyes alive with suspicion.

Julie had watched them file out onto the porch, into the back room where they slept, her heart a cold heavy lump in her breast; finished her work, set the table for breakfast, covered it with the cloth made from bleached sugar sacks sewed together, taken the milk and butter down to the spring house. Then she had sat on the porch watching the night creep down into the Hollow, her hands cold, her throat aching with tears that would not come. And suddenly it had come to her like a living growing thing inside her, and she had sat up, eyes wide, her breath coming in quick painful little gusts. The thought of running away from the Hollow had never come into her mind before. She had crept back into the cabin and stood in the middle of the floor listening to the voices beyond the log partition, where Old Doss and Doss were talking, her grandfather's voice silent, and looked around the dark room where she had been born and raised, where her mother had died and where she had lived for eighteen years. She could see without light her maple spool bed that Old Doss had made for her, the table, the cradle in the corner, the hickory chairs, the candlesticks, the mahogany clock, the letter from the government propped against it on the mantel. Then she had crept out on the kitchen stoop and waited a moment, listening, and then down the steps into the yard. The sound of a chair scraping against the pine floor caught her ear, and she ran to the corn crib, cowering down behind it. If they found her she was lost. They were hard men. If she was running away it would prove what Old Doss said—she was bad.

Julie leaned her burning forehead against the rough boards and pressed the dog closer to her side, eyes straining into the black shadow of the cedar on the steps.

"They'll call Kilgore, then they'll find me," she thought.

She heard their heavy boots on the porch floor. Then they stopped. She caught her breath and waited, cold and tense. It hadn't occurred to her that her grandfather might look in the open door to see if she was in bed, this one night, just to tell her. Then she breathed again. He wouldn't . . . it didn't matter what she wanted, she was just a girl, to do as she was told.

8

She could see them dimly in the shadow of the cedar. Then her grandfather came slowly out into the white moonlight and stood looking up at the sky, tall and gaunt, his face raised in the night. Julie could see the ragged black hat, the checked wool shirt, homespun breeches and high rough boots without moving her terrified glance from the glittering eyes sunk deep beneath the shaggy brows, and the long sharp nose and thin stern lips over the snuff-stained iron-gray beard.

Nathan Currier moved down a step and stopped. Behind him Doss emerged from the dark, his father close behind him. None of them spoke. Doss's head was thrown back. His feet were wide apart, his shotgun resting lightly on his shoulder. Julie knew he had won at last, and bent her head, biting her lips to keep the blinding tears back. Then through the rustling corn up from the narrow bed under the cypress she seemed to hear her mother whispering softly in her aching heart, a faded voice dimly remembered. "Never let them know you're afear'd, baby lamb. Never let them know." Suddenly she found her heart was quiet, the ache in her throat had eased. "It's like being dead," she thought. "They can't hurt us when we're dead, Kilgore."

The dog moved. He had heard the low whistle before Julie. Her heart stopped beating again. As she unloosed her hold on the dog her cramped foot in its heavy boy's shoe dislodged a stone. It rolled down the bank and into the branch with a muffled splash. Her eyes widened with terror. Nathan Currier's hand went back into the shadows of the porch, and she saw the barrel of his shotgun glisten in the moonlight.

"Now they'll come," she whispered, fighting back the cry bursting in her throat. Kilgore moved out from behind the shadows, stretched on his belly, ears drooping, fawning. Then they were coming down the steps, and Julie waited for the sharp scrunch of hard boots in the dirt, iron fingers gripping her shoulder, accusing eyes boring into hers. They'd never believe she wasn't out meeting the boy from the CCC camp. She leaned against the boards, sick with hopelessness, listening for the sound of their steps. There was no sound.

She braced her foot against a clump of coarse grass on the edge of the bank and peered through the boards. Old Doss was on the bottom step, as thin and dry as a lone cornstalk left in a parched field. He was looking back, gun over his shoulder, at the cabin. None of them had spoken, they only stood, waiting, it seemed to Julie. Then fear greater than the fear for herself crept into her heart. Fear of the unknown. The fear that frontier women have when their men go out into the night, stern-faced and silent. The white face and black shiny hair of the CCC boy floated through her mind. She shuddered, looking through at them, standing motionless in the white light, like the wax image of Jess Kilgore that Mis' Mincey made for Old Doss to burn so Jess would waste away till he died.

Julie's tongue flicked her dry lips, watching. Maybe it wasn't the white-faced boy, or Jess Kilgore. Maybe it was the men who came late at night and drove down to the workshop with the truck and talked to Doss and his father. She had never seen them, they never spoke of them, but they came, once a week now, never oftener and sometimes not so often. She had never asked why, she was afraid to ask even her grandfather.

She waited silently. After a moment her grandfather moved towards the gate that led into the narrow backwoods road, Doss and the dog Kilgore following, Old Doss a step behind them. Julie closed her eyes, counting the dry scrunch of the hobnailed boots on the ground. She could tell without looking when her grandfather stopped, waiting for Doss to open the gate, and then to close it again and fasten the rusty chain to the cedar post. In a moment she could not hear them, but she waited, counting slowly one, two, three . . . until she had counted one hundred and ninety-nine, two hundred. That would take them down the road into the wagon tracks across the cornfield. She counted fifty more, then relaxed her tense body and stepped out into the yard.

She stood for a moment looking up at the long straight stem of the cedar tree outlined against the clear sky. The dark branches at the top were like the flame of a candle. Julie smiled suddenly. Beyond the tree, high tonight, shone her star. She raised her delicate face with its pointed chin and wide-set haunted eyes deeply fringed above the high pale cheek bones and whispered, "Star light, star bright, first star I see tonight." When she had repeated the lonely ritual she stood staring up, strangely unhappy, poignantly longing for something she could not name.

"You can't wish for something when you don't know what there is," she thought. "I wish I knew what there was to wish, out there where we've got to go when the water comes. I wish I wouldn't have to marry Doss. No—I wish the government wouldn't cover up the Hollow with water. Please, God, don't let them cover up the Hollow. For Gran I wish it, not for me. It'll put out the fire if they do."

She looked back at the cabin. The thin smoke rose out of the chimney like the smoke of incense from an altar. The fire on the Currier hearth had never been out; it had burned there night and day, winter and summer, lighting birth and

10

death, for over a hundred years. People came from miles in the summer to "borry" from it, new married people "borried" it too, to start their own hearth fires in their cabins in the hills . . . though some said it was bad luck, because Nate Currier's wife had run off and Doss Currier's wife had died in childbirth.

She stood a moment looking down the Hollow as the three men had done. A single faint beam of light shone from the door of Doss Currier's workshop, almost a quarter of a mile down the branch. She ran across the yard and started to climb over the gate. She was on the top rail when her quick ears caught the twang of a guitar coming plaintively out of the darkness. She clung to the rail and raised her head. Edrew Mincey was somewhere in the hills. She could close her eyes and see the staring china blue eyes and dark lank hair of the afflicted boy, the loose hanging lips, the buck teeth showing in his simple terrible grin as he hopped along the roads on his twisted foot, picking at the guitar hanging from his neck. She shrank back, remembering the steel grip of those moist skeleton fingers buried in her shoulder once when he had jumped at her from behind a tree in the road. She could still feel her heart pounding again in her throat as she tore silently, terrified beyond belief, down the steep deep-guttered road towards the cabin, and stopped to hide at the foot of the hill while she got her breath back, knowing she must never tell the two old men. Because . . . she couldn't say why. But she knew instinctively that she mustn't tell what Edrew had done. She knew in some way that they were always thinking about something else when she spoke of a boy at school, or even the mail carrier. She didn't know what it was, but she knew it wasn't anything that really touched her, except in their own dour minds.

She hung poised on the gate for an instant, listening, trying to bring her courage to the point to carry her away from the moonlit hollow across the hill where Edrew Mincey was wandering somewhere, picking out his sad melodies to the things that moved at night. Edrew could see in the dark, they said, and also he had some way not given to other folk of going quickly from place to place. Everyone had heard his guitar far in the distance and then suddenly a few yards away.

Julie held her breath to keep from drowning the soft whisper of the notes disappearing in the white night. She straightened up, slid down on the other side of the fence and ran up the gravel slope to the road, her head thrown back, listening for any strange sound coming out of the night. Most sounds she knew. A startled bird, a weasel or a rat slipping through the brush, the low cry of the pigmy owls, the wind rustling

11

through the ripening corn. She ran along the edge of the road trying to stay in the grass so her clumsy shoes would not grate on the dry dirt. About a hundred yards along the road that curved round the base of the hill, a lane cut off through Nathan Currier's cornfield to the farm road that ran down to his workshop on the branch, where she had seen the lantern hanging in the door. She knew they were waiting down there for someone, her grandfather and Doss and Old Doss, and maybe the other men, the ones she had never seen.

The moon was high over the Hollow. The road ahead of her curved and was lost in the deep shadow of the woods, beyond the spring. Julie looked back. The white smoke fingers, waving her an eerie farewell, drew her back longingly. She stood a moment, irresolute, her lips trembling. Then she stretched up on tiptoe, straining to make out the shadowy patch with the cypress tree and the white marble shaft to the Nathan Currier who had brought the fire over the mountain.

"Good-by, Ma," she whispered. "I'm goin' away, but God'll go with me, Ma, like you said."

She spoke softly to her mother, trying to make her understand. The tears rolled down her upturned face, welling out of the loneliness in her heart. She knew her mother and God were always there with her, but now they seemed very far away, and she was small and frightened and alone.

The dark figure of a man standing in the shadow of a redbud tree tangled with honeysuckle, not twenty feet from her, moved out into the road. Julie did not see him until she turned with a passionate little sob. He was standing there, the moon full on his face.

"Don't be afraid," he said quietly.

For a moment she stood rooted to the spot, all the muscles of her lithe young body turned to water. Then she had a quick instinctive knowledge that the man would not hurt her. She came slowly to where he stood, her lips parted, her breath coming quickly.

"What are you doin' here?" she whispered.

"What are you doing?" he asked. His voice was deep and kindly. She could not see much of his face except his jaw. It was clean-shaven and firm. The man was short and thick-set, and he was not one of the mountain folk.

"I'm going away . . . to Mis' Kilgore's." She stopped suddenly. She didn't know why she had said that. The Kilgores were the Curriers' enemies. Young Jess Kilgore had killed her father. It was the first thing she could remember. Her mother had dreamed of crossing a muddy stream, a dove flew low over the cabin, and three days later they brought him home. They tried Young Jess at the county seat and let him off. That week they found him dead and Old Doss was tried and let off. Then some said Old Jess Kilgore tried to kill Doss, others that Doss had tried to kill him. But nobody knew. That was why the only time Julie had ever heard her grandfather laugh was when the mastiff bitch dropped a litter half mastiff, half pointer, and Nathan Currier said they would call one of them Kilgore. So maybe the Kilgores wouldn't let her in, except that everyone knew Mis' Kilgore was a good woman.

The man looked at her silently. "You can't go that far tonight—alone," he said.

"I'm not afear'd."

He looked at her a long moment.

"Are you Julie Currier?"

She nodded. It didn't seem strange that he should know her name. No one else lived within five miles of Currier Hollow.

"I'll take you across the hill, if you're bent on going. Get in my car. It's along the road."

Julie drew a quick sharp breath.

"I've never ridden in a car." She looked up at him, her face grave and lovely in the white night.

"Sure you want to go?"

"I've got to go. There's nothing else I can do."

"Run along, then," he said quietly. "I'll take you to Mrs. Kilgore."

She started forward, and stood motionless, rigid with terror. Above her in the trees, out of the shroud of moon-pale leaves, came the sharp sound of thin fingers slashing a sudden warning across the strings of a guitar. Julie shrank back at the low urgent call, turned to fly back to the cabin, her heart pounding with terror, and halted again, staring hopelessly. Across the cornfield, down the path, her grandfather was striding towards her, gaunt and terrible, his gun in his hand.

She stared at the field blindly for a moment, then turned back to the man in the road. He must run, quickly, she thought; they'll kill him. But there was no one there. The man had gone as silently as he came.

She stood alone, waiting, in the middle of the road in the white moonlight. Nathan Currier strode up the narrow wheel tracks onto the road. His eyes glittered, they seemed to pierce the terrified girl with splinters of fire.

"Jezebel! Git back!"

The words ripped out of the old man's mouth, savage with pain and anger.

Julie's eyes clung to his in an agony of terror. "Don't never

13

let 'em know you're afear'd," she whispered. She wanted to run, but she couldn't. She couldn't leave her grandfather there with the man hiding in the trees. He'd kill him.

She swallowed desperately.

"I . . . I won't," she whispered through her dry lips.

Her grandfather seized her arm and walked on, dragging her up the road to the cabin.

3

Ben Davidge rested his elbows on the barrier of the observation plateau and gazed down on the vast construction of the Norris Dam below, smoking his pipe with the tranquil self-contained air of a man completely at home in the world. Not far from him a desk-pale young man in a perfectly laundered white linen suit, with an air of the classroom about his rimless spectacles and precise flat smile, was explaining the workings of the Tennessee Valley Authority to two women obviously important enough to be shown the works. All in all he made a good job of it. Ben listened idly to him reducing nitrate fertilizer, flood control and yardstick electric production to an understandable business.

"It's simply wonderful!" the woman in the green print dress said. "Don't you think so, Dora? Just imagine the government going to all this expense so these mountaineers can have electric washing machines. My dear, it's too marvelous."

The pallid young man looked a little uncertain.

"Er . . . yes," he said. "Of course it's vastly more than that, you know, Mrs. Armitage. It's really a tremendous program. The first really scientific attempt at social planning on a big scale."

"And brick houses instead of log cabins," said Dora. "You'll do away with the mountaineer life entirely, Mr. Havens?"

"Oh, well," Mr. Havens said hastily, "you understand we're preserving certain aspects of their native culture."

Ben Davidge shifted his pipe to the other side of his mouth and grinned sardonically. "You and who else?" he thought. A light shone for an instant in his frosty blue eyes. He wondered if Mr. Havens had ever spent a night in a cabin on a pine ridge. A sideways glance showed that he was much too well-washed ever to have done that. Perhaps if he had he wouldn't talk about the oldest and purest stock in the United States as if they were a Bantu tribe. It gave you a pain.

"They're appallingly ignorant in most ways, you know,

14

Mrs. Armitage. Superstitious, illiterate, practically uncivilized from our point of view. Asafetida bags round their necks to keep whooping cough away, and all that sort of thing."

The precise young man lighted a cigarette and tossed the match out over the barrier.

"But of course some of their activities are almost unique. And quite indigenous. Spinning and weaving, and cane work. We intend to encourage that sort of thing. Not that it has any commercial value. It's what we might call cultural or folk value."

The light shone again for a moment in the frosty blue eyes.

"But you'd be astonished at the squalor and poverty in these hills."

"I know," said Mrs. Armitage brightly. "I saw *Tobacco Road* in New York. It must be simply dreadful."

"I wonder if I could get a maple poster bed very cheap," Dora interrupted practically. "I suppose they'd rather have a shiny brass bed themselves. Or maybe we could get some quilts. I've seen them on exhibition in New York and they're terribly expensive there."

Ben looked around at her. She sounded exactly like half a dozen of his mother's friends in Philadelphia. Looked like them too. A long predatory upper lip, two extra chins held in place by a half-inch lavender velvet band anchored with a pearl crescent.

Mr. Havens smiled a flat patient smile. He would inquire of some of the field workers. "They might know somebody. Many of these mountain families have been pretty substantial in their day, before they wore out the land."

"But you can't really do anything to help them," Dora said. "I have a friend who sent some money to a family through a welfare worker and the woman went to town and bought a secondhand piano with it. What can you do?"

Mr. Havens's smile was a little flatter. "It's a great problem," he said tactfully. "You see, I don't think many of these people are exactly like the ones in *Tobacco Road.* They're quite independent, and inordinately proud. They cling to their land. That's what they understand as wealth. Some of them up here own over a thousand acres. They resent any interference in their habits and customs, very intensely. We've had plenty of trouble with that sort of thing in the pool area. That's the part the water will cover."

Mrs. Armitage shook her head.

"It's a funny thing," she said. "Wouldn't you think they'd be glad to have the government take their land off their hands? Most people I know would be glad to sell for any price. We've got a farm we've been trying to get rid of all

15

through the depression. I was telling my husband just the other day I certainly wished we could find somebody to take it off our hands. The taxes are simply terrible."

She leaned closer to the barrier and glanced curiously down at the construction below her. "But I must say I can't see how that little muddy river is ever going to store up . . . did you say three million acre feet of water? Do you, Dora?"

Dora looked down doubtfully.

"Oh, well, the river's low now," Mr. Havens said. There was a trace of apology in his voice. "And the pool absorbs the Powell River too. Of course it stores up over a long period of time. That's just the maximum capacity."

"Well, it certainly is marvelous."

Ben Davidge shifted his pipe again and ran the fingers of both lean strong hands through his shaggy sun-bleached thatch of brown hair. His clear blue gaze moved across the grinding din in the pit below him to where the Clinch River crawled along its shallow bed, a sluggish putty-colored ribbon disappearing a mile or so down into a tunnel of dry dun foliage. Waves of heat rose from the gravel-faced banks of the pit, scarred by the clutched iron fingers of the giant shovels. Dusty cars creeping across the temporary bridge, slowly like winter flies; men pigmy-small against the great concrete pipes lying beyond the quartermaster's long unpainted barracks. Trucks, dirt-colored, lumbering in and out like gigantic mud-caked beetles. Conveyors running the living rock to the crusher grinding out sand; machines mixing the cement, the peaked gigantic silo that stored it, six hundred tons of it, until they were ready to dump it into the great cofferdams. Ben's eyes wandered up the scarred slopes to the head tower of the cable system and the cars swinging along the black lines like tight rope walkers over a grotesque circus pit. Men and their skill pitted against the sluggish putty river. Men throttling a crawling stream to turn fertile valleys and wooded hills and sun-baked rain-guttered slopes into eight hundred square blue miles of inland sea.

He looked back down the gulch. He had taken a plane once over the pool area with a young engineer from Cornell. That was six months before, when he first came down as a forester attached to the CCC, helping to clear those eight hundred square miles of woods, watching them stuff up gullies so that the soil wouldn't wash down and fill up the dam when it was finished. It was spring then. In the plane he had listened to the engineer talk about cheap power and flood control. Stretched below them were the hills, young green, white with dogwood. They could see it up there like snow, on the hills above the Clinch River and the Powell River, running together like silver threads. The Tennessee lay coiling back and forth through its green valley cradled among the hills that flattened under their wings. Ben had a sharp quick sense of men like ants striving against the everlasting hills.

He shook his head. This was the most tremendous— and tragic—thing going on in the United States today. It *was* marvelous . . . and Mrs. Armitage would think a pêche Melba was marvelous. The dam wasn't anything you could dismiss like that. The people out in the hills being uprooted by the thousands weren't to be tossed aside with a few clichés about native industry and folk culture. It was more than that. It was the whole vast problem of progress against the individual. A tremendous project of brains and steel and concrete against aching hearts and simple souls. Ben thought of Mrs. Kilgore setting her fresh gingerbread and new sweet milk in front of him on her porch steps and stopping to look out over the green pasture with the little graveyard in the middle of it. "My granpappy used t' say, 'The dog barks, but the caravan moves on.' I reckon that's the way hit is with us'n an' the dam."

Mrs. Armitage turned away. "They say it's going to be the finest resort spot in the country when they get it all done," she said. "Now, who are those people? Would they be what the radio calls hillbillies?"

The pallid Mr. Havens looked around. Ben looked too. Two men had come onto the dusty plateau from the road and were leaning over the barrier looking down. One of them, in overalls and blue denim jacket, was tall, rangy, with iron-gray hair. He had shrewd small brown eyes, a prominent nose and heavy lines at the corners of his mouth. He looked over at Ben, pushed the dusty black-brimmed hat back from his forehead, spat deliberately to one side, nodded, and came over followed by the other man.

"Howdy," he said.

Ben nodded. "Hello, Mr. Loftus."

"Make you acquainted with Mr. Speer, Mr. Davidge. Mr. Speer's one of them there TVA appraisers, out from Washington. Kinda lookin' things over."

The two men shook hands.

"How are you," Ben said. "Saw you down by the Curriers' place day before yesterday."

A quick light flickered in the appraiser's fish-gray eyes for an instant. Mr. Speer was short, thick-set, square-jawed, clean-shaven, quiet.

"Do tell," said Ed Loftus. He tipped his black hat back on his head and spat into the dust. "Understood you to say you'd jes' got down thisaway yestiddy, Mr. Speer."

17

"I guess you must have seen me yesterday, Mr. Davidge," Speer said. The signal showed in his eyes again.

Loftus nodded. "Reckon one day's purty like the one before fer a young feller like Davidge. Mr. Speer's goin' to stay on at our place," he added. "I was tellin' him hit's only a little piece from there to most places he'll be wantin' to go to. Curriers', fer instance. Hit ain't more'n ten mile to Curriers', I reckon, is hit, Davidge?"

Ben grinned. "Not more than fifteen. You've got a nice central location, Mr. Loftus."

Loftus nodded soberly.

"That's what I was tellin' Mr. Speer. I was tellin' him we ain't very fancy, but we got good vittels and plenty of 'em, and a wide bed. I reckon that's about all a feller asks when he's out appraisin' land all day. Hit ain't everybody that's got that."

He rolled a small brown pellet of snuff on his tongue and spat it out.

"Reckon you'll be wantin' to have a look at Kilgore's place. They tell me none of you fellers been down there yet. Reckon you'd a heap better go there an' keep away from Curriers' Holler as long's you kin. I reckon Nate Currier ain't one to take kindly to people comin' messin' round his place."

He glanced at Ben. A shrewd twinkle lighted his faded eyes.

"How about hit, Mr. Davidge? They tell me him an' Old Doss run some of them CCC boys of yourn off with shotguns t'other day."

Ben nodded. "I heard they did."

Mr. Loftus grinned and took a pinch of snuff.

"Reckon he figgered they warn't up to no good. Reckon he don't aim to have none of 'em comin' courtin' that there gal of hisn."

Ben knocked his pipe out against the barrier.

"I've never seen her," he said. "They say up at the camp that they keep her locked up in the room where that fire is, the one that's never gone out. I forget how many years."

"Hit's a mighty good many. They're real old timey over at the Curriers'. I reckon they're still wearin' the clothes they wove on that there loom they got in the loft. They put hit up there 'cause Julie never learned to do nothin' much but cook and take care of the house. Nate never let her work in the fields. Don't know whether hit was 'cause he thought some feller'd take a shine to her an' cut Doss out, or whether he jes' naturally thought she was too good to use fer a plow horse."

He spat over the barrier.

18

"Course Julie ain't strong built like most gals up here. The spit of her ma, an' she warn't good fer much."

Loftus wiped his mouth with the back of his hand.

"Them Curriers has had a heap a' trouble with their women," he said. "First Nate's wife run off with a feller that peddled calico through thisaway in the spring. Old Doss's wife she died and left 'em with Young Doss. Then Nate's boy took up with a gal from Jacksboro—purty as a picture, smooth yaller hair and little feet. An' *she* run off, but they got her back. Then Julie was born. I reckon she was goin' on five when Jess Kilgore's boy got provoked an' shot Young Nate. After that Julie's ma jes' naturally couldn't stand livin' in the Holler with the old fellers, an' she took sick an' died."

He shook his head.

"They riz the young 'uns theirselves, not askin' nothin' from nobody. I reckon they was plenty a' women that would 'a been glad to have 'em, but the Curriers was always perticular."

He spat again and shook his head meditatively. "I reckon Old Doss's aimin' fer Doss to marry Julie. Nate he don't seem to care. Looks like he'd jes' as soon she'd die an old maid. He jes' nat'rally ain't aimin' to lose her, I reckon."

"Is that why they keep her locked up?" Speer asked quietly. "Frightened out of her wits?"

Loftus looked at him.

"Hit's worked fust rate—so fer," he said coolly. "Most gals as purty as Julie would 'a been married or off to town long afore this. Julie's eighteen. I reckon Nate knows what he's about. He ain't aimin' to lose Julie."

He glanced at the backs of the departing Mr. Havens and the two women.

"I don't reckon none a' the Curriers'd think twice about shootin' anybody they thought was foolin' round Julie," he said.

Speer nodded.

"It's O.K. by me," he said. "I'm a married man myself."

Loftus shook his head. "They already been three shootin's up thisaway th' last month. Reckon that's plenty fer a while."

Ben looked out at the tiny car swinging along the cable over the pit, wondering a little. Loftus was a typical product of the mountains, shrewd as a fox and as indirect, until you got on to the fact that he never wasted words. At home, like most of the mountaineers, he was apt to sit taciturn or silent, rocking on the porch, punctuating his sister's ceaseless rattle of talk with occasional nods or projections of tobacco juice, usually aimed at a duck waddling down to the stream. Away from home or with company he was genial and even talkative, but his talk always wrapped something up like a chrysalis in a cocoon, for you to unravel or not, as you chose. That was what he was doing now. He had never talked about the Curriers or the Kilgores before. Ben Davidge threw a curious sidelong glance at the two of them, wondering what Loftus was getting at. Was the cocoon being handed over to Speer to unwind? But why should Loftus think he had to warn a newcomer, a land appraiser just out from Washington, about the Currier girl? He grinned suddenly. Maybe the warning was meant for him. Which didn't make sense. He had never seen the girl. Moreover, he wasn't interested. He had seen plenty of the mountain girls. Red-handed, heavy-hoofed, muddy complexions, always giggling, always chasing after the CCC boys. The older people were different; he liked them. The girls were movie mad, all they wanted to do was get away from the land into the towns and hang around the corner drug stores. The little towns were full of them. He hardly blamed the Curriers for keeping their girl locked up. She was better off than running around the countryside half the night.

He realized that Speer was talking to him.

"Is your crowd working round the Kilgore place?" he was asking.

"We've cleared the brush out a couple of miles above the house. They're on the edge of the pool. The water hits their beehives. Kilgore won't settle till they do something about his graves. Otherwise he doesn't seem to care how soon he leaves."

A twinkle appeared in Ed Loftus's eyes.

"I reckon all he cares about is seein' that him an' Nate Currier don't get settled next door to each other again," he said. "Don't know what them two'll do if they ain't got the other to law with. Only trouble's you cain't get 'em in the same courthouse 'thout havin' 'em start shootin'."

"That so?" Speer asked. "What's the trouble?"

"Well, they say hit's mineral rights. Kilgore's granpappy bought the land from Currier's granpappy, an' they say the Curriers kep' the mineral rights on every foot a' land they ever sold. An' they sold a heap of hit. But nobody's ever noticed any Curriers shootin' the Kilgores till Jess Kilgore's ma took in Nate's wife the night she run off, an' kep' her there a week while they was huntin' her all over the country."

Speer gave a sudden amused chuckle. "Went to Mrs. Kilgore, did she?" he said. "Must have been a long time ago."

Loftus wiped his mouth on the back of his hand.

"Year I was born."

"You'd think they'd have forgot it by now."

Loftus shook his head.

"They ain't got enough to remember to ever forgit nothin'," he said.

Ben knocked his pipe out against the barrier. He had heard part of that story from Mrs. Kilgore the day after he had first seen Currier Hollow, how her mother-in-law had taken the girl in one bitter March night. It was hard to blame the girl after Mrs. Kilgore's account of what the cabin in Currier Hollow was like then. "You could 'a throwed a dawg through th' cracks."

"I have to be shoving off," he said. "See you tomorrow, Speer. Tell Miss Elly I won't be home for supper, will you, Loftus?"

Loftus nodded. "If you're goin' t' Knoxville, you kin bring Elly out somethin' to stop her tooth achin'," he said. "Mis' Mincey don't seem to be doin' hit no good, with all her palaver."

"Thought it was rheumatism Mis' Mincey cured."

Loftus shook his head. "She ain't even had so much luck with that, not since th' revenuers broke up her still."

He spat reflectively over the barrier.

"She used to say Edrew was queer turned, like he is, 'cause his pappy sold licker to th' preacher's wife, but I reckon he didn't make as much trouble doin' that as Mis' Mincey makes tellin' th' women what th' tea leaves says their husbands are doin' when they ain't home."

Ben grinned as he went along the barrier. He knew Mis' Mincey. Mis' Mincey read cards and tea leaves, sold charms and love philters and was the proprietress of a whitewashed two-room roadside shop. Inside it was one dingy showcase half full of stale discolored chocolate bars and warm soft drinks. Outside was a single rusty gas pump, always empty and always "aimin' t' be filled tomorrer." In the daytime Mis' Mincey sat placidly in front of her shop in a rocking chair, chewing snuff. Sometimes her afflicted son Edrew was there too, stretched out on a dilapidated bench, sleeping or picking softly at his guitar.

Ben looked back out over the grinding laboring turmoil below him, piling up its giant concrete wall that would bury Mis' Mincey's whitewashed shack, her patch of corn and her gas pump with the yellow honeysuckle growing over it, under sixty-five feet of water. He wondered what people like Mis' Mincey and Edrew would do . . . where could they go when the TVA turned them out? He thought suddenly of Edrew in the hills early in the morning, slipping in and out, seldom visible, following the details of workers from the CCC camps like a shy small bird among the branches. Or at night coming suddenly out of the darkness somewhere, like a lost child's soul wandering along the narrow roads, sometimes so close he could not be ten yards away, sometimes very far off, lost in the stars.

Ben Davidge's frosty blue eyes flickered. He wondered what Mrs. Armitage and Dora, and the serious pallid young man in white, would think of Edrew and Mis' Mincey, Jess Kilgore, Nate Currier and Old Doss, if they knew them as something alive and very human, instead of pawns in their giant chess game with the waters of the Tennessee.

"Most a' the young fellers has jobs in th' TVA," Loftus was saying. "You cain't get nobody t' plow a field fer you."

"What about this Doss Currier, the young one? Does he work on the dam?"

Loftus pushed his hat back off his moist forehead and scratched his thatch of curly gray hair.

"Th' Curriers air farmers," he said slowly. "I reckon Doss would think workin' in th' road warn't good enough fer him."

He spat in the dust between his two arms resting on the barrier.

"Th' Curriers air proud as Lucifer. They ain't good people t' start quarrelin' with. Most people give 'em all the room they want. They're likely t' shoot without askin' questions. People don't like questions, up thisaway—neither questions ner people that ask 'em."

He grinned amiably.

"I ain't sayin' that perticularly t' you, Mr. Speer. Jes' tellin' you what's a fact."

A dour twinkle flickered in the appraiser's eyes. He glanced after Ben.

"That goes for Davidge too?"

"That goes fer practically everybody in th' United States," Loftus chuckled. "Perticularly if they happened t' be revenuers."

4

Ben turned sharply off the paved road into the Loftus front yard and stopped his car under the apple tree at the end of the porch. It was after midnight. The yellow moon, riding high in the narrow ceiling of the valley, drenched the house, the corn crib, the vegetable garden sloping down to the low spring house under the weeping willow at the bend in the creek, with light as white and dense as hoar-frost.

He got out of the car. A chicken roosting on the fence flew down and scrambled across the porch, the white cat disengaged herself from the shadow of the geranium tub and came mewing to rub against his leg. He leaned down to stroke her with a sudden sense of the warmth of another living thing in the eerie white stillness of the night.

He glanced back at the two cars parked in the yard, Ed Loftus's old Buick sedan and a black Ford coupé. Speer's, he thought, seeing the Washington tags. He bent down again to stroke the cat and raised up quickly, his senses sharpened and alert, puzzled by a sound that was odd but familiar. It was the sound of a very hot radiator cooling after too long a strain. He glanced at his own car and shook his head. He hadn't been making over thirty on the winding mountain road. He looked at the house. The windows facing the road were blank dark oblongs glittering in the moonlight like shallow sightless eyes. He walked over to the drooping tree at the end of the picket fence, pulled off a large ripe pear, stood leaning for a moment against the black coupé and moved quickly away. It was much too hot.

He stood for a moment eating the pear. Two things seemed both obvious and queer. One: Mr. Speer could not have been in more than a very few minutes. Two: he had either been going very fast in high, or going in second for some time over rough roads. In either case, it was a queer thing for a TVA land appraiser to be doing . . . at midnight in a region where most people were in bed by eight o'clock. Ben shook his head, threw the pear core over the fence into Miss Elly Loftus's flower garden and went round the end of the house to the side porch.

It ran along under the roof of the log cabin that had been Loftus's home long before the clapboard front wing had been added and was still the only part of it ever used except for company and boarders. Ben sat down on the steps in the shadow of the overhanging roof and looked out over the cornfield, down at the silver halo of the mist undulating above the river, outlining its bending course like white smoke from a moving train.

A rocking chair on the porch creaked. Ben started and turned sharply around, then cursed himself for a jumpy fool. Loftus's black collie, Prince, seventeen years old, lumbered down out of the hickory chair and waddled over to him, wagging his tail. He stretched out comfortably on the floor. Ben rubbed his soft fat neck. "You scared me, boy," he said.

He pulled the dog closer to him and rubbed his ears. The idea of sleep was as remote as the moon. Something deep inside him seemed to have waked up and to have stirred in him some sharp instinctive sense of uneasiness. He took his pipe and pouch out of his pocket and stuffed the warm brown shreds into the caked bowl, wondering about it, trying to analyze it. He shook his head impatiently. None of it made sense.

The dog beside him stiffened and growled. Ben struck a match and lighted his pipe.

"Been out appraising?" He asked quietly, without turning his head. "You TVA fellows never let up, do you? And why don't you get 'em to give you the TVA white license plates like the rest of the boys?"

He looked around into the shadow of the porch. Speer was standing there, fully dressed. A long gray object was in his hand by his side. He took two quick silent steps across the porch and bent down.

"Listen," he said. "Take this."

He thrust a stiff manila envelope into Ben's hand.

"The first morning I don't show for breakfast, open it and use your head."

His voice was low and crisp. Before Ben could speak he had straightened up and disappeared noiselessly through the door at the other end of the porch.

Ben shifted his pipe to the other side of his mouth and looked at the envelope, turning it over in his hands. It was an ordinary long manila oblong, blank, the flap still damp.

"Made up your mind in a hurry, old fellow," he thought.

Loftus's conversation at the dam came back into his mind, the veiled warning, apparently so amiable and garrulous that a stranger would probably never have caught it. There was something queer about the whole business. Speer's giving him a high sign when he mentioned having seen him near Currier Hollow. Loftus's long-drawn-out account of the lives and sorrows of the Curriers and their women. The hot engine showing that the land appraiser had been out appraising land at midnight.

He shook his head and scowled down at the envelope in his hand. What business of his was it if the fellow didn't show at breakfast? What did he think was going to happen to him?

He drew at his pipe and blew a gray plume of smoke out, shrugged his shoulders and put the envelope in his pocket.

Prince's tail struck sharply on the floor. Ben looked around.

"You're settin' up mighty late, young feller."

Ed Loftus came out of the old part of the house, his dungarees pulled up over a flannel nightshirt. He sat down, pulled a round box of snuff out of his pocket and opened it.

"What's that other feller doin' up this time a' night?" he asked curiously. "He went t' bed same time as I did."

24

"Couldn't tell you," Ben said. "Maybe he can't sleep in the country. Lots of people can't at first. Maybe he had a nightmare."

Loftus nodded soberly. "Maybe he did an' maybe he didn't."

They sat in silence for a while.

"They say you all air aimin' t' cut down th' big cedar up yonder tomorry."

Ben nodded. There was no sound for a while except the rhythmic creaking of Loftus's rocking chair.

"I don't reckon Nate's aimin' to make no trouble fer you," Loftus said. He hunched his angular body forward and spat neatly through the rails. "When we was boys Old Doss Currier was th' best shot in th' country. They say he still don't think nothin' a' bringin' down a squirrel fur's he kin see hit, an' some say further'n that. An' there's them that hold young Doss he's a better shot'n his pappy."

5

Ben Davidge was still thinking about that left-handed warning when the CCC truck carrying the detail of ten boys from the camp lumbered down the narrow rain-guttered road into Currier Hollow the next morning.

"You pull up here a minute, Mike," he said. "I'll go in and speak a friendly word. Just to be on the safe side."

The driver, squint-eyed, hard-mouthed, broken-nosed, shrewdly amiable, grinned at him cheerfully. "You wearin' your bullet-proof weskit, Mr. Davidge?" he inquired. He put on the brakes and stopped at the incline running down to the cabin gate.

Ben lifted the rusty chain from the cedar post and pushed the wide rail gate open. As he shut it behind him he had a weird sense of closing out the present and entering into a different time, remote and isolated. The smoke house and corn crib on one side, the rude low stable on the other; an ancient ox cart, an old buggy with broken shafts propped against it, a rusty-geared grindstone, a blackened iron hog kettle, all lay jumbled together, dilapidated and primitive, in the sunbaked dirt courtyard. At the end of it lay the log cabin. Six clean pine steps led up to the cool vine-covered porch, and the two old Curriers were waiting there, silent, gaunt and hostile.

Beside them, a few steps apart, stood a young man. That would be Doss Currier, Old Doss's son, the one who was going to marry the girl. Ben shot him an oblique scrutinizing glance. He saw a hard proud mouth, black hair, cold gray eyes, a proud thin nose. Leaning against the vine-covered porch post, aloof and uninterested, Doss Currier had an air of somber power in every inch of his lithe strong body. You didn't see many like him in the hills, Ben thought, or anywhere else.

He came on towards the steps with a certain sardonic satisfaction that none of them had a gun in his hand. Mingled with it was a sharp sense of uneasiness. He didn't mind Doss Currier. It was the two old men that made the whole thing seem weird as hell. There was something savage, almost sinister, about them—the way their eyes, Nathan Currier's black and glittering, Old Doss's colorless and dead, were fixed on him with enmity and suspicion. He heard his boots striking the dry caked earth, and the idling truck motor out in the road, aware that except for them the Hollow was as silent as death and as grim. The atmosphere was taut and sharply ominous.

He was halfway across the yard when a loud and alarmed shout rose from the truck behind him. He turned sharply. Ten feet away and coming silently towards him was a huge gaunt dog, eyes bloodshot, jowls dripping, yellow fangs bared. Startled for a moment, Ben stood still, staring at it. The dog stopped, growling deep in his throat, as gaunt and hostile as the two old men on the porch, waiting for a signal from them. Out of the corner of his eye Ben could see the boys standing on the truck, frozen rigid, staring down.

The old Curriers were motionless on the porch. Doss leaned his head to one side and spat through the vines without moving a muscle of his body.

For an instant a wave of white fury blazed in Ben's brain, not at the dog but at the men on the porch, particularly the young one. He wondered for a split second what to do, and grinned at the dog.

"Hello, boy!" he said. "Nice boy!"

He turned and walked on. There was nothing else to do. His boots scrunched in the hard dirt. Out of the corner of his eye he could see the giant half-mastiff move with him, tense, ready to charge. He did not see the girl who came to the kitchen porch with a pail of water and stopped to look, wondering, down to the road at the truck full of staring boys. She looked back into the yard. Then she dropped the pail and ran down the steps to the corner of the cabin. Ben saw her, white-faced, eyes black with anger, poised there an instant; then with a lightning dash she was at the dog's side, her two hands buried deep in the loose skin at his throat, her face

26

flushed, breath coming quickly, eyes blazing with anger at the three men on the porch.

The dog snarled, jerked back, reared on his hind feet, growling. She struck him sharply across the nose. "Peace, Kilgore!" He cowered, still quivering, at her feet. She bent down. "Peace, boy," she said softly, her hand on his muzzle.

"Thanks very much," Ben said. "You're very brave."

She looked up quickly, a friendly smile in her eyes.

"No, I'm not. He just won't hurt me, that's all."

As her eyes met his the smile faded out of them.

"But you're not—"

She stopped as suddenly as she had spoken. "I thought you . . ." She smiled again. "It's all right. He shouldn't bite strangers."

Ben stared at her. She wasn't like any other girl he had seen in the backwoods. She was lovely, with long deep-fringed gray eyes and smooth shining hair, combed in two sleek gold wings into a knot on the nape of her neck. But it wasn't that as much as the way she spoke. She did not speak the mountain dialect, except that she spoke slowly, with a little of the slow rhythmic cadence of the hills.

He did not realize that he was staring at her until he saw the expression in her eyes change from frank naïve friendliness to shy perplexity. She stood up quickly.

Ben smiled. "Sorry!" he said.

The warning frightened flash in her eyes stopped him. She moved backwards a step, then turned and went quickly back the way she had come, without a glance at the men on the porch. When Ben turned to face them they had not moved or changed expression. He went up to the steps.

Inside the cabin Julie Currier lifted the stove lid and put two clean sticks of oak on the fire. She watched them catch and flare up, put the lid back in place and stood gazing down silently at the top of the stove.

She turned at a sound behind her. Old Doss was standing in the door, his colorless eyes boring into hers, his gaunt face dark with suspicion. Julie saw him as she had seen him all her life, his thin beard straggling about his chin like dry swamp moss, his hair hanging in graying wisps about his ears, wisps of it coming through the rents in his old felt hat. It had been sandy-red once, but she could only remember it as yellow-gray. He seldom spoke, and now he only stood a moment, haggard and gray in his faded homespun shirt and yellow pants flapping around his thin hairy legs, staring at her with pale questioning eyes, before he turned and went back on the porch.

Julie's head drooped a little. Why did Old Doss watch her

like that? Why did everyone look at her—even the man out there that they'd set the dog on—as if she were a ghost? She put her hands to her flushed hot face.

"I can't be as homely as that," she thought.

Her heart was a hot aching lump inside her.

"If I could only *see*, just once!" she cried to herself. But Old Doss had taken the little looking glass the lady from Nashville had given her and shattered it to bits with the ax.

Her hands were cold against her cheeks burning like fire. She stared out of the door across the kitchen stoop into the green hillside with dry listless eyes. They wouldn't let her out now, not even into the yard while the camp boys were working on the place, and when they went back over the ridge she could go out in the yard but not outside the gate. And Saturday night they'd bring preacher Tower and marry her to Doss. Her grandfather had told her so when he brought her back to the cabin. This was Tuesday. There were three more days.

Outside she could hear her grandfather's familiar singsong voice rising and falling. She didn't try to listen to what he was saying. The young man was just another agent from the government, talking about how fine it would be to have things they'd never heard of before, lights that went on when you pressed a button on the wall. Asking questions, prodding at them as if they were possums on a hickory limb. It didn't matter. Then her whole heart cried out that it *did* matter. They had no right to take the land. If they'd never come, then her grandfather would never have made her marry Doss.

She turned around abruptly, choking back the hot tears that stung her cheeks. Her grandfather's voice rose harshly.

"Yer aimin' t' cut down my tree today?"

Julie's body stiffened sharply. She stared at the open door onto the porch, her breath coming in sharp broken gusts. She crept to the foot of the maple bed and looked out through a chink where the mortar had fallen from between the logs.

The stranger was standing on the top step, the sun beating down on his head. Julie looked at him, trying desperately to tell herself that he couldn't mean what she was able to make out of his strange clipped speech, so sharp and fast compared to the slow easy talk of the Hollow.

"I'm afraid so, Mr. Currier. I hate to do it. It's my orders from the government."

Gover-ment, gover-ment. Julie's heart cried out in protest against the word. That was what they all said, when they talked about moving her mother's grave, when they talked about covering the Hollow with water. No, no, it couldn't be gover-ment. That was something far away, in a place

28

called Washington, and it was good. It wasn't something to hurt people who paid their taxes and sent their men to war. She had never really believed they would really let the water come. She would have to marry Doss, but still the water wouldn't come. One day they would wake up and find it was all a dream, their ridge would be covered with oak again, oak that the boys at the camp hadn't really cut. Something would happen, so many of them believed it would. The President would find out about it—Julie knew two people who had written to him, telling him, so that he must know.

She gripped the bed post more tightly. Even if they had to go her grandfather would not let them cut down their tree— not the Currier cedar. But why was he just standing there not saying a word?

On the porch Nathan Currier moved a little so that she was able to see his face. For a moment she stared, bewildered, at what she saw in it; and then the truth came to her slowly, creeping over her the way she had seen the crust of ice creep over the dark surface of the rain barrel at the corner of the cabin in the winter. Her grandfather couldn't help it. He had to let them cut down the tree, because they were stronger than he was.

She looked at the tall bronzed stranger, a sudden bitterness aching inside her. Her grandfather's slow voice rose and fell in monotonous cadence.

"They tell me that there tree's about seven hunderd year old," he said.

Ben Davidge nodded.

"It's all of that and more," he said.

"When my great-great-granpappy brung his fire over the mountains from Virginny after the Revolutionary War, he put hit down here, an' built this yere house so he could see that tree from this yere porch," Nate Currier said. It was hard for him to speak. He was not used to speaking so many words to a stranger.

Julie saw his eyes move out over the yard, across the rail fence over the bright corn, and climb slowly, as if they were too old and heavy for the task, up the hill to the great cedar, towering tall and strong against the cloudless sky. A tear glistened and furrowed down his gaunt cheek into his grizzled beard. Julie's eyes filled with sudden bursting tears of pity. "Oh, Gran, poor Gran!" she whispered. The years of fear and aching dread of the stern iron old man melted away. Hot rebellious anger at the government surged in in its place. In an instant she was out on the porch, standing straight and slim beside the gaunt gnarled old man, her gray eyes dilated black with anger.

29

"You shan't cut down our tree!" she cried passionately. "It's our tree! It's not your tree or gover-ment's, it's my grandfather's, and you can't cut it down!"

Ben moved down a step. It brought his head even with the proud little head thrown back, defending her home against the government.

"I'm sorry," he said gently. "I've got to do it. It's a government order. I wish I didn't have to."

She flashed back to her grandfather.

"It isn't true, is it, Gran? He can't do it, can he?"

The defiance in her face turned up to her grandfather's faded slowly. The haunting terror of the fear that brooded over the valley crept into her eyes.

"Are they making us go too, Gran?" she whispered.

A slow tear coursed down the grimy furrows of the old man's grizzled cheek. He jerked his arm up and encircled the girl's slim shoulders, quivering under the rough homespun of her old-fashioned dress. A gnarled hand unfamiliar with caresses trembled over her smooth gold hair, stern lips mumbled, seeking long-forgotten words.

Ben looked away for an instant. "I understand that all the people who settled for their land before October first have until January to leave," he said after a moment. "Otherwise it's thirty days. You knew that, didn't you, Mr. Currier?"

"I knew hit," Currier said quietly. "I never told the girl."

Julie shrank away from him. She was white to the lips, staring urgently at his face.

"Gran . . . have you sold our land?"

For a moment there was no sound in the tragedy of exile. The old man nodded slowly.

"But, Gran, you—you said you'd never sell, you'd never let them take our land."

"Hit's gover-ment, Julie. Men ain't go no rights when gover-ment wants their land."

She stood silent for a moment. Her gray tear-washed eyes moved from her grandfather to the steps and out over the courtyard to the stable and the corn crib as if she were seeing them for the first time. She looked up at the cedar, a little smile in her eyes. "It's a pretty tree, isn't it, Gran?" she said softly.

6

Mike Shannon maneuvered the truck off the guttered backwoods road and into the wagon tracks across the Curriers' bottom field.

"Looks like somebody been across here since yesterday," he said.

"TVA men probably. They're coming up to get a round of this cedar for the museum."

Mike shook his head. "Looks like a truck tire to me, Mr. Davidge. Hello, there's that halfwit."

He nodded down the branch and listened to catch the sound of Edrew Mincey's guitar somewhere at the edge of the Hollow.

"Wish he'd play somethin' cheerful once in a while."

Ben nodded absently. He was thinking of something different.

"Beats me how that guy gets around. He was layin' on the bench in front of the store when we came by, dead to the world, and that's damn near twelve miles off. And there he is now."

Ben looked back down the road. Edrew was leaning against the shed built over the branch, picking at his guitar. The drone of his voice weaving out words of old songs reached them across the yellow field.

"Say, what is that place down there, Mr. Davidge? Ain't a still, is it?"

"That's a workshop, Mike. Doss Currier has a lathe. He's the old man's brother. Makes wagon wheels and things like spool beds. Loftus says they used to have a good business thirty years ago."

Mike nodded. "I know. That's where they run the TVA guy off when he was lookin' for 'examples of native industry.' "

He chuckled.

"Jeez, does that burn these guys up. You oughta hear 'em when they get a jolt of white mule in 'em. That an' movin' the graves. I say what the hell, they're dead, ain't they? But these guys look at it different."

He swung the truck off the road and threw it into low to make the steep grade up the cleared path towards the tree.

Two cars were parked in the Currier road. One had the TVA white license plate, the other was a Ford coupé. Mike leaned out.

"Jeez, there's a Washington tag. Don't suppose Mrs. Roosevelt's dropped in to watch us cut it down, do you?"

"That's a fellow named Speer. Land appraiser."

"Yeah? Somebody said they'd already given the old Currier guy twenty grand for his land."

Ben looked quickly at him. "Where'd you hear that?"

"Hell, I don't know. Funny thing the way news gets out around these hills."

"Who told you, Mike?"

Shannon scratched his head. "Let's see. It was in a crap game the other night. I know, it was this berry Sisky. He'd been down to Mis' Mincey's to get his fortune told. That's where he got it."

The truck was climbing slowly.

"Say, I wanted to tell you something, Mr. Davidge. You ever notice that guy?"

"Sisky?"

"Yeah. Notice the kids don't like him? Notice he's always bellyachin' about the grub an' gettin' out of the work?"

Ben nodded. He had noticed it. He had also noticed the East Side accent, the fat city-pale face, thick moist lips, patent-leather marceled hair, and particularly the cocky self-assertiveness of the guy.

"You ever notice he's always got money?"

"The folks get the allotment from Washington and send it back to him, I suppose."

Mike shook his head.

"I happen to know Sisky's folks don't send it back. Fellow named Kurtz lives in the same block, and Sisky's old man ain't had a job in a year. Anyway, it looks queer to me. This O.K.?"

"This'll do."

A group of men were already standing by the big tree. Ben shook hands with Anderson, one of the head foresters, and nodded to the others. Two were men he knew from the TVA. The other was Speer. He was standing by the tree, silent and self-contained, looking down into the Hollow. Ben turned around. The sunlit cabin lay nestled in the little valley, its long ridgepole swaybacked against the hills. The stable and corn crib, the smoke house and beehives clustered around it like pieces around the manger under a tree at Christmas. Smoke circled up out of the broken-lipped chimneys at either end of the low lichen-stained roof. One of the TVA men pointed to the farther chimney where faint wisps scarcely seen vanished in the air.

"That's the fire that hasn't been out for a hundred and forty years," he said to Speer. "There's another place further up where they say their fire hasn't been out for a hundred and sixty. The old fellow won't move till we find a way for him to take his fire with him."

He shook his head, smiling. "You'd think they'd be glad to get out of these God-forsaken hills. It's funny. A fellow that runs a store down the bend blew his brains out night before last, with a check for $500 on the table right in front of him."

Speer nodded. "I guess he didn't want to leave."

"Crazy, of course. No wonder, living out by themselves in the woods. Look at this young Currier. You'd think he'd have got out by the time he was eighteen. Most of the young ones do."

Speer said nothing. Ben went up to the tree. The blaze for the undercut was on the great shaggy trunk facing the Hollow. He looked down there again. The two old men were standing motionless, like toy figures, on the porch. Doss Currier was still leaning, apparently not having moved a muscle, against the vine-covered post. The slim gray figure of the girl was nowhere to be seen. "Doesn't want to see it," Ben thought. He was glad Anderson was there, glad he did not have to cut her tree down. He looked up at the straight brown column towering green-tipped into the blue sky.

One of the CCC boys was standing beside him looking up, his eyes wide.

"Jeez, that's a big one. I guess he's been here one long time."

Ben shook his head involuntarily. This tree had been here a long time when Columbus landed. It was a giant tree when Chaucer died. When it was a sapling thirty feet high ironclad men were pouring into the Holy Land. Richard the Lion-Hearted was alive, no stone had been laid on those age-old buildings he had seen in France and England, Dante was not yet born. For eight hundred years perhaps it had stood here above the Hollow, and ten boys were cutting it down before lunch. It was a kind of murder.

He looked down at the cabin again. A lithe gray figure tipped with gold flashed across the yard. Ben stared down at it.

The sound of the guitar came suddenly from above them on the hill.

"Well, for God's sake," Mike said. "Here's that damn doleful halfwit up here."

The melody rose and fell to the rhythmic whirr of bright teeth biting into the live red wood, singing a plaintive accompaniment as the saw bit deeper and deeper into the great tree. The sun climbed high in the Hollow between the ridges, the smell of the red dust rose like the smell of church incense.

Ben saw Speer again, standing off a little, by himself, still looking down at the cabin. He went over, wondering if Speer had come back or had been there all the time.

"Hello," he said. "Well, you showed, this morning."

Speer's eyes flickered an instant and were dead gray again. He nodded coolly and glanced around.

"That kid down there's having a bad time," he said quietly.

"Look out for her if you get a chance. There's something up. If anything breaks you've got the story."

He nodded again and moved away. Ben looked after him for a moment. When he looked back at the Hollow a quick movement in the thicket below caught his eye. A slim streak of gray wove quickly in and out in the underbrush. He looked hastily up at the tree, already swaying, and down the hill where it would fall. Julie Currier was already far out of its path. He saw her slip behind a clump of young dogwood and stand, her foot braced against the trunk of a hickory sapling, the pale oval of her face raised to the sky, watching the shivering mast with great unhappy eyes.

He looked back at the men around the tree. None of them had seen the girl. Something almost instinctive made him turn his head and look behind him. Sisky was sitting, head bent forward, watching her out of the corner of his eye, a little smile in the corner of his full red mouth. Ben felt a little wave of cold anger. He looked around for Speer, but Speer had disappeared.

"That's enough," the head forester said sharply. The two boys disengaged the saw and stood back. Ben could feel the shiver that ran up and down the great stem. It trembled a moment, crackling. There was a stentorian shout: "TIM-BER!!" Far above their heads the green plume bent forward a little, paused, leaned out again and paused, as if gathering strength or courage, before it swept down in a gigantic arc and hurtled to the ground in a crashing of great branches. For an instant no one moved; then a great shout went up. Ben had not seen the tree fall. He was looking across at the dogwood thicket. He had seen Julie Currier's face just before she buried it in her raised arms. She was clinging to the tree trunk, only her fingers moving, opening and closing convulsively against the smooth bark.

7

A few straggling groups of khaki-clad boys were wandering aimlessly along the road in the cool dusk, killing time until midnight when they had to be back in barracks at the CCC camp on the hill. Ben nodded to them and strolled along almost as aimlessly. There was nothing to do unless he went up to the camp for bridge at the officers' quarters. He didn't particularly feel like it. He did want to get away from Miss Elly Loftus's ceaseless ribald chatter. It was shrewd and racy, but it got tiresome. Tonight she was rattling on about the Curriers, and Ben had heard enough about the Curriers to last him the year. What interest was it of his whether Julie Currier married Doss or whether she didn't? Or whether she was "carryin' on," as Miss Elly put it, with another fellow.

He wondered idly about it. It was hard to think of Sisky as a successful rival of Doss Currier, but obviously there was somebody else about, or he would have had to put on an exhibition match with the dog, with Queensberry rules off, that morning in the yard. She evidently thought he was the other fellow, hadn't seemed surprised that the old men put the dog on him.

However, it was none of his business, and he would probably not have thought of it again if it hadn't been for the Loftus's conversation during supper. He picked up a handful of gravel from the pile at the edge of the road and stood leaning against the white culvert, dropping the pebbles one by one into the clear shallow stream below. He was thinking of Miss Elly's malicious and slightly obscene grin when she said, "If hit warn't fer her ol' fool granpappy, Old Doss'd take Julie Currier down off'n her high horse mighty quick. He'd whip th' stockin's off'n her. They ain't many'd put up with a scrawny no-account piece like her. Doss'd beat the life out a' her."

"I reckon he'd do worse'n that if anythin' was t' happen t' Nate." Ed Loftus stopped rocking long enough to lean forward and spit under the porch rail. He shook his head a little.

Ben shook his head, thinking of it. It was probably just a manner of speaking and they meant nothing by it. Nevertheless it stuck in his mind. If it hadn't been for the business of the dog and the three Curriers standing calmly on the porch, perhaps he wouldn't have thought that Old Doss Currier's dead hooded eyes were so malignantly hostile. Perhaps it was like the pictures of men wanted by the F.B.I. that he had looked at, tacked up in the Bradleyville Post Office the morning before. They looked so definitely and obviously criminal. Then he thought of his own passport pictures, which certainly made him look like a mobster of the worst sort. Perhaps it was like that with Old Doss. Perhaps setting the dog on him was just a bit of quiet mountain humor. Ben grinned sardonically.

He strolled on up the road. On the whole he felt sorry for Julie Currier, or anybody else who had to live with those two savage old scarecrows. On the subject of Doss Currier he reserved judgment. A savage too, with something cool, ominous and deadly about him, but still more human, some way, than Old Doss. A queer feeling came suddenly to him that in spite of the fact that one of his first duties to the government was to avoid friction with the mountaineers, he and Doss had not seen the last of each other.

He wondered where Julie Currier had learned to speak. That was probably why Miss Elly thought she was on her high horse. And what did Speer have on his mind when he had told him, this morning by the big tree, to look out for her if he got the chance? He grinned, shrugged his shoulders and lighted his cold pipe, a little annoyed at the irritating sense of foreboding that had begun to nag at one corner of his brain.

A shrill voice from the side of the road interrupted him.

"Howdy, mister!"

He looked up, surprised to find himself in front of Mis' Mincey's whitewashed vine-covered shack.

Mis' Mincey was rocking back and forth, her bony claws folded in her lap, peering at him out of watery blue eyes, like Edrew's except that a crafty low-grade mind looked out from behind them, cunningly shrewd and watchful.

"How're you, Mis' Mincey?"

"Tol'able. Hunt yerself a seat."

Mis' Mincey's thin beaked nose and her chin were like ice tongs trying to meet and not quite making it. Two trickles of brown juice ran down the corners of her toothless mouth and dried in little deltas on her chin. A few wisps of dyed hair, mossy brown, hung down her hollow cheeks and escaped from under her black head kerchief like fetlocks around the back of her neck.

Mis' Mincey spat with great precision at the base of the gas pump, set like a lighthouse on an island of flat whitewashed rocks from the branch, and wiped her mouth with the back of a scrawny freckled hand.

"Some several of th' ladies from Norris come down yestiddy fer me t' read th' tea leaves fer 'em."

"I guess you gave them all rich husbands. Throw in a dark woman to devil 'em?"

Mis' Mincey caught her face in her hands and collapsed, rocking back and forth, in a grotesque spasm of giggles. She peered out at him through her fingers.

"Be hit a dark 'oman devilin' ye, Mister Davidge? Be she this yere color?"

With incredible dexterity the gnarled old hands dived into her voluminous rusty black serge skirt and whisked out a pack of unbelievably filthy cards. Her pale eyes fastened avidly on Ben's, she flicked off the queen of hearts and placed it face up on the three-legged stool in front of her. She grinned up at him. Her hands moved again. The jack of hearts turned up beside it.

"That there's her," Mis' Mincey announced shrilly.

The jack of spades turned up.

"There's the dark feller that's devilin' ye, mister. An' he's devilin' her too."

The hands moved again like lightning. Four successive black cards appeared: the king of spades, the jack of clubs.

"There's another of 'em that's devilin' her too."

She turned over the king of diamonds. "An' he's devilin' her. They be all devilin' her, poor mite."

Mis' Mincey's face clouded, she huddled down over her stool and shook her head, mumbling, wiping her mouth with her grimy hand. Her game seemed to end suddenly.

She stared down at the ground.

"Trouble. Trouble," she muttered. "Fer ye, but more fer her, mister. There ain't nothin' but trouble fer her, mister."

There was a curious convincing tone in Mis' Mincey's voice. Ben gripped his cold pipe between his teeth, interested in spite of himself. The old eyes shot him a crafty glance. She hesitated a moment and threw off the top card. It was a red jack. Mis' Mincey gave a quick jerky nod of satisfaction, mumbled to herself and spat at the pump without looking up. She dealt the rest of the cards and squatted forward in her chair, fingering them lovingly. Then she squinted up at Ben.

"Money," she said. It was almost a whisper. "Hit's all round a light 'oman. Hit's a right good-sized pile a' money. But they's a heap a' trouble round her too, a whole heap of hit. Money ain't no use if they's nothin' but trouble an' heartbreak. Is hit, mister?"

She pointed to the red king, and shook her head slowly, a long time.

Ben sat down on Edrew's bench and filled his pipe. Mis' Mincey watched him silently. He pointed to the red queen entirely surrounded by black face cards.

"The Currier girl?" he asked quietly.

Mis' Mincey spat at the pump and creaked back and forth in her rocking chair in the fading mountain light.

"I ain't got no way a' namin' names," she said after a while. "Hit's jes' in th' cards. Julie Currier's got purty yaller hair."

They sat there silently. When it was too dark to see the cards any longer Mis' Mincey gathered them together slowly and put them back in the mousy folds of her black skirt. Ben got up and stood for a moment leaning against a whitewashed upright, his head bent forward to keep from scraping against the roof. Was this again some of the almost childish deviousness of the mountain folk? Was Mis' Mincey trying to tell him something, as Loftus apparently had done? It was the first time she had ever acted this way, and he had known her for six months. One thing was sure. She meant something, and she meant it in earnest. But there was no use asking her to explain it. She would not tell him any more.

Ben nodded and walked back towards the Loftus place. Mis' Mincey sat there creaking back and forth in the dusk . . . biting her grimy finger nails in a sudden fit of terror at what she had tried to do.

8

Ben did not hear the people talking on the back porch until it was too late to go back. He groaned inwardly. The Curriers seemed to be pursuing him relentlessly in one way or another. This was Jess Kilgore, their greatest enemy. He was talking with Loftus and his sister on the porch.

"Howdy, Mr. Davidge."

"Hunt yerself a seat," Miss Elly said. "Law me, hit's gettin' so's we don't see hair ner hide a' Mister Davidge, the way he's taken t' runnin' off. Ye'd think he was a-courtin' Mis' Mincey."

Miss Elly laughed until she choked on her pellet of snuff and finally had to go inside.

Neither of the men smiled. Neither did they seem concerned about Miss Elly.

"They tell me yer aimin' t' clear my place over th' ridge next week, Mr. Davidge," Jess Kilgore drawled out. His round pleasant face, open and heavily-lined, and his thick white hair shone in the path of the moon coming up down the valley.

"I think we'll get up there Tuesday," Ben said.

There was a silence.

"Hear'd anythin' 'bout movin' th' cemetery?" Kilgore asked.

Ben shook his head.

"They tell me they's some talk 'bout lettin' you move jes' the ones that belong to you," Kilgore said slowly. "I reckon we wouldn't like t' leave any a' the folks there. Don't look as hit would be right. We'd hate t' leave Aggy Currier there. Not after she come to us to die like she did."

Loftus nodded.

"I reckon Nate Currier's never goin' t' forgive you fer takin' her in a second time," he said.

38

"Nate Currier's a ———— ———— ————," Jess Kilgore said peaceably. "So's Old Doss, an' so's Young Doss. Where they aimin' t' go?"

Loftus shook his head. "They was some talk a' gettin' Julie married off, so's they wouldn't have t' worry 'bout anythin' happenin' to them."

Kilgore nodded. "They're purty well along."

"Nate was born in 18 and 58. Doss ain't so old. They's some years difference."

"I reckon if anythin' happened to 'em, Julie and Doss'd be alone."

Loftus nodded soberly. "I reckon nothin' ain't aimin' t' happen to 'em."

He spat out into the yard. "I reckon you see right many a' th' boys from th' camp down your way?"

Kilgore's face showed no surprise at the sudden change of subject.

"Th' old woman don't do nothin' but make cake an' pies fer 'em. Most of 'em don't act like they'd ever had a bite t' eat."

He chuckled quietly.

"Th' old woman was hoppin' round like a chicken on a hot griddle t'other day. Found out one feller, that feller name of Sisky, was buyin' her pies fer a dime an' sellin' 'em up to th' camp fer half a dollar."

Both men laughed.

"Saw him headed over there this evenin'," Loftus said. "Wouldn't surprise me none if th' old woman snatched him baldheaded."

The two settled into a judicial and deliberate discussion of state politics. Ben looked at his watch.

"I think I'll run up to the camp for a while," he said. "Good-by, Mr. Kilgore."

Kilgore nodded. "Ain't seen much a' you lately. Th' old woman was sayin' somethin' 'bout hit yestiddy."

"We'll be over your way next week. Good night."

Neither of them spoke until Ben had backed his car into the road and was gone.

"You ain't hear'd if Julie's made up her mind t' marry Doss, I don't reckon?" Jess Kilgore inquired indifferently.

Loftus spat over the rail and shook his head.

"I'd mighty hate t' see Aggy's granddaughter to marry Doss's boy," Kilgore said slowly. "Seems like Julie allus favored Aggy, an' her own ma—like she didn't have no rotten Currier blood in her. I'd mighty hate t' see her marry Doss. Doss's the spit of his pappy."

39

9

Just why Ben thought he had to go to Currier Hollow that night he could not have told. It would be dark before he got there. The chances were ten to one that if the Curriers saw him they would shoot, and apparently a hundred to one that if they shot they would hit. But the vague uneasiness that he had felt while dropping the pebbles over the culvert had become sharper and sharper, until he had to do something . . . anything, just to prove it didn't make sense, if nothing else.

The Curriers lived five miles from the Kilgores, along the so-called river road. It was a bad road in the summer, with dozens of little bridges over tiny streams that overflowed with the heavy falls of rain in the hills. From the Loftuses to the Kilgores it was ten miles, because the old bridge across the river had never been repaired since the spring floods of 1931. Ben thought suddenly of Sisky, whom Loftus had seen headed towards the Kilgores'. He was nearer to the Curriers, because the camp was across the river. Ben suddenly wondered if it was because of Sisky that he was now setting out. He didn't like the man. On the other hand it wouldn't do to have him hanging around Currier Hollow and getting shot. It wasn't the sort of publicity the CCC wanted.

At the three-storied flour mill at Jones Crossroads he turned to the left off the paved highway and slowed down, his tires plowing through the loose gravel. It was a lonely road through the valley. The family on the farm above the school house had already left. The cabin door creaked mournfully back and forth on one rusty hinge, the porch had fallen in at one end. A gourd vine sprawled desolately over the broken-down steps.

Beyond the cabin stretched barren fields, dry and deeply grooved, like sheets of corrugated iron, or like the relief maps in old-fashioned geographies. These were the fields that the TVA talked about, that had been planted in tobacco and corn so long that they were worn out, where farmers did not make fifty bushels of corn a year or a hundred pounds of tobacco.

He turned at the Methodist meeting house at Swallows Bend and crossed the branch to the narrow road through Murray's Hollow to the spring under the big white oak. From there the road was rough, with ruts so deep that once the car slipped off the hard ridges it would have stayed there, resting on the axles. It was narrow too. Ben hugged the bank to keep from sliding off the edge. He could see the bottom of Murray's Hollow, and he still had the hairpin bend where the road turned on itself to climb the rest of the way to the top of the ridge. How Mike could get the truck up there had always been a wonder to him; it was hardly short of miraculous driving. He slipped into low and cautiously made the almost impossible bend, with a sheer drop of six hundred feet below and nothing but a single redbud tree between him and whatever there is when it's all over.

No one lived on the top of the ridge. The twin beams of his headlights made it darker and lonelier. On this side the ruts were deeper still. He stayed in low, closed in to the up side, made another sharp bend. Below him was Currier Hollow, stretching down from the ridge top beyond the cornfield and Old Doss's workshop to the Powell River.

The car fumbled along on top of the dry hard mounds, like raised tracks in the road. Ben brought it slowly to a stop, looking down in the dark closing in on the Hollow, wondering what he was going to do now he was here. He slipped the car into neutral, slid it over against the bank at the bottom of the road where it widened at the foot of the hill, switched off the lights and sat there a moment, wondering whether it wouldn't be wiser to go straight ahead and leave the lights on. Nobody with a grain of sense, he thought sardonically, would be fool enough to wander about Currier Hollow at night. He looked at his watch. The moon ought to be up; in fact it was coming up, its bright rim rolling over the far ridge like a moving target in a shooting gallery.

He got out of the car, stepped out of the tunnel of trees overhanging the road and stood there a minute looking around. The cabin was dark, of course. He could have known it would be. People in the hills went to bed with the sun and rose with it in the morning. He stopped abruptly. Further down the Hollow a faint light shone out across the cornfield. It looked as if a lantern was hanging in the door of Old Doss's workshop. Ben hesitated. For the first time he had a sharp sense of something definitely queer about Currier Hollow. It was odd for the mountain folk to be at work late at night.

He fumbled in his pocket for his oilskin pouch, filled his pipe and looked back at the cabin. Surely they didn't leave the girl there alone. Then he remembered the dog.

The sound of quick steps in the road around the curve made him move back into the shadow of the trees. They were furtive illicit steps, and they were coming towards him, towards the Curriers' gate. He put the pouch back in his pocket and waited, intent and alert. Suddenly an unexpected thing happened. A little clump of straggling cornstalks growing up

41

against the rail fence beyond the gate moved almost noise-lessly. A voice, plaintively quavering above the low thrumming of a guitar, rose up like mist above the river, and a narrow twisted little form came out from the leaves and hopped along the fence to the gate. Edrew Mincey stood there, picking dolorously at the guitar. The steps in the road stopped abruptly a moment, came slowly along towards the gate. Ben waited. The monotonous melody sounded quaveringly on.

Then it happened suddenly as Ben watched. A dark crouching figure appeared before the gate, an arm lashed out. The crippled boy went down without a sound, the guitar catapulting off to the side. The dark figure looked down at Edrew Mincey for a second, pushed the crumpled little body aside with his foot, opened the gate and went silently into the yard.

Ben put his pipe into his pocket, slipped down the road and across the grassy edge of the incline and bent over the boy. The man crossing the yard had not heard him; he went on towards the house. The dog was nowhere in sight.

Ben put his hand down on the frail bony chest. He could feel the slow heartbeat. "You'll be all right," he thought. He went through the gate into the yard, keeping in the shadow of the smoke house.

The man had his foot on the bottom step when a gray figure came out from the shadow of the porch. Ben drew back against the whitewashed wall. It was Julie Currier, and she had been waiting there on the porch.

"I'll be damned," Ben said silently. A sardonic grin twisted his mouth; he took a deep breath and relaxed his taut body. Miss Elly was right. Little Julie was carryin' on. Speer had known it too.

"What a prize innocent moron *you* are, old fellow," he thought. He reached for his pipe, put it in his mouth, took it out. It tasted bitter. Somehow, she hadn't seemed that sort.

He looked back at the porch before slipping away. The man was going confidently up the steps. Then in the half-light of the rising moon he saw Julie Currier bend forward, then straighten up sharply. It was an odd startled movement. Ben came back to attention. He saw her draw back, turn for an instant towards the cabin door, then, lightning swift, break past the man on the steps to fly down the yard towards the gate.

For an instant Ben stood motionless. He saw her white face and the blind terror in her eyes. The man on the porch had turned and was running after her. "Hey, wait a minute!" he whispered hoarsely. Ben heard the little cry strangled in Julie's throat as her shoe struck a rock on the baked earth and she stumbled. He sprang towards her and caught her

42

arm. She gave a quick aching sob of relief and drew her body erect.

The pounding feet behind him stopped short. Ben turned around. Ten feet away Sisky was standing, staring at him open-mouthed, his face slowly turning a sickly gray. Ben let go the girl's arm gently and walked towards him, suddenly cold with fury.

Sisky's eyes shifted from side to side. He licked his thick lips.

"Listen, Mr. Davidge—you got me wrong!" he cried hysterically. "I wasn't goin' to do nothin' to her. I didn't mean to scare her. I'm . . . I'm goin' to marry her."

Behind him Ben heard a sharp intake of breath. He looked around at Julie. "Is that true?" he said quietly.

"Oh, no!" she cried.

He turned and walked up to Sisky.

"This is for the crippled kid," he said coldly. A smashing straight left with a hundred and eighty-five lean and muscular pounds behind it caught Sisky on the point of the jaw and went on. Ben looked down at the whimpering figure on the ground.

"Get up and get out," he said. "If I catch you here again I'll break your neck."

He watched Sisky stagger to his feet and through the gate, looked around at Julie, staring at him white and shaken, and grinned cheerfully. "Just a minute," he said. He went to the gate, picked up the boy lying there and carried him to the branch. Edrew stirred, moaned softly and was quiet again. Ben dipped his handkerchief in the cold water, started to lay it on the boy's swollen face, and stopped. The empty china blue eyes were wide open, staring up at him. They looked past him. Ben turned. Julie had crept up behind them and was looking down at the boy. Ben smiled and turned back.

"She's all right," he said. "And you'll be all right in the morning."

The boy wriggled painfully to his feet and looked over the ground by him.

"It's over by the gate," Ben said. Edrew hopped off slowly, like a wounded rabbit. Ben saw him reach down and pick up the guitar, strum carefully at it for a moment, then hop off down the road.

He turned back to Julie.

"You're all right?"

She nodded.

"Well, we're even. You drag off a dog, I drag off a rat. Where is he, by the way?"

"Kilgore?"

43

"No, the dog."

"That's Kilgore. That's his name. He's mean, but it isn't his fault. They fed him gunpowder and raw meat when he was a puppy."

"Is that why you call him Kilgore?"

She nodded. "We don't get on with the Kilgores."

She said it simply. It was an accepted fact, understated, as Ben knew.

"Why did you come here?"

She looked up at him with wide serious eyes, frank and curious, like a child's.

He smiled down at her. "I don't know," he said. "I'm glad I did. You didn't expect that fellow to come here, did you?"

"No."

She turned away for an instant, a guarded mountain look in her eyes.

"He came before and they ran him off with a gun. They didn't think he'd come back again. You'd better go too, before they see you. Doss shoots without thinking what he's doing, lots of times."

"Did they raise him on raw meat and gunpowder too?"

A quick smile stirred the calm depths of Julie's eyes and deepened for a moment in the corners of her red mouth.

"All us Curriers were," she said very soberly.

"You too?"

She nodded. The smile died in her eyes. "That's why you'd better go . . . quick. Honestly."

"You haven't told me where Kilgore is."

"He went with Doss."

"And you're supposed to be in bed, asleep."

Ben smiled to himself involuntarily. "I'm damn near as paternal as if I was head of the TVA," he thought.

She nodded. It didn't seem to her that it was an odd question at all.

"And instead you're waiting for somebody, and that's why you want me to go."

He grinned cheerfully down at her.

"It isn't safe for you to stay here."

"But you are waiting for somebody."

She nodded. "I'm waiting for a man to come and take me away," she said simply. "Before Doss gets back."

Ben looked at her seriously. "Who is he? Where's he going to take you?"

"I don't know. I just thought if he was going to Knoxville he might take me there. There's a lady there, she came here once but Old Doss drove her off and wouldn't let me talk to

44

her. She was a friend of my mother. I don't know where she lives, but I reckon I can find her."

"What's her name?"

"I don't know. But she knew my mother. Couldn't I find her by asking for somebody that knew my mother?"

Ben stared at her, curiously touched in a way that he could not understand.

"Good Lord, no. Child, there are thousands of people in Knoxville."

His eyes met hers, looking gravely up at him. Moved by a sudden impulse he put one hand on her slim shoulder and tilted up her soft pointed chin.

"Look here. You can't go away with a man you don't know to hunt for a woman you don't know who lives in a place you don't know. You just can't do it. Do you understand?"

She drew away from him quickly.

"It's you that don't understand," she cried softly. "I've got to go away. I can't stay here."

"Why can't you?"

She hesitated a moment. "Because they're going to make me marry Doss," she cried passionately. "I can't do it, I won't! I tried to run away the other night. I was going to walk, but the man said he'd take me to Kilgores'. Then I knew I couldn't go to Kilgores' because that would be going against my people, and you can't go against your people even if they was—were to kill you. Then Gran caught me and made me go back."

She looked away.

"The man was here today. I think he'll come back tonight."

"Do they know you tried to run away?"

He understood that "they" meant Old Doss and Doss, not Nathan Currier.

She shook her head. "Gran didn't tell them. They'd tie me up. Gran don—doesn't like that."

"Tie you up?"

She smiled. "Like a colt. I didn't use to mind, because then they'd have to cook and wash the dishes, and I'd read my books."

The smile faded quickly. "Old Doss burned them. I had three. They belonged to my mother. She was from back East, Charleston. That's in South Carolina, a long way across the mountains. She taught school over at Jackboro."

"Is that why you don't talk like the rest of them?"

She nodded simply. "Doss makes fun of the way I talk, but I don't care. Gran was going to send me to school, but they wouldn't let him, not after she died. There wasn't anybody else to do for them but me. I said when we had to go away from here maybe I could go to school, like the TVA lady said, but Old Doss said I couldn't."

"Why not?"

"He says I'm too old and ugly."

Ben laughed, and stopped abruptly, seeing the hurt unhappy tears spring to her eyes.

"I'm sorry, Julie," he said. "Listen. You aren't too old, and you're not ugly at all. In fact, you're very pretty."

"Me . . . pretty?"

"In fact, I think you're really beautiful, Julie."

He smiled. Her cheeks flushed warmly. "Oh!" she gasped. Then she shook her head. "You're like Iago. You try to deceive people by telling them lies."

She smiled with shy gaiety.

Ben shook his head soberly. "Haven't you got a mirror?"

"A mirror?"

"A looking glass?"

"Oh, no. I had a little one once, but Old Doss smashed it because I was a vain wicked girl."

"Good God," Ben thought. "Anyway," he said, "nobody's ever too old to go to school. They have schools for people as old as I am. And your looks don't matter. You ought to see some of the people that go to schools."

Then I can go, and learn all about everything?"

Her eyes were wide and radiant.

"Oh, you know when the airships fly over the Hollow I look up and think if only one of them would come down and pick me up and carry me away and away! Maybe to Rome, and all the places that there's pictures of in my book."

She looked up at him. "Have you been to Rome?"

"Yes. I've been there."

Ben reflected that the only real memories he had of it were the fleas, and the cats yowling at night in the Colosseum. But there was no use saying that.

"And have you been to the movies? Gran went to see one in Knoxville, five years ago. He told me about it. He brought me a paper book called *Movieland*, but Old Doss burned it up too. I'd like to go to Knoxville, just to see what it's like."

Ben was silent a moment. Then he said gently, "Haven't you ever been to Knoxville?"

"I've never been out of the Hollow," she said. "Except the year after Mamma died. I went to school over the ridge, until a boy walked home with me one day. They didn't let me go back after that. Once Gran was going to take me to a church supper way over at Jones Crossroads, but he didn't do it."

"They wouldn't let him?"

She shook her head. "I reckon I must have been vain and wicked. I put on Mamma's silk dress that was in the trunk. It just fit every place."

The tears welled up in her eyes again.

"They wouldn't let me go, and Old Doss tore it trying to get it off me."

"Then he burned it too, I suppose."

She shook her smooth gold head. "Gran wouldn't let him. I've got it up in the loft, and sometimes when they tie me up I put it on and play like I'm Rosalind or Juliet. They're in my Shakespeare book that Old Doss burned up. I've still got the Bible—he didn't dast burn it. So I can read it and play like I'm Ruth, and sometimes I play like Gran is Samson and I'm Deborah, and I cut his beard and the whole house falls down like the walls of Jericho. That's not what it is in the book, but that's what I play."

Ben nodded gravely. "What's your other book, Julie?"

"That was a dictionary, but Old Doss thought it was vain and wicked too, most because it had pictures of all over the world in the back of it. He said I hadn't any call to be reading about Rome, because I wasn't ever going to leave the Hollow."

She looked up at him, her face a pale wistful oval in the white moonlight, her fingers tracing the charred outline of the big "C" burned in the gate post.

"The Curriers haven't ever left the Hollow. That's what makes Old Doss so hard now, because gover-ment is driving us out."

"But you want to go, don't you?"

She raised two puzzled eyes to his.

"But I want to come back! I don't want to go and have the Hollow where I was born all covered with water so I can't ever see it again. It's just like cutting the roots away from under a tree. It isn't so bad for me, because my roots will grow again, but Gran and Old Doss can't grow new roots in a new soil. Like my tree."

She looked up at the empty sky against which the great cedar had stood almost ten centuries long.

"Trees are better than people. They're clean and strong, and they don't get cruel when they're old, like people do."

They stood looking up at the hill. Neither of them spoke for a long time.

"That's why I have to marry Doss," she said slowly. "Be-

47

cause the gover-ment is tearing up my roots like they cut down my tree. Gran is old, he'll die pretty soon, and there isn't anybody to take care of me out there where we're going."

She turned away, choking back a quick anguished sob.

"Oh, I'm afear'd of Doss. The way he looks at me . . . I always was afear'd of him, when I was a little girl. That's why Old Doss hates me so."

She looked up quickly, her eyes wide again with sudden terror. "That's why I've got to go! I don't care where it is just so they don't let them find me!"

She brushed her smooth hair off her forehead with a terrified helpless gesture.

"But you've got to go, quick. They'll come back and they'll kill you. They won't kill me—I wish they would!"

Ben hesitated a moment, wondering if the imperative thing for him to do wasn't to mind his own business. Then a strange feeling that he had never felt before impelled him. He reached down, took her cold hand and held it firmly in his own large warm hands.

"Look here," he said. "You said a while ago that you couldn't go against your own people."

"It's not the same—I just can't go to Kilgores'!"

"Yes, it is, if you run away from your grandfather. Listen, Julie. When are you supposed to marry Doss?"

"Saturday. They're going to get a preacher."

"All right. Now listen. You go back in the cabin and go to bed. Something will happen before Saturday. If it doesn't, I'll take you away myself."

He hesitated again. The idea came to him that having gone so far there was no use in stopping short.

"We'll get your grandfather to let you go visit my mother for a while."

She stared at him open-eyed, and shook her head slowly. "They'd never let me."

"Forget about them. Promise me you won't go, Julie."

He looked down at her for a long time, seeing beyond the clear gray eyes and pale lovely face, to the face it would be after a year in the maelstrom of the life she would find, lost and rootless in a great city.

"You'll . . . you'll help me?"

"I'll help you. Promise you won't run away."

She smiled shyly, and nodded. "Cross my heart!"

"All right. Then run off to bed. Scoot. Good night!"

"Good night . . ."

She hesitated.

"Ben Davidge is the name, ma'am."

She laughed. "Good night, Ben Davidge." She ran across the hard-caked courtyard to the cabin.

Ben closed the gate behind her, stared after her until she had disappeared into the darkness of the porch, and stood there, his hand still on the gate, silent and motionless, wondering at the person called Ben Davidge whom he had never known before.

At last he straightened up.

"My dear fellow!" he thought. "I hope you haven't—as Miss Elly would say—bit off more'n ye kin chaw."

He looked back again at the silent cabin, and went up the wagon road. The lighted lantern still hung in the door of the workshop across the cornfield on the branch. An owl fluttered softly through the trees overhead. He could hear his heart beat in the utter silence of the night. At the entrance to the dark shadows he looked back again. Julie was standing on the steps, lithe and slender in the moonlight. He waved to her. She waved back and disappeared. When he turned back the light in the workshop door was gone. There was nothing but empty blackness where it had shone.

He thought suddenly that he really had better get out. It would be pretty hard on the girl if they found him there. He went quietly up the road to his car, put his hand on the handle, started to open the door, and stopped sharply, every muscle taut. He turned around. A dark figure was standing silently against the leafy bank. Stray moonbeams filtering through the trees glinted on the cold blue steel in his hand. A dog scratched suddenly, thumping his hind foot against the ground.

Ben knew it was Doss Currier standing there, shotgun in his hand. He felt a sudden wave of cold fury, and controlled it with a violent effort. He moved back from the car.

"I'm waiting, Currier," he said curtly.

"I *bin* waitin', stranger," Doss Currier said. His slow drawl was as cold and deadly as the gleaming blue barrel in his hand.

10

The road was very quiet. Ben stood there a moment, hesitating. There was no sound from the cabin or from Old Doss's workshop across the cornfield. The dog Kilgore edged across the road and sniffed at Ben's boots. Doss Currier's dark figure was silent and motionless, the blue gleaming barrel of the shotgun in his hands was unwavering, deadly.

Ben stifled the impulse to leap across the ten feet between them. It wouldn't do. The shooting was too good in these parts.

"Well?" he said curtly.

Doss Currier's drawling sing-song rose again. 'Whar's yer gun, stranger?"

"I don't carry one."

The blue gleam lowered, pointed towards the ground.

"I ain't aimin' t' kill gover-ment men," Doss said slowly. "Not th' fust time they come hangin' round the Holler. Might be a mistake th' fust time. Git along now."

Ben hesitated, wondering how much of Julie's outburst Doss had heard, hating to leave her alone with him even if he had heard nothing, only seen her here alone with him in the moonlight.

"I ain't aimin' t' wait much longer, stranger."

Ben grinned suddenly in the dark.

"Davidge is the name," he said. He opened the car door. Down in the road across the cornfield he could see two dark figures moving slowly towards the cabin. Old Nate Currier was coming, it was all right. He slipped in under the wheel, switched on the ignition and turned the car round. Doss stood at the roadside, watching him silently. Ben waved cheerfully and put the car into second and up the guttered road to the top of the ridge.

He braked at the top and switched off the motor to cool after the heavy climb. The clock on the dash read ten minutes to eleven. The smile had faded from his lips as he slowly filled his pipe. He stopped and listened. From somewhere down below him, in the night as silent as the stars, came the soft halting thrum of Edrew Mincey's guitar. Ben rested his pipe and pouch against the wheel and listened. It had gone already; there was nothing now in the soft air. Perhaps he had just imagined it.

He finished filling his pipe, put the pouch in his pocket and struck a match. His hand stopped before the tip of flame reached the bowl. From below in Currier Hollow came the clear loud report of a shotgun. There was a second shot, then silence.

Ben sat perfectly still, waiting. After a moment he opened the door and stepped out into the road, looking back down the narrow black tunnel towards Currier Hollow. He stood there several minutes, then got back in the car and headed on towards Loftus's.

It was 6.30 when Miss Elly called him the next morning. He got up and dressed, and went out onto the back porch to wash in the tin basin on the bench. The girl brought him a cup of hot water to shave in. He tilted the cracked mirror hanging on the upright under the roof to try to see his chin, and rinsed his face off in a dipper of cold water from the tin bucket.

Miss Elly was scolding the farm hands for being late—it was 4.30 when they had started milking and chopping wood. Ed Loftus was at the table, chewing reflectively when Ben came in. He looked up and nodded, passed the platter of fried chicken, passed the platter of fried ham swimming in red gravy.

"Help yerself t' the corn bread," he said. "These here's biscuits, even if they do look like rocks." He pushed a plate across the table with a broad wink.

Ben smiled. It was the daily bait to rouse Miss Elly and she always rose to it. Loftus shook with laughter at her shrill anger. It was the sort of joke all mountain people loved, and never tired of, as far as Ben could see. He passed his cup to the girl for coffee. When she came back with it she took up the platter of chicken.

Loftus stopped her halfway to the door.

"Where you aimin' t' go with that there chicken?" he drawled.

"Miss Elly said bring hit out t' keep hit hot fer Mr. Speer."

Ben glanced at the empty place across the table, with the plate turned down between the bone-handled knife and fork.

"Tell her she don't need to. He'll prob'ly be gettin' his breakfast the same place he slept. Doggonedest feller fer stayin' out all night I ever did see."

Ben put his cup down. "He didn't come in?" he asked.

"Might have," Loftus said. "His car ain't out there, an' his bed ain't been slept in, an' I cain't see him round no place."

"Thought I heard him last night."

Loftus speared a piece of ham with his fork.

"Then he must 'a went out again," he said. "I reckon maybe hit was Prince you hear'd. Elly she taught him to sleep on that there chair when he was a pup, an' he still does hit. I reckon Speer's got the right t' stay out if he wants to. Only hit ain't recommended by most, up in these yere parts."

Ben pushed his chair back and got up. A curious chill ran down his back. At a single stroke the whole thing had fallen into place like the pieces of a jigsaw puzzle and lay flat and perfectly lucid in front of him. Loftus's conversation on the barrier overlooking the dam. Speer's boiling engine. Julie's vigil in the shadow of the porch. Doss Currier's silent presence in the road, gun ready. The two shots in the night.

"Ain't finished, air you?" Ed Loftus asked, looking up from his plate.

51

Ben nodded and reached in his pocket for his pipe and tobacco. He went out on the porch as casually as he could. There was no use rousing Loftus's insatiable curiosity. What he wanted to see was the letter. "You've got the story," Speer had said up at the tree.

He went into his room and closed the door. The flannel jacket he had worn on Sunday was hanging in Miss Elly's pine wardrobe. He took it down and reached into the pocket. Then he stood motionless for a moment. The manila envelope that Speer had given him was gone.

11

For an instant Ben stood staring blankly at the empty pocket of his flannel coat. He looked on the floor of the wardrobe to see if the letter had fallen out when he hung the coat up. There was no letter there. The letter was gone.

He put the coat back and stood looking out of the window. Why had Speer given him the letter in the first place? Why should anyone in the house take it, in the second? Loftus and Miss Elly were the only ones who had access to it. The half-witted girl and the three hired men could be disregarded, no one else would be likely to be in his room. Unless it was Speer, and that was nonsense. But it was all nonsense. None of it made sense, not any of it.

His room was one of two downstairs in the front clapboard addition to the old house. Speer had the other. Each room had doors opening onto the front and back porches and into a tiny enclosed landing from which steps led to the upper floor. His room could be entered from either porch, from the stair entry or from Speer's room. But by well-established usage the door to the back porch was the only one that was ever used.

He tried the doors. The front door was locked, the stairs door was not. Quietly he tried the door leading to Speer's room. It was also open. He went in. Speer's room had been the dining room of the enlarged house. The bright quilts were still neatly drawn up to the feather bolster. The clock on the small square table had stopped at three. Speer's suitcase lay closed on the mission sideboard, reflected in the mildewed mirror. He tried the other doors; the door to the back porch was locked, the front door was not.

"This gets us exactly no place," Ben thought. He listened a moment to be sure Miss Elly was still scolding the hired girl, and opened the suitcase. Shirts, collars, socks, underwear and handkerchiefs. Nothing else.

He closed the suitcase, went back to his own room, sat down on the side of the high bed, stared at the enlarged crayon portraits of Ed Loftus and Miss Elly in their youth, and tried to figure out what it was all about. Speer's giving him the letter, whatever reason he had had for doing it, was not important; it was the fact that the letter was missing. It was that that gave importance to Speer's having thought it worth his while to write a letter after a hard drive at midnight and give it to a complete stranger.

"He said open it and use your head," Ben thought. It was hard to use your head when you hadn't the faintest idea of what to use your head about.

Loftus was sitting in his rocking chair on the porch when Ben came out. He spat over the rail and looked inquiringly up.

"I reckon you got th' letter Speer left fer you yestiddy evenin'?" he said.

"What letter?"

Ben's answer was sharper than he had meant it to be. It didn't do to speak to these people that way. They drew back into their shells.

Loftus looked away. The injured air on his face seemed strange in a grown person if you didn't keep in mind that they were really children. Shrewd, even savage, but children.

"I mean I didn't see any letter," Ben said hastily. "Where'd he leave it?"

"Couldn't tell you."

Loftus spat again with elaborate indifference.

"All I know is I seed him comin' out a' yer room, an' he says, 'I jes' lef' a letter'—a note, I reckon he called hit—'fer Mr. Davidge.'"

"What time was that?"

"What time would hit be, Elly, when Mr. Speer come back yestiddy?"

Miss Elly looked up from stringing beans.

"Hit was after we cleared up an' put away," she said. "He come up an' says, 'I'm hungry as a b'ar, Miss Loftus,' an' could I fix him a bite to eat. Hit'd be about th' middle a' th' afternoon."

Ben nodded. "Thanks. He probably changed his mind. See you later."

He went round to the road and stood waiting for the truck. What Loftus said put a new angle to things. Speer had not left a note. At least none was in sight. It was perfectly possible that he had changed his mind about the letter, come into the room, hunted round till he had found it, and taken it along with him. It was not only possible, it was the simplest and most reasonable thing to assume. For one thing, there was no reason to assume that the two shots he had heard the night before were fired at Speer. Or that all shots were necessarily fatal. Speer might, as Loftus said, be having breakfast somewhere else. Perhaps Sisky had still hung around Currier Hollow. That could easily explain a couple of shots without reference to Speer.

And yet . . . there were still all the points that had struck him as strange when he thought about them before. It was perfectly obvious that whatever he was Speer was not a TVA land appraiser. Land appraisers were not usually of that square-jawed, resolute type. Neither did they appraise land at midnight. Neither were they in any danger of not showing for breakfast. This was a district in which human life was not held very sacred; there had been two killings, back out in the hills, within the last three weeks. But they were family affairs. One mountaineer shot another, everybody knew all about it. They did not shoot outlanders like Speer. There was no record of the shooting of a TVA land appraiser.

A sudden thought came into Ben's mind. These people did shoot "revenuers." Most of the prohibition agents who were killed in line of duty were murdered in cold blood in places like this—not in Chicago and New York as people believed. But Speer's operations, whatever they were, seemed to concern Currier Hollow, and somehow it didn't seem possible that the Curriers were moonshiners.

The truck came around the bend. Ben got in the cab. The driver looked at him with a grin. "Heard about Sisky, Mr. Davidge?"

"What about him?" Ben said hastily.

"He goes out and gets in a fight," Mike said with a chuckle. "Man, did that baby take a beating. Comes back an' says he hurt his hand and his leg in a barbed wire fence. Barbed wire fence, for Cripe's sake. The Captain says, 'Look more like dog bites to me, Sisky.' You know what I think? I think he ran into that damn dog at Curriers' place. Then there's something else funny. He ran into a lollapalooser right on the jaw. You know that ain't right, these guys up here fight with guns. I never heard of 'em usin' their fists, no more'n I ever heard of 'em havin' any barbed wire up here."

"It is funny," Ben said. "What's happened to him?"

"They got him in bed. He won't take the pasture shots. I guess he'd rather go mad an' bite a few folks before he'd say it was the Currier dog, after the way the gal there jumped in fer you yesterday morning."

"He wasn't shot, though?"

Mike shook his head.

"Naw. Captain says he's lucky not to have his pants full a' buckshot."

"He is, if he was around the Curriers'."

When Ben had met Sisky last night the dog Kilgore was nowhere in sight. Sisky must have met him later, then, after Ben had met Doss Currier. Doss probably had set the dog on him and fired into the air, just for emphasis. Speer was probably all right somewhere.

12

The leader of the CCC detail trimming the fallen trunk of the great cedar, an up-state New York farm boy named Dave Phinney, stopped by Ben for a moment.

"They're sure getting a big kick out of this fellow Sisky, Mr. Davidge," he said. "You know he told somebody he was going to marry this Currier girl?"

"He did?" Ben said.

"Yeah. You know one of the fellows married a girl who's been teaching school over the ridge. I guess that's where he got the idea."

The boy turned back towards the tree, his clean sunburned young face troubled. He stopped and came back awkwardly.

"I didn't like to say anything to Captain Dell about it," he said, "but don't you think something ought to be done about it?"

"I guess we can leave it to the dog, Dave."

Ben remembered as soon as he had said it that Kilgore had not been in the yard, wherever Sisky had met him.

"You can poison dogs, if you're that kind of a guy," the boy said. "All I mean is, she's sort of different from most of the girls up here. She's . . . she's more like she was just taking the part of a mountain girl, in a movie."

He fumbled for the words, blushing a little. "If you get what I'm trying to say, Mr. Davidge."

Ben nodded. "I get it. I'll see if we can do anything."

He looked over across the dip to the Currier cabin, with the tendrils of white smoke rising against the green wooded hill behind it. He had already looked down there several times during the morning. Kilgore was lying in the middle of the yard asleep. Old Doss was sitting on the porch. He got up every few minutes to go inside or down to the low stable, and came back to his seat. A queer shambling scarecrow of a man, too ravaged-looking, Ben thought, to seem very dangerous, except that every time he passed Kilgore the dog raised himself and moved a few feet away. After a while Young Doss came out too, and sat with his father on the porch.

Nathan Currier did not appear; neither did Julie. At first Ben thought she was probably cleaning up inside the cabin. As the sun rose high and higher over the Hollow and neither of them appeared, a vague feeling of uneasiness grew in him. He wondered if she was being punished for talking to him last night. He had counted on Nathan Currier for saving her from that, and Nathan apparently was not around.

It was nearly eleven o'clock when he looked down and saw Doss Currier closing the gate and fixing the looped chain back on the post. He went up the gravel incline followed by Old Doss and disappeared under the hill in the direction of the workshop. Ben looked expectantly back at the cabin porch. No one was there, no one came out. Only Kilgore was in sight, still asleep in the yard in the sun. Ben waited fifteen minutes, and called Dave Phinney.

"I'm going down to the Curriers' a minute," he said. "You know what's got to be done before lunch."

The boy nodded. Ben went down to the truck.

"I want you to come down to the cabin with me," he said.

Mike scratched his head with a grin.

"I ain't got the drag with that hound that you've got, Mr. Davidge," he said. "We startin' now?"

Ben nodded. "Hand me that lunch box."

As they went in the gate Kilgore got up and came slowly towards them, growling softly, the hair rising on his neck.

"Hello, boy."

Kilgore advanced slowly. Still no one appeared on the porch.

"Nice boy!" Ben said. He held out a leg of Miss Elly's fried chicken. The dog sniffed at him, wagged his tail gently and took the chicken. His great jaws closed twice on it and it disappeared.

"I'm a son of a gun," Mike said. "He knew you."

"I counted heavily on it," Ben said. "Here, boy. Have all of it. This is what you call making character."

He emptied the box on the ground. They went across the yard and up onto the porch. Ben knocked on the wall. He waited a minute and knocked again.

"Guess there ain't nobody home," Mike said.

56

Ben looked around. It was the first chance he had had to look at the cabin. It was like something of a different age. The porch was ten feet or so wide, not separate; its roof was the sloping cabin roof; it was floored with the wide pine planks of the cabin floor. It ran the full length of the building and was nearly enclosed by sweet-smelling flowering vines that Ben had never seen before, full of drowsy yellow bees and brilliant butterflies. At one end there was an old-fashioned loom, and near it, against the rail, three great gray sacks of raw wool. Benches and hickory rocking chairs stood along the rail. There were two door frames set in the pine logs of the cabin, but neither of them had a door. Between them hung rude farming implements of all sorts and an elaborate Spanish tooled leather saddle with tarnished silver and red velvet trappings, the leather dried and splitting. From the slanting beams of the roof hung bunches of dried herbs, onions, red and yellow ears of corn, a bunch of everlasting flower and sweet clover. Two big crocks of sliced apples stood on the bench, between them a homemade knife and a basket of russet apples.

Ben knocked again, then went to the nearest door and looked in. A fire was burning in the old cook stove, a long table in the middle of the room was covered with a white cloth made of hemmed sugar sacks. There was a cradle in one corner, in it a gray cat with six sleeping kittens. A single bed with an elaborate red and white quilt spread neatly over it stood in the other corner. The room had no windows; the sun streamed in through another empty door frame opposite him and through the chinks around the fireplace chimney.

He went along the porch to the other door and knocked. There was still no answer. He looked in. There were two double poster beds in this room, neatly made up with quilts over the high feather beds. In the end of the room was a fireplace, and burning in it was the fire that had not been out for more than a hundred years. In a corner was a large old-fashioned safe, above it a small shelf with two tattered books.

Ben looked around. Perhaps it was the fire, or the neatly made beds, that gave the dark room—it had one tiny paneless window set in the far wall—an air of having someone in it.

"Hello!" he said. There was no answer.

"Hello! Mr. Currier!"

A faint grating sound above him made him look up. Over one of the beds was an opening into the loft. The trapdoor moved a few inches. Ben went over to the bed and looked up into Julie Currier's white startled face.

57

Her lips moved noiselessly as she stared down at him, her eyes wide with bewilderment. Then suddenly she turned as white as death.

"Please, help me loose!" she cried softly.

Her voice throbbed in his ears. He sprang up on the bed, pushed the trapdoor back, put both hands on the sides of the opening and swung himself up into the half-light of the loft. Julie Currier drew back against the log partition and looked silently at him, her eyes pleading, anguished. Beside her was a chipped granite pie plate with a piece of cornbread on it, and an earthen jug of milk. There was a straw pallet in the corner with a quilt folded across the foot. A painted wood trunk with a rounded top stood in the middle of the floor. Behind it was the stump of a white tallow candle.

He looked back at Julie. She moved her foot out from under her skirt.

"I've got to get down . . . please let me loose," she said.

A rope was tied round her ankle, the other end made fast to a bolt in the log wall.

Ben took out his knife silently, slashed the rope in two and untied the knot. He rubbed her ankle briskly through the coarse woolen stocking.

"All right," he said quietly. "See if you can stand on it. Give me your hand."

She shook her head. He saw that her hands were tied too. A second wave of cold fury swept over him. He cut the rope around them. She leaned against the glossy pine logs and closed her eyes wearily.

"I thought they killed you," she whispered.

He helped her to her feet and rubbed the red welts on her white wrists.

"Did they do this because Doss saw you talking to me?"

"Partly."

"But your grandfather . . ."

"He's not here."

"Where is he?"

"He's in Knoxville."

Ben looked at her.

"Are you sure he is?" he asked slowly.

She nodded. "Help me down, please. I've got to find out . . ."

She stopped as if frightened to go on. Ben let himself down through the trapdoor and lifted her down after him.

"I've got to find him," she said quickly. "You can't come with me. You must go, quick."

"Where are you going, Julie?"

58

She caught her under lip between her teeth and shook her head.

"Then let's go."

She shook her head quickly.

Ben looked at her. There were two shots last night. He had seen two men coming up from the workshop. He was beginning to understand. The same curious chill ran up and down his spine for an instant.

"Listen," he said. "Go on. I'm going with you. Where is he?"

She turned desperately to him and looked up imploringly into his eyes. "Please!" she said. "I don't want anything to happen to you. It doesn't matter about me—they won't really hurt me—but they'll kill you if they see you. You're not brave, you're just foolish."

Ben nodded.

"No doubt," he said. "I'm going with you, Julie. Come on."

She turned and went slowly out onto the porch.

Mike Shannon was sitting on the top step, hat jammed down over his broken-nosed face. He was looking at Kilgore. Kilgore was sitting on his haunches at the bottom of the steps, looking at Mike.

"Glad to see you, Mr. Davidge," Mike said over his shoulder. "Jeez, I started to take a drink outa that gourd dipper, an' I thought this—— —— dog was goin' to take my leg off. Wish you'd use your influence."

He looked around and got hastily to his feet, face purple.

"This is Mr. Shannon, Miss Currier."

Mike pulled off his hat.

"Is he going with us?"

Ben nodded. "He'll come along."

"All right, then. We've got to hurry."

Ben took the chain off the post and held the gate open, and closed it again, leaving Kilgore standing in the yard. Julie ran up the incline to the road and hurried along the curve past the path through the cornfield without a glance towards the workshop. Her feet stepped quickly and surely on top of the deep-grooved wagon tracks. The road bed grew damper and softer under their feet.

Suddenly Mike dug Ben in the ribs with his elbow and pointed down to the dirt.

"There's that truck again, Mr. Davidge. Remember? It's got a couple of treads shaved off, just like the one I was showin' you across the cornfield."

Ben looked down and nodded absently. He glanced up and saw Julie's face. She had stopped a little ahead of them and was looking at Mike, her lips closed firmly, her eyes fixed on him with a level scrutinizing gaze. It was not hostile, Ben thought, wondering, but it was not friendly. It had more of the mountains in it than he had seen there before. She hesitated for a moment as if uncertain whether to go on or not. A struggle seemed to be going on behind her cool gray eyes.

Ben looked at her, puzzled. Her face had a calm loveliness that few of the mountain faces had. She was not looking at Ben; her gaze rested steadily on the truck driver bending down over the tire track. After a moment she turned and hurried on along the road.

Ahead of her the cornfield came to an end. The road made a sharp left turn into a leafy thicket. Over the tree tops Ben could see a solitary towering sycamore. The road was softer, the ruts deeper. Julie hurried on. They followed her into the sudden cool of the narrow shady wagon lane.

Mike whistled softly. "Hello, there's that car with the Washington tags."

Ben nodded. The road curved again down a gentle slope. At the bottom of it, opposite the sycamore, was a cleared spot, and in the clearing stood the black coupé with the Washington license plates, run off the road into the soft ground. They went towards it across the oak logs laid against each other across the wet ground at the bottom by the spring. Near the sycamore was a crude shed, five feet high, three or four feet wide, propped up against the bank. A yellow gourd dipper with a string through a hole in the handle hung by the door, on the leather latch. The water flowed out under the door into a crystal pool that spread out over the road.

Julie Currier stood looking for a moment, then pointed to the spring house. Ben slipped the slit leather strap off the bent nail on the door. Two thin streams of water fell down a moss-green rock into an old oak trough. Ben looked at Julie. The spring house was empty. She was looking across the road at the thin trickle of dark brown in the mud under the black coupé.

Mike followed her glance and whistled again.

"That car never got stuck there by itself," he said. He pointed to the rear wheels, sunk over the rims in the mud.

"Jeez," he said. "He didn't even try to get it out. You see that?"

Ben nodded. He was looking at the single set of tracks filled with clear water in the swampy ground. However the car had got there, it was certain that no attempt had been made to get it out.

He went across to the edge of the log road and looked at

the back of the car. The curtain was drawn. He looked around. Mike had already rooted up a log out of the road. Ben took it from him and let it fall across the mud to the car. He walked out on it and looked through the closed window.

Speer was in the car, lying with his face on the seat, knees thrust against the gearshift, feet crumpled up against the closed door. The back of his coat was a mass of torn wool, drenched and black with drying blood.

Ben turned and stepped back over the log onto the road, thinking for a moment that he was going to be actively sick.

Julie was standing there white and rigid. "Who is it?" she whispered. Her lips barely moved as she breathed the question.

"It's a TVA land appraiser," Ben said quietly. "His name's Speer."

She leaned against the spring house for an instant and closed her eyes. Her hand trembled as she smoothed a wisp of pale gold hair away from her forehead.

"I was afear'd it was my grandfather," she whispered.

She straightened her slim body, lithe and graceful under the old gray homespun dress buttoned tight at the throat. Ben watched her step across the wet logs in the spring bed and run swiftly up the slope towards the cabin. She had not meant to say what she did—he could see it in the way she suddenly caught her under lip in her teeth.

Ben turned back to the coupé. Mike was coming across the log. "There ain't a coroner inside a hundred miles, Mr. Davidge," he said. "There's a fellow named Fairchild, he's a sheriff, about a mile the other side of the Crossroads."

"Take the truck and get him. I'll stay here. Tell Phinney to keep the detail. He knows what to do."

"O.K."

Ben started across the log, stopped, pulled his leather gloves out of his pocket and put them on. Not that it would matter much about finger prints, he thought. Nobody interested in such things would get there until everything was smeared up. Still it was worth being careful about. He opened the car door. The crumpled body did not move when the pressure was removed. Rigor mortis. Ben tried to remember how long it took to set in. It began in three or four hours and was complete in eight or twelve. Vague memories of something he had read came back to him. It came on faster in hot weather and there were other factors that affected it, like fatigue and age. Funny how little you really knew about that sort of thing.

In this case he didn't need to know about it, because he already knew when those two shots were fired. When he looked at his car clock on top of the ridge it was ten minutes to eleven. The shots were fired just after that. And just after that they had stuffed Speer's body into his car like a bag of meal—after they had shot him in the back.

He thought over what must have happened the night before. Speer was there, by the spring house. Sisky had probably passed him; he therefore had not come to meet Julie, waiting for him on the porch. When Sisky left, Ben was there, talking to her by the gate. And Doss Currier was waiting for him, as he was waiting for a chance to see Julie. Only Doss had waited by the wrong car. Or perhaps he had thought Ben was going to take her away, which was why he didn't shoot when he saw him alone. Then he had gone back and found Speer. Ben wondered if Julie had come out again to meet Speer, if that was why they had tied her up.

"I should have come down," he thought. But he knew it would not have done any good. If he had, he would probably have been there too, crumpled up in the same fantastic, grotesquely huddled death that imprisoned Speer.

He took the dead man's hat off the shelf behind the seat and looked at it. It was mashed flat, covered with dust-grained blood stains. Inside it the initials R. J. S. were perforated in the sweat band. It came from a men's furnishing store on F Street in Washington. He put it back on the shelf and opened the compartment in the dash. There were a few road maps there and a couple of cards of matches from a Knoxville hotel.

Ben leaned into the car. Speer's coat was unbuttoned, the right side of it hanging down in front of the seat. Ben lifted it gingerly until he could get at the opening of the inside breast pocket. He reached in, pulled out what was in it, and stood looking at it. There was a worn brown leather wallet, and a plain sealed manila envelope folded in the middle. The end had been torn off and the envelope was empty. Speer had taken it after all . . . and consequently all this that had happened must have been unexpected.

Ben opened the wallet. There were fifty dollars in bills, fives and tens, membership cards in the AAA and two fraternal orders, and a driver's license showing Speer's address as Rittenhouse Street, Takoma Park, Maryland. There was a picture of a sweet-faced middle-aged woman, her arms around two small boys looking down at a picture book open on her lap. The boys' faces were exactly like the face of the man on the seat in front of him.

"Poor little devils," Ben thought. He slipped the wallet and the envelope back into Speer's pocket, went back into the road and stood looking helplessly at the mired car. Its dusty surface was certainly alive with evidence, perhaps definite proof. It was useless up in the hills with no photographers, no finger print experts, none of the paraphernalia of modern crime detection. It would be another hour, perhaps two, before Mike could get there with the sheriff. When he did get there with him nobody would be any forrarder. Not if the sheriff was anything like his neighbors.

Ben walked back along the road. Speer's car was headed away from the Curriers', along the river road, but he could not find any impression of the tires in the damp part of the road behind it. Speer must have come by the river road, not over the ridge as Ben had done. It would indicate that he knew his way better than Ben did. The river road was like a labyrinth without markers, but shorter by five miles if you knew it—unless its dozens of little bridges were washed out by recent rains. No one but the postman ever went that way. And another inconvenience besides losing the way was possible; there was always the danger of a Currier or a Kilgore bullet zinging through the windshield. Loftus had warned him about that when he first came in six months before.

Along the bend by the sycamore tree there were tracks where Speer had backed off the road and turned. He had intended to stop here, then. Ben bent down and looked at the moss by the road. It was spattered with dark brown spots. The leaves low on the alder bushes were streaked with brown.

"They brought his body here and stuffed it in the car," Ben thought. "Then they slid the car off the road into the mud."

He went back towards the Curriers' field, out of the woods along the road. He could see the smoke coming out of the chimney of Currier's workshop across the field, and hear the whirr of the saws and the ringing axes up on the hill where his detail was working on the cedar. As he walked along the road he could see a brown splotch now and then on the purple ironweed or the yellow black-centered daisies. If it had not been for the track of that truck tire they were looking at before they could have seen them then.

He looked down suddenly towards the river. Someone was moving through the corn, back from the direction of the spring. At first he could hardly make out the tall emaciated figure of Old Doss, it was so much the color of the drying corn. He was moving slowly, bent a little. Ben took out his field glasses. Old Doss was carrying a large bundle of some kind. It couldn't be cat-tails, Ben thought. He swept the glasses around to the direction the old man was coming from, and rested it on the level marshy area spiked with the brown heads.

63

"Cat-tails it is," he said to himself. "What in God's name is he picking cat-tails for?"

The primary grades and the Gifte Shoppes were the only places outside swamps that he had ever seen them. It was hard to associate Doss with either. He watched him plod steadily back to his workshop and disappear through the black oblong of the open door.

Ben lowered his glasses slowly. "I'd like to go down there," he thought. He wondered if that rather than Julie could have been Speer's mistake.

He turned sharply at a sudden noise behind him, a curious chilly sensation tingling along his spine. An elder branch moved, the leaves rustled as if a cat had passed through. Ben waited, looking down the road. The leaves parted silently, the thin bruised face of Edrew Mincey peered out, staring loose-mouthed around him. He saw Ben and disappeared. It was exactly like the Cheshire cat, Ben thought; he could still see the vacant stare hovering there in the leaves. He moved on down the road and sat down on a log with his back to the boy, a little puzzled. There was something about Edrew he did not understand. Afflicted—queer turned, they called it in the hills—he nevertheless was not a complete idiot. He knew some things. Ben remembered Ed Loftus's opinion that Edrew was brighter than he looked or Mis' Mincey's fortunes would not hit the mark as well as they often did. Then suddenly he remembered that he had heard Edrew playing, or thought he had, before the two shots the night before.

He looked around at the sound of a low sad thrumming, hardly louder than the air in the corn ribbons. Edrew was hopping slowly, like a sparrow dragging a hurt wing, through the field. Ben watched him making his way towards Old Doss's shop.

He got up and went on down the road looking for the brown splotches. They were more frequent as he went along, and they were larger. He stopped suddenly. At the edge of the road to his right, near a little clump of trampled ox-eyed daisies under a white oak, lay a small red object. He crossed the road and picked it up. It was an emptied shotgun cartridge, and there was a second lying a yard off in the dry leaves under the oak. "We're getting somewhere," he thought. He picked up the hollow red cylinders and put them in his pocket. It was from here that the shots that had killed Speer were fired.

But the dark splashes of blood were across the road. He looked across and down farther than he had gone. Ten yards from him, on the opposite side of the road on the bank of the shallow ditch, two broken stalks of ironweed leaned out.

He went over and looked down. The stagnant water was dark and stained. The scar of a heavy boot was sunk deep in the muddy bank. Ben got down on his hands and knees and peered down at the bottom of the ditch. Speer must have fallen backwards into the shallow trough; the footprint would have been made when they—or he, Ben thought—pulled him out. There was blood in the water and on the near bank, none on the other side. Speer had been standing there, looking down, probably, towards the workshop.

A sudden glint at the bottom of the ditch caught Ben's eye. Something was shining under the stagnant blackened water. He reached down with a stick and worked it up out of the mud. Even before he had it in his hand he saw that it was a shield-shaped badge, on it engraved laconically "United States Treasury Department Agent" and a number.

Ben wiped it off with a faded stalk of the ironweed and held it in his hand looking at it. He looked back up the road to where the black coupé was half hidden in the leaves.

"So you *were* a revenuer," he said to himself. "It wasn't the girl you were after. You were just trying to give her a hand."

He nodded and got to his feet, and stood there. Finally he looked back towards the black coupé again.

"All right, old boy," he said aloud. "We'll make 'em pay up for this."

The blue eyes glinted like icy steel. He walked back up the road.

13

The truck stopped in the cornfield road. Mike jumped out.

"Fairchild's at court," he said. "Loftus's deputy. He's comin' down the hill now with a doctor. They was on my tail all the way over."

The old blue Buick pulled up at the foot of the hill. Loftus got out, followed by a white-haired, tired-eyed old man in an old-fashioned frock coat and frayed starched linen.

Loftus nodded to Ben and looked curiously at the black coupé.

"I reckon you know my cousin, Dr. Corbin, Mr. Davidge," he said. They shook hands, the doctor awkwardly, as if he had forgotten how, it was so long since he had shaken hands with anyone but death, out there in the hills.

"It's Speer," Ben said. "Shannon told you?"

Loftus nodded again.

"Whar is he?"

"In the car. He's been dead for hours."

The two men looked at him.

"Dead?" Loftus said.

"Dead. Shot in the back."

Loftus shook his head.

"That feller said he was shot, didn't say nothin' about him bein' dead. I reckon you come all this way fer nothin', Will. If you'll hold on a mite I'll carry you back."

He turned to Ben.

"A doctor ain't much use if a feller's already dead," he said. His voice had a quiet tone of reproachfulness, as if Ben had allowed a foolish thing to be done.

Ben stifled a quick gust of anger, reminded himself that he had got to remember this was not in Philadelphia. It was out in the hills. People looked at things differently here.

"Since he's here he might as well look at him," he said. He tried to speak as calmly as he could.

"I reckon there ain't no call for you to look, Will," Loftus said imperturbably. "You better rest yerself. You was up all night with Preacher Lane. Ain't no tellin' whose goin' t' be took bad t'night."

By an effort Ben kept himself from saying anything. There was nothing he could do. It was not the first time he had run into the maddening and invincible deliberateness of the mountaineers, their steady clinging to the old ways.

Loftus spat into the dust.

"We only got one doctor between here an' Bradleyville," he said. "We ain't aimin' t' get him wore out 'fore his time."

Ben nodded. "All right," he said. "Come down here, will you?"

He led the way down the road and stopped at the broken stalks of ironweed.

"This is where he was shot," he said. "He fell in the ditch. You can see the blood here. I found this in the mud at the bottom."

He handed Loftus the badge. Loftus looked at it and nodded. "I'd figgered he was a revenuer," he said.

"These two cartridges were across the road, below the oak there. He was shot from the foot of the tree, through the back. He fell in the ditch, or on the near bank here."

He handed the shells over. Loftus turned them over in his hand.

"Law me, you sure been usin' that there head of yourn, Mr. Davidge," he said. He pushed his hat back off his forehead and ran his fingers through his thick iron gray hair, his eyes moving slowly from the white oak to the ditch. A

66

look of bland amusement appeared for an instant in his eyes.

"I reckon some people'd think you was on hand when hit happened."

He looked at the spent shells and tossed them down in the ditch. "I reckon they ain't no further use fer them? You cain't shoot with a used cartridge, now, can you, Mr. Davidge?"

Ben flushed at the drawling calculated irony. "I guess you can't," he said.

Loftus nodded.

"I reckon hit's your idea they carried him along here, where the brown spots air, an' stuck him in his car, an' rolled the car down in the mud," he said. A twinkle appeared again in his shrewd eyes.

Ben nodded. "I think so," he said quietly.

"Maybe so," Loftus said. "Reckon I'll take a look at him."

They went back to the coupé. Loftus stepped on the log, placed a large hand against the rounding top and looked through the window. He stepped back and stood looking at the mired car.

"Reckon you got some rope on that there truck we could pull hit out with?" he said. He shook his head. "Too bad Fairchild ain't here. I'm the dep'ty, but hit ain't a job I crave, gettin' cars out 'a th' mud."

Mike backed the truck out of the cornfield. When the wheels of the coupé were clear of the clinging mud Loftus untied the rope and handed it back. He opened the car door.

"He was a nice feller," he said soberly. "Revenuin's a dangerous business. Allus was, I reckon, an' hit ain't improved none as long's I can remember. Will, I reckon you'll have to help a body out, after all."

Ben turned away. He did not want to see the old doctor's hands unloosening the stiffened joints. He was thinking of the picture in the dead man's pocket.

"Thar he is," Loftus said. "I reckon you could drive him to the mill at th' Crossroads? Lem there'll take care of him till Fairchild gets back, I reckon."

Ben turned back. "I'll drive him," he said. "Look here. Aren't you planning to do anything?"

Loftus ran his fingers through his hair. "Don't reckon there *is* much I can do, Mr. Davidge."

"What I mean is this. Aren't you going to try to find out if anybody heard the shots, or saw the killing?"

Loftus spat thoughtfully at the coupé and nodded deliberately.

"I reckon I know what you're talkin' about," he said. "Different folks have different ways a' doin' things, Mr. Davidge. Now you been doin' a mite a' detectin' fer yerself. Jes' like

67

th' fellers in th' movin' pictures. An' I ain't sayin' hit ain't a good plan."

He took out the box of snuff.

"Hit's your way, now. Up here folks is different. I reckon we don't hold with all these here newfangled ideas. Reckon we don't need to."

He grinned at Ben.

"You could go on with the detectin' fer a week," he said, "an' all you'd find out's what every man an' woman in th' whole country'd know soon's they hear'd about hit. I reckon, till you got through with hit, you'd be about th' only feller in the county didn't know the Curriers killed this here feller Speer."

"Then why don't you arrest them?"

Loftus shook his head patiently.

"They ain't no use in doin' a fool thing like that," he said. He spoke slowly, as if explaining an obvious thing to a little child. "They ain't goin' no place. Don't see's much'd be gained by havin' 'em up in court. Ain't no jury's goin' t' convict a man fer shootin' a feller that's been hangin' round his place fer a week or more. An' I reckon if that there feller turns out t' be a revenuer, hit ain't goin' t' make a heap a' difference to folks up here."

Ben nodded helplessly. He knew it was true.

"What if he'd found a still?" he asked.

Loftus shook his head.

"If you went an' told a jury that a revenuer had found a still in Currier Holler," he said, "they'd sure know you was lyin'. The Curriers is strong temperance. Took the pledge way back, the time after the election, Nate an' Old Doss did, an' Young Doss foller'd 'em afterwards. A parcel of 'em drunk too much an' cut th' tails off'n all old Judge Miller's pigs, an' spent a week in th' jail at Bradleyville. The Curriers is strong temperance. They ain't no still inside miles a' here, Mr. Davidge."

"This man Speer must have been on the trail of something," Ben said quietly.

Loftus spat and nodded. "I reckon hit wouldn't take th' jury five minutes t' decide who hit was he was on th' trail of . . . now you speak of hit."

Ben kept himself from answering.

"Different folks got different ways, Mr. Davidge," Loftus said. He was speaking with a kindly earnestness. "I done my level best t' tell Mr. Speer t' keep away from Currier Holler. I reckon you hear'd me. Anybody could a' told him hit warn't healthy. I told him Nate Currier warn't aimin' t' lose Julie."

68

"It wasn't Nate Currier," Ben said. "He wasn't here when it happened. Nate Currier's gone to Knoxville."

The words were not out of his mouth when the memory of his leaving the Hollow that night came flashing into his mind. There were two dark figures coming up through the cornfield towards the cabin, not one. It was only because he thought Nate Currier was there that he had gone. Yet Julie had said he was not there.

He came out of a trance of bewilderment to find Loftus looking quizzically at him.

"Sure nuff?" he said slowly. "I reckon you must 'a been listenin' t' Mis' Mincey. Reckon they ain't so many people that knew Nate was goin' t' Knoxville."

Ben flushed. "That was a mistake," he thought. Loftus went on.

"Anyhow," he said, "hit don't make no difference where you hear'd hit. They ain't no way a' provin' when Speer was killed, even if you could prove what time hit was Nate Currier lef' th' Holler."

"Dr. Corbin could tell when he was killed, or pretty close to it."

"Maybe he could an' maybe he couldn't. I don't reckon th' jury'd put much stock in that kind a' nonsense. Anyhow, Mr. Davidge, I reckon hit don't matter so much *when* a revenuer's shot as *why* he was. An' I reckon nobody'd put much stock in the idear that th' Curriers was doin' anythin' wrong. Hit jes' ain't like th' Curriers. Nary a soul round thisaway knows Mr. Speer. I reckon everybody knows Nate an' Old Doss, an' th' trouble they've had keepin' their women folks."

He spat slowly with an air of complete finality.

"I reckon you'd jes' as soon drive him over yonder to th' Crossroads? Hit ain't but a little piece."

"Right," Ben said. He opened the car door and turned back. "Just one thing more, Mr. Loftus. Have you got any objections to my notifying the United States Treasury Department about this?"

Loftus shook his head. "I was jes' aimin' to ask you if you'd send a telegram from Bradleyville when you was through this evenin'. I'd shore appreciate hit an' thank you too."

14

It was after three when Ben drove Speer's coupé into the Loftus yard and parked it under the pear tree at the end of the picket fence. He had deposited Speer's body at the Crossroads mill and gone on to Bradleyville to telegraph the Bureau of Investigation, Treasury Department, in Washington. That was done, and there was nothing else he could do. In face of the slow-motion mountaineer indifference he was powerless.

He was tormented with an impotent rage that made him want to cut loose and force somebody to do something—anything, so it was action. If the revolver slung under the Treasury agent's left arm had been drawn out of its holster, if he had even been facing the ambush, there would have been some excuse for the killing. But to empty two charges of buckshot into a man's back was indefensible, by any standards, mountain, plain or coast.

The one thing that he ought to do was perfectly clear to him. He ought to sit tight, keep his mouth shut, do his own work, wait for the arrival of a government agent. He should then put what information he had in his hands and pass out of the picture. It was equally clear to him that that was the one thing he could not possibly do. He was in it. Speer had given him the letter, even if he had changed his mind about it later. But it was not Speer as much as it was Julie Currier. If Speer had thought she was in trouble, and had been willing to compromise his own reputation as a government agent, even to risk his life, in helping the girl to get away from the Hollow, then there must be a reason for doing it that would apply just as well to him.

He got out of Speer's car and into his own, and sat there, trying to figure out some answer to the questions that had kept coming into his mind all day.

What was Speer after? What was so important in Currier Hollow that a Federal agent should wait secretly there night after night? It certainly was not Julie Currier, even if in the end it turned out that the Curriers had thought it was, and if that idea cost Speer his life. Ben wondered suddenly if that explained why he was killed the night Nathan Currier left to go to Knoxville, and wondered again if Nathan Currier had gone to Knoxville, or at any rate had gone before Speer was shot.

In any case, the secret of Currier Hollow remained. Had Speer taken the letter back because he had solved it? Another question, grotesque and trivial, flashed into Ben's mind. What was Old Doss gathering cat-tails for and carrying them by the armful into his workshop? There was still another queer thing: the marks of the truck tire that Mike Shannon had pointed out to him twice in the road. And finally, where was Julie Currier in all this?

The idea of her alone in the Hollow with the two Doss

70

Curriers, young and old, and with her grandfather away, disturbed him. She was safe in one sense . . . in another cruelly and pitifully vulnerable.

He chewed the stem of his pipe and wondered what it was about her that seemed to make people who had work to do quietly give up minding their own business and start meddling in hers. Just a mountain girl who happened to speak English and who combed her hair and washed her face. If she hadn't lived way out in the hills she would have been like every other girl in the world. Ben shook his head.

A big red oil truck lumbered by on the way north. Ben looked at it in the mirror over the windshield. He was staring after it absently when he sat up with a start. For the first time the significance of the empty manila envelope in Speer's pocket occurred to him. The Curriers had taken the letter out of it, from the dead man's pocket. They therefore must have known that Speer had left someone to carry on. Did they know who it was? What had the letter said? Had Speer put his name in it? If he had, could they read or write, for that matter? If they could, and if Speer had included his name in the letter, then that obviously complicated matters.

Ben put his foot on the clutch and hesitated. His detail, trimming the cedar, would be there till four o'clock. It was now twenty minutes past three. He backed into the road and headed towards the Hollow.

At the top of the ridge he edged the car off the road and walked down the hill. The detail was clearing up to lay off for the day. As he came out into the clear road the thin film of smoke from the fire burning forever, and the smoke coming from Old Doss's workshop, were the only signs of life visible to him. The cabin was silent. Kilgore was asleep on the top step. The sun had gone down behind the ridge, early twilight was falling in the Hollow.

He walked down past the cabin and along the lower road until he came to the place where Speer had toppled backwards into the ditch. He got down on his hands and knees. The two red paper shells were still there. He fished them out, sodden with the discolored water, wiped them off on the grass and put them in his pocket. He went back up the road, up the hill through the undergrowth, until he came to a narrow opening in the leafy screen where a tree had fallen. Down below him he could see the gate and the cabin at one end of the Hollow, and the road leading down through the corn to the workshop at the other. He sat down to wait.

He had to assume that Julie had gone back to the loft and was safe there. Nothing would happen to her if the two Curriers were marrying her to Young Doss. Therefore it was

71

the workshop that mattered. Speer's interest had centered on it, it was there that the secret of the Hollow, whatever it was, was to be found. With the field glasses he could see Edrew hopping back and forth across the open door. He seemed to be carrying small pieces of plank. No one else was visible.

The detail left at four. At half-past, Edrew came out of the workshop, took his guitar from a nail on the wall and came hopping painfully up the road through the field, picking lightly at the strings. In the deep quiet of the Hollow Ben could faintly hear the notes. Then they were lost in the shadows of the trees. Doss Currier came out of the door. He stood there a few minutes, looking up at a plane so high above the Hollow that it seemed scarcely moving. Old Doss came out, the two of them moved slowly up behind the yellow corn towards the cabin.

Ben watched them through his glasses in the fading light. Hard, colorless, furrowed, scarcely human, Old Doss came slowly along, shuffling, looking straight ahead of him, until he came to the road. There he stopped and stood, staring down towards the place where they had found Speer. Doss Currier, tall and straight as a sapling oak, stood beside him. Neither seemed to speak. After a long time Doss turned and went on towards the cabin, his father following him.

15

Julie sat in the back room of the cabin, waiting. The hours before her grandfather would come stretched ahead of her, endlessly dark and foreboding. Part of her brain was numb, the part that had tried to think what was in store for her when they found she was not in the loft. There was no use going back up there, they would find the cut ropes.

It was the dead man she was thinking of. He had come back for her . . . and they had been ready for him. She hadn't even warned him that Doss knew a stranger was hanging around.

She got up and went over to the little shelf above the safe. Her mother's Bible was there, between the McGuffey's Blue Backed Speller that belonged to Nathan Currier and an almanac for 1896. She took the Bible and sat down again. She didn't open it. It was too dark to read. She held it in her hands, waiting.

It was almost dark when she heard their slow heavy boots mounting the steps. They moved about the other room, fixing their coffee and ham without saying a word. She could tell what they were doing. Doss was bringing water from the branch. Old Doss was feeding the chickens. She could tell by the sudden flurry of noise in the courtyard. The warm fragrance of coffee and frying ham wafted through the door. After a while she heard Doss come out on the porch, and gripped the book tight in her hand, waiting. He stood in the doorway looking up at the trap door.

"Julie!" he called.

She stood up in front of the fireplace, her eyes great pools in the fading light. The flickering embers smoldering on the everlasting fire threw her pale cheek bones in high relief.

"Yes, Doss."

He stood looking at her a long time.

"He hadn't ought to tied you, Julie," he said finally.

It was the first kind thing he had ever said to her. She blinked back the hot tears stinging her eyelids.

"When's Gran coming back?"

"Tomorrow mornin'."

Doss looked at her silently a moment. "Ol' Doss said I was to go git th' preacher tonight, while Gramp's away," he said slowly.

The embers in the hearth flared up redly a moment and died down again. There was no sound in the dark room. They stood motionless, looking at each other.

On the hill above Ben shifted his position, peering down through the leaves at the cabin, waiting for Julie to come out on the porch. Old Doss came out. Young Doss went down to the branch for a bucket of water. Still Julie did not come. The odor of frying ham stole up the hillside. Ben tightened his belt. After a while Old Doss came out on the porch and sat down in the hickory rocking chair by the steps. In the gathering dusk Ben could see him polishing and cleaning his gun. After that it was too dark to see. No lamp was lighted in the Hollow. He heard the chain on the gate post rattle, and heavy steps grating on the graveled incline. Then the Hollow was silent. He waited for a light to show in the workshop, but no lantern appeared in the dark patch in the field.

At half past ten he got to his feet and came down the hill as noiselessly as he could. Kilgore, prowling in the road outside the gate, growled deep in his full chest. Ben spoke to him quietly. He came up sniffing and thrust his wet muzzle into Ben's hand. The moon was slowly rising over the ridge, the cabin was perfectly silent.

Ben stepped quickly across the hard dirt road into the lane through the cornfield and hurried along the dry soft earth. No sound behind or in front warned him of danger. The horror that Old Doss Currier's workshop was to hold before he was through with it had no sign that went before. He felt none of the nervous tenseness that he had felt only watching the old man methodically cleaning his gun on the cabin steps.

The corn stalks were taller near the river. He kept close to them, moving in the shadow. Around him were the faint noises of the night things. A belated rabbit scampered across in front of him into the bracken, an owl flew past on noiseless wings into the oak tree at the edge of the branch. He came silently out of the road into the clearing in front of the workshop and stood looking around. The moon was clearing the ridge. He could dimly make out a pile of cat-tail stems lying on the ground, their brown candle heads stripped off, near the black oblong of the open workshop door.

He took his flashlight out of his pocket, glanced back for a moment at the cabin, white in the rising moon, and the white weaving strands of smoke from the near chimney, then walked quietly towards the workshop. It was a low log building, with a narrow porch rising one step from the ground, thrown into shadow by the low overhanging roof. On each side of the door were neat piles of sawed boards, and Ben could smell the odor of charred wood. He stepped up on the porch, flashlight in his hand, hesitating a moment; a chance watcher from the cabin could see the beam. The little hut was utterly silent, there was no sound back of him in the Hollow. He felt for the open door with his free hand, groping in the darkness of the porch, found it and stepped over the threshold into the pitchy blackness inside, his foot reaching down until he felt the solid earth.

He raised the flashlight, but before his thumb could move on the switch a small hard circle, cold and deadly, was pressed into his back without a sound.

16

Ben halted abruptly, staring into the warm darkness of Doss Currier's workshop, the cold steel boring into his back. After the first instinctive shock he was cooler than he had ever been in his life, with the dispassionate coolness of the man who knows death hangs in the balance and holds himself taut and controlled to meet it. Furthermore there was nothing else to do.

He stood motionless. There was no sound from behind him.

74

"Well?" he said.

There was no reply. He waited coolly, wondering. The shotgun muzzle on his spine moved slowly to the right of his back and pressed sharply.

"I get you. I'm to turn around and get out?"

He lifted his foot over the raised threshold and turned his head slightly to see if he could see the silent figure behind him. The pressure quickened sharply. He took a step forward. The gun was again hard against his spine. No word had been spoken, none was needed. The command was as plain as it was deadly. For one instant his muscles tensed; then he shook his head. The odds were hopeless.

"Well," he said, "what do you want? What's the idea?"

The pressure increased.

"Is it the idea that I walk ahead and get out?"

The gun prodded twice into his spine, thrusting him forward.

A wave of choking anger swept over him. Then he laughed.

"O.K. I'll be back. Get that straight."

A rough boot grated on the floor of the porch, the gun prodded again. He hesitated, standing there. Suddenly the idea came to him that this was all right, in a sense. The workshop and Julie Currier were apparently separate parts of Currier Hollow, wholly disconnected. He had been caught at the workshop. It might make it easier for Julie than if he had been caught at the cabin again.

Suddenly he grinned cheerfully in the dark.

"If you don't mind," he said, "I think I'll just rush along. See you later."

He took a first deliberate step away from the gun muzzle, holding his breath a little in spite of himself. There was not much point in shooting him out in the open rather than in the workshop. Cleaner, though, he thought suddenly. A sudden vision of the torn back of the Treasury agent flashed into his mind. He looked steadily ahead along the wagon tracks through the cornfield and walked slowly towards the road. At ten yards a charge of buckshot would make a fairly regular pattern, quite circular and just twenty inches in diameter. It would include most of an ordinary man's back, and was not pretty. He downed an impulse to break and run and a second to turn around, and walked as slowly as he could towards the end of the field.

It seemed half an hour and probably was two minutes before he crossed the field into the road. In the shadows he turned and looked back. No one was in sight, the log hut was as silent as before. He hesitated a moment and went on up

75

the hill. The cabin yard as he passed the slope to the gate was quiet, the porch, as far as the moon lighted it under the low roof, was empty. In the shadow of the trees on the hill road he turned around and looked back down into the Hollow. Kilgore was there in the yard, the workshop was there at the end of the cornfield, with the moonlight heavy as frost on its sloping roof. There was nothing else. His eyes rested for a moment on the slow wisps of smoke faintly visible below him.

He turned his car off the road at the Loftuses' and parked at the end of the porch by the geranium tub. Speer's car was still where he had left it. It might have been that other night when Speer gave him the letter. The three cars were there now in the same places. The only difference was that Speer's car was cold and Speer was dead. It came to him with a little shock that this night he had taken Speer's place. It was his car that was hot, he had received a silent but hardly mistakable warning. He wondered if he ought to carry the similarity a little further and write a letter for the next Treasury agent, in case he himself did not show for breakfast the next time he went back to Currier Hollow. Another flash of idle reading came into his mind. A shotgun fired at four yards makes a quite neat pattern six to eight inches in diameter.

He undressed in the dark, opened the window, sank down in the soft feather bed and went to sleep. A shotgun fired against the spine would have made no pattern at all, only a large ragged hole with ruptured edges burned and blackened. He drowsily remembered Ed Loftus's slow voice saying, "Nate Currier ain't aimin' t' lose Julie."

17

He was up and shaved next morning before Miss Elly called him. Loftus came out on the porch to throw a handful of cold water into his eyes and run a wet comb through his thick iron-gray hair.

"You're sure mighty cheerful, Mr. Davidge," he drawled.

Ben broke off whistling and grinned.

"Morning. You look sleepy yourself."

"Reckon I got a call t' be, with my boarders comin' in all hours a' th' night, an' night before comes a night they don't turn up at all. I reckon hit ain't easy fer people t' learn hit ain't healthy fer to stay up late, not in these yere parts. I reckon most of 'em don't learn th' night air ain't healthy till they're so fur gone hit don't make no difference."

His small eyes twinkled shrewdly.

"Hear'd many a feller whistlin' cheerful as a lark when he didn't know what he was aimin' t' get into. But there, I reckon hit's human nater. Comin' t' breakfast, or air you too light-headed t' eat?"

Ben grinned.

"Elly says this feller Sisky was down lookin' fer you, last night. She figgered he had somethin' t' say t' you."

Loftus looked at him quizzically.

"You ain't aimin' t' let anythin' he's got t' say make you quit bein' cheerful, air you, Mr. Davidge?"

Ben grinned again and shook his head. "I think not," he said. But for some reason he could not put a name to he went into breakfast with a strange uneasy feeling he could not throw off.

Miss Elly nodded at him severely.

"Hit's what I allus say," she remarked. "Whistle afore breakfast, cry afore supper."

Loftus shook his head at her. They ate breakfast in silence for the first time since Ben had been there.

He left as soon as he had finished, without waiting for the detail to come by. A red gasoline truck was drawn up at the mill at the Crossroads, blocking the entrance to the gravel road. Ben came to a stop and sounded his horn. Someone was getting down from the cab of the truck. It was a funny thing how much these mountain people traveled back and forth in gas and bread trucks, and a friendly thing. Very few of them had any other means of getting out.

When the truck moved on Ben saw that the man who had got out of it was Nathan Currier. He still wore the checked wool shirt and homespun trousers tucked into his high rough boots, and the tattered black hat. He was carrying a heavy paper bag with a cord handle.

Ben sent the car forward twenty feet and stopped beside him.

"Hello, Mr. Currier," he said. "Going up to the Hollow? Can I give you a lift?"

Nathan Currier turned a slow bewildered, even startled, gaze on him. He stared suspiciously a moment. Then his eyes lighted faintly.

"Thank ye kindly," he said. He got in, very gingerly, like a child getting into a fascinating but dangerous contraption, and held tightly to the door strap, watching Ben anxiously.

"Ain't never rid in one a' these yere but twicet afore," he said in his curious sing-song, when they had started. "Ain't been away from th' Holler fer two year now. Used t' go t'

77

Court oncet a year till the rheumatiz got me all crippled up."

"Does your brother go?"

"I reckon Old Doss ain't been out a' th' Holler fer nigh thirty year."

Ben remembered what Loftus had said. "Not since he shot Jess Kilgore's boy," he thought.

"Young Doss, he goes off'n on," the old man said. His voice increased and diminished in volume like an accordion that had not been used for many years. "I ain't been t' Knoxville since th' hard times in 19 an' 11."

"Most of the young fellows like Doss have got out of the mountains, I guess," Ben said. "Especially now. They're all working for the TVA."

Currier nodded.

"Doss he ain't never wanted t' leave th' land," he said.

They were passing the tumble-down cabin with the gourd vine sprawling over the step.

"I see the Blisses have gone already," Ben said. Nate Currier nodded slowly.

"They tell me they gave him twenty hunderd dollars fer his place, but his debts et hit all up, an' he ain't got none left t' buy no more land with."

"He's still got his thousand dollar homestead right. They can't take that away from him."

"I reckon maybe he didn't know about that," Currier said. "They's a heap a' things folks don't know about till hit's too late." His eyes were fixed unseeing on the parched rain-guttered fields.

They drove in silence past the meeting-house at the bend. Ben stole a glimpse at the furrowed grizzled old face beside him. Nathan Currier did not look savage . . . only old and lost and a little tragic. It was that that gave Ben the courage he needed. He breathed deeply and made up his mind to it.

"I had a talk with your granddaughter yesterday," he said.

Currier let go the door strap and turned his glittering black gaze full on him.

"You war talkin' with Julie?" he demanded hoarsely.

Ben nodded coolly. He apparently had not realized, it seemed, how unorthodox such a proceeding would appear to the old man. There was nothing to do but go on with it.

"She said she'd always wanted to go to school," he said. "And see the world. It occurred to me you might be willing for her to have a go at it before she marries and settles down."

Nathan Currier shook his head.

"Julie ain't ever goin' t' settle down. Julie's like her ma an' her gran'ma. They warn't made t' live hard. That's what killed th' life out a' them."

He stopped a moment and went on awkwardly.

"I never seed hit till Julie commenced growin' up. I ain't never let her work in th' fields. Maybe I been hard on her other ways, but I done th' best I knowed."

Ben hesitated a moment. There was no use beating about the bush.

"Would you let her go to Philadelphia to visit my mother?" he said. "She'd like to have her. After a while she'd probably want to come back . . . and marry Doss."

He said it in as matter of fact a way as he could.

"Julie ain't goin' ever t' want t' marry Doss," Nate Currier said slowly. "She don't now, when she ain't never seed another feller. She ain't likely t' change her mind. Julie's hard-headed as a mule."

"Then I should think it would be a mistake to force her to marry him. She'll just run away." He glanced at the grizzled old man. "The way her mother did."

Currier took it without offense.

"Her gran'ma too, she run off. We ain't never let Julie know they run off, but I reckon they don't have t' have nobody show 'em th' way if hit's in their blood."

He was silent, as if he had thought it over so many times that there wasn't any more to say.

"When you leave the Hollow, she won't have anybody to run to," Ben said.

"She ain't got nobody to look to, if anythin' was t' happen t' me."

"Why not let her go see my mother? You can look us up. Judge Winters at Bradleyville can do it for you. Mother would come down and get her."

No other possible conduct on the part of his mother occurred to Ben. That was the sort she was.

Nathan Currier turned his head and looked at Ben a long time. The glittering black eyes searched his face, bewildered, deeply troubled, as if he did not understand.

Ben ran the car off the road and stopped it. He turned to face the old man. Nate Currier's bewildered gaze traveled slowly over the bronzed clean-cut face and firm strong jaw, and bored for a long moment into the frosty intelligent eyes that met his without wavering. Then he looked away, rubbing his knotted hand trembling across his face, shaken with emotion, his head bent forward on his breast.

The CCC truck came around the bend and passed them, gathering speed for the hill. Mike leaned out of the cab and waved. Looking out, Ben saw his face change suddenly as he saw Nathan Currier bent forward in the seat. The CCC detail, shouting and waving, suddenly stopped and stared silently. Ben paid no attention to them. The idea did not for an instant enter his head that this too was a part of the chain of evidence being forged about him with damning tenacity.

He sat there waiting. Nate Currier looked up after a long time. Ben was hardly able to believe the change he saw in the old man's face. The glittering eyes were wet with tears, the hard furrowed cheeks and stern iron lips had softened.

"Would ye do that fer Julie, Mr. Davidge?" he asked huskily.

"Sure. We'd be glad to. She's too nice a person just to . . . to trample down."

Currier repeated the words slowly. "Trample down." He nodded. "That's what we did to 'em, Aggy an' Big Julie. Trampled 'em down like they was hogweed."

He shook his grizzled head. "I don't know what Old Doss'll say."

Ben started the car and drove up the hill. They both knew what Old Doss would say, and Ben had a pretty good idea what Young Doss would say too.

"Would you have to tell him?" he asked.

"I'd have to tell Old Doss."

At the top of the ridge, looking down into the Hollow, Ben suddenly remembered.

"I forgot to tell you," he said. "A man—a revenuer, Speer —was shot down the road here, night before last."

He turned and looked squarely at Currier. There was no doubt that Nate had left the Hollow before Ben had heard the two shots, and that he had only imagined he had seen two dark figures crossing through the cornfield. Nathan Currier turned quickly and stared at him, his mouth dropping open. He wetted his snuff-stained lips. Ben did not understand the horror in his eyes until he made out the whispered syllables.

"Whar's Julie?"

He knew then that Nate Currier was afraid, for Julie; and he sensed for the first time that it was Old Doss he feared.

"She's all right. At least she was yesterday."

Currier sat erect in the seat, moistening his lips, his hands trembling. They went down the hill and clear of the trees overhanging the path into the open road in front of the cabin gate. Ben heaved a sigh of relief as he jammed on the brakes. Julie Currier was standing on the porch. He heard her cry of delight as she flew down the steps and across the courtyard, starry-eyed and breathless, to meet her grandfather.

The old man leaned back a moment in the seat, then struggled blindly with the door. Ben opened it.

"Good-by, Mr. Currier," he said.

18

He parked the car at the foot of the hill and walked up the cleared trail to join the detail. If he had been less preoccupied with the four people down in the cabin yard he would have noticed that the CCC boys were quieter today. The shouting and wisecracking were gone. A curious uneasiness seemed to hang over them. Sisky was not there. Ben did notice that and wondered where he was. He did not see the questioning earnestness in Dave Phinney's blue eyes or the curious glance that Mike Shannon gave him as he came up.

It was nearly lunch time when he stopped to look at an oddly-shaped knotty branch that Phinney was lopping off a big branch near the butt of the tree. He stooped and picked it up. It occurred to him that it would make an offering for the Currier fire. When the detail knocked off for lunch he went down the hill with it under his arm.

Kilgore thwacked the ground with his tail and looked at him hopefully. Nathan Currier and Old Doss were sitting on the porch, Young Doss was nowhere in sight. Julie was coming up from the spring house. They met at the bottom of the steps. The color deepened in her pale lovely face and she smiled. Ben was acutely aware of the two pairs of ancient eyes watching them. He looked down at the jug of cold buttermilk in her arm.

"Hello, Julie," he said. "Carry it for you?"

She shook her head quickly and hurried past him to the kitchen porch.

Ben held out the heavy cedar knot. "I brought this down for your fire," he said.

The old man made no move to take it. He sat perfectly still, staring at Ben with strange hostile eyes. For a moment Ben wondered if the morning's event had really happened, not four hours ago. Then he looked past Nate Currier and saw Old Doss shift his colorless eyes from the piece of wood he was whittling and rest them for an instant on him with silent concentrated hatred. In that moment's glance there was all the venom of a nest of copperheads.

Ben tossed the cedar knot onto the pile of wood on the ground against the rough stone chimney and brushed off his hands.

"My mistake, I guess," he said. He started down the steps. Before he had moved Nate Currier's slow voice stopped him. He looked up again. The same hostile eyes were fixed steadily on him.

"I'm an ig-norant man, Mr. Davidge," Nathan Currier was saying. "I only got one book. I reckon you ain't never seed hit, have ye?"

Ben looked at him curiously. "I don't know. What is it?"

"Julie, git my book."

Ben heard her quick step on the bare cabin floor and looked up expectantly. Old Doss's mouth hardened to a thin bitter line. He got slowly to his feet. As Julie started to come through the door he thrust her back and took the book out of her hands. He handed it to Nate and leaned back against the pine door frame, silent, hardly human, Ben thought; more like an evil scarecrow come to life. Ben flushed, realizing that there must have been some kind of eager anticipation in his own eyes. He looked at Nate Currier. He had taken a pair of thick-lensed spectacles with heavy silver rims from a battered tin case in his pocket and put them on. He turned the pages of the tattered blue-covered book with awkward unaccustomed fingers until he came to the place he wanted.

"I reckon you kin read that, Mr. Davidge?" he asked. He handed Ben the book. There was no smile on Ben's face as he saw it was McGuffey's Fifth Reader and read the title of the story Nathan Currier held open to him. It was called "Meddlesome Tom." Ben read it through with Nate Currier's glittering eyes fastened on his face. He had heard the story before. Theodore Roosevelt had used the part about Meddling Sally in an early campaign. The moral was simple. There is nothing but grief for people who meddle in other people's business. It was Nathan Currier's way of telling him to mind his own business and let theirs alone.

Ben read it carefully, wondering about it and the old man's sudden change. Was it because of his hopeless and unfortunate trip to the workshop the night before? Because he had cut Julie loose? Or was it the letter taken out of the manila envelope in Speer's pocket?

He closed the book and handed it back, meeting the old man's sardonic glance with a steady gaze.

"They was an eddicated woman here from th' East last spring," Nathan said. "I showed her that book, an' when she left she said, 'I thought you said you was an ig-norant man.' "

Ben smiled.

"I never thought you were an ignorant man, Mr. Currier," he said quietly. "I thought you were an honest one."

The smile on Currier's face faded to slow angry surprise.

Ben turned and strode across the dirt yard. He was annoyed not so much at Currier's having put him neatly in his place with a moral tale out of a blue-backed speller as at himself for laying himself open to such treatment. This was the sort of a joke that would go the length of the valley in two days. And it wasn't that he minded that so much. What had Nate Currier heard since he got out of the car and went into the cabin? How was it going to affect Julie Currier . . . before Saturday night? He remembered the promise he had made to her here by the gate.

He laughed suddenly in spite of himself. The night before he had been routed with a shotgun pressed into his spinal column, now with a blue-backed speller thrust into his hands. It would now appear, he thought ruefully, that in setting out to help the Currier girl he had succeeded in making enemies of all three of the Curriers.

Outside the gate he lighted his pipe and strolled down to the spring under the sycamore tree. The gourd cup had fallen to the ground. He picked it up to rinse it off and stopped, listening. A car was coming over the ridge above the cabin. He turned back. It was probably someone from Norris to look over the cedar again. He stood in the road waiting. The long dried form of Old Doss was moving deliberately through the field towards the shop. Ben glanced at the cabin. Nate Currier was sitting on the porch, Julie standing beside him. Both of them were looking up, waiting for the car to come out of the wooded hill road.

Ben recognized the old Buick before he saw who was in it. As it stopped at the incline by the gate Loftus and another man got out. They came towards him.

"Howdy," Loftus said. "Mr. Davidge, make you acquainted with Mr. Wade, from Washington. He's come out thisaway t' see about Mr. Speer."

Loftus spat thoughtfully between his solidly planted feet. Ben shook hands with a middle-aged, sandy-haired man with cold eyes. He had a firm jaw and a quiet manner, much like the dead Treasury agent's.

"I been tellin' him you an' Speer was right friendly," Loftus said. "I reckon maybe you can tell him what happened better'n any a' th' rest of us."

Ben looked at him. He wondered if he was being taken for another ride, or if the blue-backed speller was making him as suspicious as all the rest of them.

He watched Loftus take the chain off the gate post and turned back to meet the cool scrutiny of the Treasury agent standing beside him. Mr. Wade had very bright and very sharp eyes, and there was no gleam of friendliness in them.

"You're a forester with the CCC," he said. He had a flat indefinite accent that placed him anywhere above the Mason-Dixon line. "Cold," Ben thought. He nodded.

"You found Speer?"

"Down the road here, by the spring."

"Shot in the back, from behind a tree?"

Ben pointed down the road to the oak. "He fell backwards in the ditch there, by that dead stalk of ironweed."

The icy eyes shifted from Ben's face to the tree, across the road, back across the yellow field to the workshop. He hesitated a moment and nodded at it.

"Been down there?"

"Last night. Somebody was down there with a shotgun. Old Doss is my guess. I came away."

A cold light flickered in the agent's eyes for an instant.

"Who's Old Doss?"

"The old man's brother. It might have been Young Doss, only I think he'd have fired. The Curriers don't like meddlers. They told me so again this morning."

Wade nodded. "Most of these people don't."

"By the way," Ben said coolly, "would you mind telling me what the devil's down there? Loftus says there's no still here, the Curriers are temperance."

"So he said."

"Then what was Speer after? Or was he a meddler too?"

Wade looked at him. He had an abrupt trick of darting his bleak gray eyes from side to side without changing the position of his head that gave him an alert watchful air. There was something abnormally impersonal about him.

"Where's the letter of instructions he gave you?"

So Loftus knew that too, Ben thought. Crafty old fox.

"He took it back again. The envelope was in his pocket when I found him."

Wade's lips hardened.

"Did Loftus tell you about that?"

"No."

Wade's answer was brief and final. Ben got the idea. His job was to supply information, not to ask for it.

"How long have you been down here?"

"A little over six months."

"Where from?"

"Philadelphia."

The agent looked sharply at him. Ben thought he looked a little surprised.

"You know Pete Hromanik?"

Ben had not thought before that it was to be a social chat. He shook his head. "No. Friend of yours?"

A sudden flicker lighted Mr. Wade's face again. It seemed to be the nearest he came to showing amusement.

"Oh, yes," he said. The eyes darted around, focused steadily on Ben. "Your home's in Philadelphia?"

Ben nodded.

"Look here," he said abruptly. "Did Speer expect to get killed down here? What did he give me the letter for?"

Wade looked at him silently for several seconds. "You know as much about it as I do," he said curtly. "The letter ought to tell us."

Ben flushed. "I tell you it's gone."

"Then I guess we won't ever know."

Wade looked down the road, at the workshop, up at the cabin.

"What about the Curriers?" Ben said doggedly. "Are you going to take 'em in?"

The agent turned back. "Not till I find out whether they killed Speer or not."

"Loftus told me I'd be the only man in the county that didn't know they did."

"That's what a fellow named Kilgore told me. If they did we'll get them. We've got laws with teeth in 'em now. It's closed season on Federals."

Wade hesitated a moment. "What makes you think they shot him?"

"Doss Currier and his father were the only ones around. Nathan was in Knoxville."

Wade shook his head coolly. He hesitated again.

"What about this half-wit. Can he shoot?"

Ben stared at him. "I shouldn't think so," he said. He realized instantly that he had no reason for thinking anything about it, one way or another.

"You don't think so?" The light flickered in Wade's eyes again. "Well, Kilgore tells me he's a crack shot. One of the best in the county."

"I didn't know it," Ben said stiffly. "Anyway, he can't shoot with a guitar. He didn't have a gun when I saw him, a little while before."

"A little while before what?"

The Treasury agent spoke sharply. Ben flushed. There was something about Wade's manner that made everything he said not only incriminating but downright stupid.

"Before Speer was shot. I was here in the Hollow. I saw Edrew. I didn't see Speer."

"You were here? In the Hollow? Where were you?"

Ben told him. When the two shots sounded in the night he was in his car at the top of the ridge.

Wade nodded. "And you're the man who just told me Old Doss and his son were the only people around here," he said sardonically. "Seems to me you spend a lot of time down here yourself, Mr. Davidge. Who else did you see?"

Ben flushed angrily. Wade did not appear to notice it. His eyes had shifted to the cabin porch, where Nathan Currier and Loftus were talking. Julie was standing for a moment by the kitchen door. She went in as Ben followed the agent's glance.

"Who else did you see?"

"Miss Currier. A fellow from camp. His name is Raymond Sisky."

Wade darted a quick glance at him.

"Anybody else?"

"No."

"Sure?"

"No. There might have been somebody else. I wasn't sure. I thought at first it was Nate Currier, before I knew he was in Knoxville."

The semblance of a wintery smile showed in Wade's eyes for an instant. He looked at his watch. "I'll be getting on," he said. "See you tonight. I'm staying at Loftus's place."

He started towards the cornfield road.

"If you're going to that workshop, I'd like to come along," Ben said.

Wade stopped and turned back. "It wouldn't interest you," he said. He went on and turned again. "It's not a still. Speer knew that."

He nodded coolly and went on through the corn. Ben stared after him a moment. He grinned. "O.K., brother," he thought. "But don't you go passing me any secret letters."

He heard a voice calling him and turned. Loftus was leaning against the Curriers' gate, beckoning to him. He went down the little gravel slope.

"I been talkin' t' Nate," Loftus said slowly. "I was tellin' him you was friendly with this feller Speer, an' you didn't mean no harm by last night."

He shook his head soberly and spat through the rails.

"Law me, Mr. Davidge, I reckon you sure ought t' know by now folks up thisaway ain't cravin' t' have people prowlin' round all night. Seems like you ought t' know better'n that. Well, I was talkin' to him, an' I reckon if I was you I'd go 'long an' have a cup a' buttermilk with 'em. I don't reckon you'll get airy thing stronger."

Ben grinned. "I had that dog set on me once," he said. "No, thanks."

Loftus chuckled. "That Kilgore's a smart dawg," he said.

He spat again. "Well, suit yerself. Reckon I'll go up an' look at that there tree while I'm waitin' fer Mr. Wade. Comin' along?"

Ben looked at the cabin. Julie was standing on the porch looking down at them.

"No," he said.

Loftus chuckled again. "Julie's shurnuff gittin' right purty," he said. "Some'd say a mite scrawny."

<h1 style="text-align:center">19</h1>

Ben crossed the dirt yard between the corn crib and the low stable. Julie was standing on the porch, the sun shining on her smooth gold hair. Her eyes were deeply troubled. So were Nathan Currier's.

"Set down, Mr. Davidge," he said. "We'll be friendly with ye."

It was very direct and simple, and it contrasted oddly with the black suspicion and hostility of less than an hour before. Ben wondered if Old Doss would relent as easily as his brother had done.

"Thank you," he said. He sat down on the top step. The spare wiry figure of the United States Treasury agent was half-way down the lane to the workshop.

"Hit was mighty nice of ye to bring down that there knot," Nate Currier said slowly. "Hit makes a right purty fire, less'n a body was t' feel he didn't have no heart burnin' hit, hit's stood thar so long."

Ben nodded, puffing tranquilly at his pipe. None of them spoke for a while.

"If they say Old Doss kilt the revenuer," Nate said abruptly, "they ain't sayin' th' truth."

Ben looked at him, surprised.

"He never done hit, Mr. Davidge."

Ben glanced at Julie. She was standing with hands folded in front of her, looking out across the cornfield. He wondered what she was thinking. When she felt his eyes on her she looked down without smiling. Her eyes were shuttered, remote.

"Old Doss he says he was most to the end a' the road when he hear'd th' shots," Nate Currier said. His voice rose and fell, harsh and grating.

Ben grinned suddenly. "Didn't know he could talk," he said.

"He don't talk much. Don't never talk t' strangers."

"Uncle Doss doesn't like strangers much," Julie said.

Nate Currier shook his head slowly. "He never kilt th' revenuer."

No one spoke again for a moment. The bees in the honeysuckle hummed drowsily, a chicken, encouraged by the silence, came hopping up the steps and wandered into the house. Both Julie and her grandfather were completely at ease. Only civilization made people unfit for silence, Ben thought. He wanted to ask, What about Young Doss? but it didn't seem quite the thing. After all, Wade had strongly suggested that he could keep out.

"Have you decided anything about leaving the Hollow, Mr. Currier?" he asked.

Nate shook his head.

Ben wondered if he could ask whether Julie was to be allowed to go to Philadelphia. He supposed that was probably out.

"Would you like to live in town?" he said.

"I ain't goin' no place without takin' my fire with me."

They sat in silence again, in the hot afternoon sun, with the drowsy bees and the clang of axes from the hill pulsing in their ears. It was very pleasant, sitting there. Ben had no desire to move. But they sat so long without speaking that he thought they must be waiting for him to go. He pulled himself back out of a warm golden haze and got up.

"I'll have to be getting along," he said.

Nathan Currier raised his head as if he had come back from a long journey somewhere.

"Why don't you walk a piece with Mr. Davidge, Julie?" he said slowly.

She stared at him, eyes wide, as if she couldn't believe what she had heard. So did Ben. He recovered quickly and turned to her with a smile.

"Please do," he said. She shook her head.

"Are you feeling all right, Gran?" she asked anxiously, bending down to look in his face.

"I thought you'd like t' walk a little piece, Julie," he said gruffly. He picked up a piece of wood and began whittling.

Julie's cheeks flushed. "All right," she said, perplexed and a little uneasy. "I'll go to the gate with you."

Ben looked at Nathan Currier. His eyes were fixed on the stick he was whittling, his hands trembling a little. Kilgore got to his feet and ambled after them, savaging a flea on his back as he came.

Neither of them spoke until they got to the gate and Ben lifted the chain from the post.

"Did your grandfather tell you I asked him if you could go to Philadelphia to visit my mother?" he asked.

"He told me. I'd like to go," she said. She looked up quickly at a tiny plane soaring through the blue field above them. "It's like wanting to go in an airship. It ain't for me."

The poignant longing in her eyes raised to the sky surprised Ben. He had been thinking of her as a child who was in a bad spot. Just now there was something extraordinarily mature in the tragic acceptance of the fact that the struggle was useless.

"Has anything happened, Julie?" he said.

She shook her head.

"No. It's just because it's like you said . . . it's going against my own people for me to go."

Ben was surprised to find himself annoyed.

"Now, listen," he said. "I told you it was against your people for you to run off in the middle of the night with a man you'd never seen before. Going to Philadelphia with my mother's different. What does your grandfather say?"

"He says maybe I could go. But . . . well, it's because I just didn't know before."

"Didn't know what?"

"I didn't know about my mother running off like she did. She ran off, with a man. That's why they've been alone here in the Hollow. It wouldn't be right for me to leave them too."

"Who told you all that, Julie?"

"Doss. He told me last night. He came to untie me and he didn't tell Old Doss I wasn't tied. He made believe I was."

Ben thought about it. It didn't sound like Doss.

"He told me Old Doss wanted him to go for the preacher then, while Gran was away."

She spoke softly and almost mechanically, looking out over the yellow corn, as if hardly aware of his presence, it seemed to him.

"He said, 'I don't reckon I'd do that. You wouldn't be so mean as to leave me when the only reason I stayed here was so I could have you when you'd growed up.' Then he told me about my mother, and about Gran's not making me do anything like the other girls had to do. He said it would kill Gran if I was to go off."

"But you'll be back."

She shook her head.

"That ain't—isn't—it."

A twisted little smile trembled for an instant in the corners of her mouth.

"I reckon I might as well say 'ain't' like the rest of them.

That isn't it. Doss said he didn't want to stay with me hating him, and Gran needed me the most. So he's gone away."

"Doss?"

She nodded. "So you see I couldn't go now."

Ben filled his pipe and folded his oilskin pouch up very slowly. There was something wrong. He had seen Doss Currier just twice, at close hand; but his giving up and wandering off sounded very fishy. He wondered about it. A Federal agent had been shot in the Hollow, another was on the job there now, investigating. Doss might very well have a sensible reason, quite apart from Julie Currier, for not being on hand. He lighted his pipe, flicked the match over the fence, and looked down at the unhappy face beside him, thinking with still more annoyance that for some reason all this seemed to mean more to him than it had any right to mean.

"It's up to you, Julie," he said. "Don't give up in a hurry."

He wanted to say more, but across the waving corn tassels he could see Old Doss's battered hat moving up towards the cabin from the workshop.

"Good-by," he said. "You ask Mr. Currier about it."

He went up the slope to the road. Loftus had joined Wade and Old Doss on their way up from the shop. There was nothing in Wade's attitude that showed any change from the cold dispassionate watchfulness that Ben had seen before. He had a narrow oak board in his hand, rudely hollowed out in the center, tapering a little at each end. Old Doss Currier was walking a step or two behind him, staring sullenly at the ground. Ben stood aside to let them pass. Old Doss lifted his short white lashes and looked full at him before he went on with the others. Ben stood in his tracks for an instant, then wiped the fine beads of cold sweat off his forehead and moistened his lips. He had seen hatred, suspicion and fear gleaming utterly naked in the dead eyes of the old man, twitching his sunken lips and dry skeleton fingers. The idea of Lazarus came into his mind. He shivered involuntarily. Someone walking over his grave, Mrs. Kilgore would say. Ben knew it was fear. Fear for Julie Currier when those obsessed eyes would turn on her and the horny yellow fingers fasten in her soft flesh.

He tried to shake it off. "I'm crazy," he thought. "She's been in the same house with him for eighteen years. She's bound to be safe."

He suddenly realized that a deep paralyzing conviction had come to him that some terrible fate, horrible because unknown, was walking close with the girl in that lonely Hollow, and that the gaunt knotted figure of her grandfather was

90

all that was keeping it from her. He shook his head impatiently, but the idea haunted him still. Speer had known it too. Ben looked down at the workshop, and back at the cabin. If only Wade wasn't such a cold fish, he thought. He took his pipe out of his mouth and put it in his pocket.

Mike Shannon was coming down the hill in the truck. He stopped it, leaned out of the cab, looking curiously at him. The flat wet end of a rolled cigarette drooped out of the corner of a mouth set crooked in a battered face.

"Somethin' screwy, Mr. Davidge?"

Ben nodded. "Plenty."

"Count me in—on your side," Mike said out of the free corner of his mouth.

"Thanks."

"Particularly if you need anybody to hang one on that berry Sisky. There's plenty of candidates, but I'm the guy."

Ben scowled. He had forgotten Sisky.

"I guess I shut him up awhile myself," he said.

Mike shook his head a little. Ben looked at him.

"What's up?" he asked.

Mike shook his head again and shrugged his shoulders. "I ain't made out exactly, but it's somethin'. Boys 'a been actin' queer. Talkin' round. Dave says Sisky told him he was talkin' to a Fed this mornin' after breakfast."

Mike's face was sober.

"You gimme the office, Mr. Davidge, and I'll turn his white belly up. That guy's a rat."

"Thanks," Ben said. He wondered what all this meant. "I'll call on you if I need anybody."

"O.K., Mr. Davidge."

The truck went on. Ben went back to his car and drove out across the fields. Loftus's Buick was gone. An old Ford with "U. S. Mail" painted on it was standing in its place. The carrier was coming out of the Curriers' gate. He stopped.

"Howdy," he said. "I reckon Jess Kilgore'll be leavin' th' next."

He patted his bag.

"Carryin' him a gover-ment letter, an' when they git their letter, I reckon hit means they're aimin' t' go right soon."

"I suppose the Curriers will be going pretty soon too."

"Reckon so. Them Curriers sure can well afford hit. I reckon most of 'em wisht they had th' money them Curriers got. Some several think they's the richest ones round yere. Been saltin' hit away a mighty long time. So's I reckon they don't have t' worry none 'bout where they're goin'."

He interrupted himself to spit.

"How's the river road?" Ben asked.

"Fair. Leastwise as fur's Jess Kilgore's. Ain't so much down yonder t'other side a' th' school house."

He climbed in his car and rattled off down the rough wagon road. After a little Ben followed him. He looked back to wave to Julie, but Old Doss was dipping water out of the oak bucket on the back stoop.

20

What it was precisely that drew him to the Kilgores' that afternoon Ben could not have told. Œdipus complex, he said to himself. He grinned at the idea of comparing his mother with Mrs. Kilgore, big-boned, broad-hipped, rough-handed. You could just as well compare a Watteau lady with an Epstein primal mother. Yet they were alike, subtly alike, for under their environmental differences both of them were wise strong women, gentle and understanding and courageous. Somewhere in the back of his head Ben had a vague notion that perhaps Mrs. Kilgore could help about Julie. She knew the Curriers, she had known Julie's mother.

He was so engrossed with the idea that he did not see Loftus's Buick parked in the Kilgore road until he came almost even with it. He was still too used to cars to notice one at a distance. The absence of them on the mountain roads was a sort of unconscious relief, and he had not been in the mountains long enough to think of the presence of one as an event.

It was too late for him to wave and drive on when he saw Wade and Loftus sitting on the porch. The Kilgores had seen him before he passed the tobacco barn on the lower road.

"Laws, hit's Mr. Davidge."

A smile of welcome beamed on Mrs. Kilgore's broad kindly face.

"Howdy, Mr. Davidge. You ain't been here fer a month a' Sundays, I do declare. Hunt yerself a seat."

Wade was eating an apple, peeling it carefully with a pocket knife, carving the shiny red skin into even spirals. He threw a piece of it into the yard and watched the chickens scrambling for it, without appearing to hear Mrs. Kilgore's surprise and pleasure at seeing Ben after so long a time.

"Thinks I'm following him," Ben thought. "Or why would I pick out today of all days to come here."

Loftus nodded to him as he came up.

"Cass was sayin' as how you'd got your letter from th' gover-ment today," he said, spitting into the flock of chickens.

Jess Kilgore's placid face lighted with annoyance.

"He ain't been by thisaway yet this evenin'," he said.

"I passed him up at Farrell's Crossroads," Ben said. "Ten minutes ago."

"Reckon everybody'll know about th' letter afore we git hit," Mrs. Kilgore said. "They tell me Farrells air aimin' t' leave next week. Well, if gover-ment seed things as I see 'em, they'd not leave Mis' Farrell sign no papers till they'd bought another piece a' land for 'em. They won't be a penny left when Joe Farrell comes back from Knoxville Sat'day night."

"Air you fixed on where you all air goin', Sairy?" Loftus asked.

Both the Kilgores sat silently looking across the road beyond the pasture to the little cemetery this side of the cornfields up the side of the ridge.

"We figgered we had six hunderd acres left, after we'd got shed a' what Sairy's pappy give us," Jess Kilgore said. "Th' way gover-ment measures hit, we ain't go much over four hunderd fifty. We cain't buy four hunderd fifty acres a' land as good's ourn fer less'n a hunderd an' fifty dollar an acre. They ain't givin' us near that. They ain't countin' the mineral rights. I could 'a got $25,000 five year ago fer th' mineral rights on th' ridge, if hit hadn't been fer that low-down Nate Currier holdin' up till gover-ment stepped in an' says they're buildin' a dam."

"Does the water come this far?" Wade asked.

"Hit comes jes' above Sairy's beehives yonder on th' hill," Kilgore said. He pointed to the row of neat white boxes against the rock. "I said couldn't I move up on the ridge, but they said no. I reckon they're after th' mineral rights fer theirselves."

He rocked back and forth.

"I reckon Sairy an' me we'll be in the pore house afore hog killin' time."

Mrs. Kilgore's broad gentle face flushed. She picked up an apple and wiped it on her checked apron.

The Treasury agent finished his apple and wiped off the blade of his knife between his thumb and forefinger. "See many trucks pass this way, Mr. Kilgore?" he asked.

Kilgore did not answer for a while.

"Some several was by thisaway last week," he said at last. He turned in his chair, facing Wade directly. "Hit ain't healthy goin' round askin' questions up in these parts," he drawled. "I reckon they ain't never been so many folks meddlin' in other folks' business as been round thisaway lately. I reckon you knowed this yere feller Speer?"

Wade nodded.

"Reckon he wisht he'd stayed in Washington."

Wade's eyes glinted. "I guess people that aren't doing anything wrong don't have anything to worry about," he said coolly.

Ben got up. "I'll be running along," he said abruptly. He liked Jess Kilgore, and he did not like Wade particularly. If Wade wanted to get all of them sore at him it was his affair.

Mrs. Kilgore walked down to the car with him. Her face was troubled. When they were out of earshot of the men on the porch she said, "This feller Speer, that was kilt—he war a revenuer, warn't he?"

Ben nodded. She pleated the hem of her apron with her big toil-roughened fingers, looking dumbly at him, wanting painfully to speak, not knowing what to say. Ben smiled and got in the car. She put her hand on the window ledge.

"Don't you go traipsin' round, nights," she said earnestly. "Hit ain't safe fer nobody, Mr. Davidge. Man air cruel hard things when they been wronged. I reckon they don't look ahead none to what's comin' hereafter."

She turned away abruptly, but when Ben looked in the windshield mirror she was still standing there looking after him. Beyond her the mail carrier's old Ford was rattling up the lower road.

"Poor devils," Ben thought.

He stopped suddenly, a quick bird-like movement in the elderberry bushes at the side of the road catching his eye. He saw the black head and pale staring blue eyes of Edrew Mincey there, crouching down behind the bending purple clusters.

"Hello!" he said. "Edrew!"

The boy got to his feet and hopped out of the bushes, his white vacant face still discolored, yellow, where Sisky's fist had caught him. His guitar hung down from his neck. Ben suddenly realized he had not heard him, near or far, for a couple of days.

He pointed to the guitar. "What's the matter?"

The boy held it up silently. The strings were snapped. He turned it over in his thin hands. The fragile wood was shattered as if a heavy fist had gone through it. Edrew's loose lips hung open; his vacant stare rested on the ruined guitar and moved off over the fields. His fingers plucked soundlessly, went limp when no sound came.

"Want me to take you home?" Ben asked.

Edrew stared at him, then hopped off and disappeared in the thick stand of corn. Ben watched the moving yellow ribbons ripple as he passed under. He remembered suddenly hearing Edrew after that night at the gate. It was after he had found Speer's body the next morning.

94

"Probably fell down and knocked a hole in it," he thought. But something troubled him.

He stopped at Loftus's to clean up, and got in his car again. There was something he wanted to get for Julie. The forty miles to Knoxville was a short ways to go for it. As he passed he waved at Mis' Mincey. She was sitting in front of her little white store, rocking back and forth. Edrew was lying on the bench behind her, picking at the broken guitar. Ben had driven five miles before it occurred to him that for Edrew to have got there in that time was impossible. He thought of the stories the mountain people told, that he had heard from Mrs. Kilgore and others, how Edrew had been given ways of getting from place to place that were not given to ordinary people. He must have come with somebody, of course. Probably with Cass the old mail carrier.

21

Ben slipped quietly out of the front door of his room the next morning before Miss Elly was stirring and opened the rumble seat of his car. He felt oddly like a conspirator as he took out the shiny new guitar he had brought from Knoxville the night before and set off rapidly up the road to Mis' Mincey's store.

Edrew was lying on his back, his white heavy eyelids closed, the broken guitar hanging from his neck, resting on the dirt against the bench. Mis' Mincey was bringing a bucket of water from the spring behind the shack. She set it down quickly when she saw Ben, and stood for a moment staring at the bright new instrument in his hands. She picked up the pail and came running up the bank, slopping the water out onto the voluminous folds of her black serge skirt, looking at him with pleading grateful tears running down her grimy leather face.

"Hit's fer him!" Mis' Mincey whispered.

Ben nodded. Her face worked convulsively. She wrung her hands in her torn apron.

"God bless ye, mister! God bless ye!"

She went over to the sleeping boy and lifted the broken guitar gently from around his neck. Edrew waked up, staring about him until his blue china eyes lighted on the guitar. The whole expression of his face changed. His two thin dirty hands reached out for it, he fell forward on his knees and lay, his cheek against it, caressing the polished wood, his fingers stealing softly over the bright strings, thrumming soft chords, his

95

idiot face radiant with joy. He was not aware of Ben or of his mother, only of the new guitar. Then, as if a wayward thought had pierced his poor brain, he pulled himself to his feet and raised the brave red silk cord to his neck. He stood there for an instant, fluttering his sensitive fingers through the strings; then hopped off down the road, quicker than Ben had ever seen him move.

Mis' Mincey stood looking after him, her eyes still bright with tears.

"He hasn't had any breakfast, has he?" Ben said.

She shook her head.

"I reckon he's off to the Holler to show hit t' Julie," she said. She looked up at Ben steadily, searchingly. A crafty flicker appeared suddenly in Mis' Mincey's eyes. She picked up the broken guitar and turned it over. Ben watched her peer down into it and prod with dirty fingers around the splintered edges.

She held up a little white fluff between her thumb and forefinger. Ben looked at it closely, puzzled. One tip was a tiny seed pod, the other tip was a darkish brown. He looked at her inquiringly.

Mis' Mincey held it out to him. She looked sharply up and down the road. Her face was suddenly quite pale.

'Hit's flaggin'," she said quickly. "Hit's fer calkin'."

She looked anxiously at him as he stared at it, not understanding. Suddenly she dropped it hastily to the ground, ground it into the dirt with her foot and picked up her pail of water. Ben turned around. Wade was coming up to the store.

"Hit's the revenuer," Mis' Mincey whispered. She scuttled into the store.

Wade nodded coolly as he came up.

"I don't suppose they'd have any pipe cleaners here," he said.

"Probably never heard of 'em," Ben answered. "Plenty of straws around."

Wade nodded. "Are you over at Currier Hollow again today?"

"Yes."

Wade drew a piece of dried grass back and forth in his squat black briar.

"Loftus says there's sort of a feud on between Kilgore and the Curriers."

Ben nodded. "That seems to be common knowledge."

"That's what interests me. You weren't up at the CCC camp last night, were you?"

"No. I was in Knoxville. I got back here about eleven."

Wade nodded. Ben looked at him curiously. "Why? Anything on your mind?"

"Nothing but my hair, as they say. Not so much of that as there used to be."

He hesitated a moment.

"There's some talk," he said slowly, "up there at the camp, about you and Speer disagreeing on the subject of that little Currier girl."

Ben stared coldly at him. "There is?" he said. He looked at his watch. "If it's all the same to you I'll be getting back for breakfast."

The Treasury agent's eyes held his steadily.

"Hold on a minute," Wade said. "I want to have a word with you."

Ben stopped. "You said you knew Speer?" he asked.

"Very well."

"Then you'd know of course what he was down here for? Whether he was doing his job as a Treasury agent or just running after a girl?"

Wade looked at him. "I knew Speer," he said quietly. "He was doing his job. What else he may have been doing I don't know."

Ben held himself in control, teeth set savagely, white ridges showing in his bronzed lean jaws.

"Say whatever you've got to say," he said curtly.

"I'm going to," Wade said succinctly. "That's why I want to talk to you. First you can probably tell me why Jess Kilgore is so anxious for everybody to know the feud between him and the Curriers is still on. Also why this half-wit kid here was hanging around his place yesterday afternoon."

"Was he?"

"You stopped your car and talked to him. You ought to know."

Ben met the steady cold gaze of the agent.

"You're going back for breakfast?" Wade said. "I'll go along with you. Now let me tell you something. You're headed for trouble, and you're just being pig-headed about it."

He rapped the words out sharply.

"They say it isn't healthy for revenuers down here. It's healthier for us than it's going to be for you, if what they're saying up at the camp gets down here—and it gets around that you're giving presents to this half-wit. Now keep your shirt on."

Ben felt the blood pounding furiously in his temples.

"All right," he said. "Go on."

Wade stopped suddenly and leaned against the concrete culvert.

"Look here," he said quietly. "This isn't my first job in the mountains. I know what I'm doing. I know what Speer was doing. I want to tell you something. Get this: the Curriers aren't running a still. What's more, the Curriers aren't doing a damn thing that's illegal or actionable."

Ben stared at him. "Then what was Speer doing?"

"That's our business. Listen. Kilgore, Loftus, the mail carrier—anybody you'll meet here—will tell you one or the other of the Curriers killed Speer. You say Nathan Currier wasn't there. Old Doss Currier says he didn't do it."

Wade hesitated an instant.

"I don't know whether you know what that means?"

"I don't," Ben said.

The agent's eyes were steadily on his.

"This will sound foolish to you," he said, "—if you don't know these people. I know them. Old Doss Currier is what they call a God-fearing man. Everybody knows that. He's shot to kill—he's done it. But he wouldn't tell a lie. They all know that. All right. Old Doss says he didn't kill Speer. He says he came up from the shop with his gun, ready to kill. Not the revenuer—the fellow that was after Julie Currier."

"It happened to be the same thing," Ben said.

"What's that?"

"Speer was going to give the girl a lift as far as the Kilgores'. She was leaving, running away because she doesn't want to marry her cousin, Old Doss's son. He was hanging around there with a gun too. In fact he ran me off, just before the shots were fired."

"What were you doing there?"

"Talking to the girl."

"He didn't like it?"

"He didn't seem to."

"How'd you happen to be there?"

Ben hesitated and flushed a little. "That's what she asked me," he said. "I told her I didn't know. I guess it was the same sort of thing that Speer was thinking about. He'd told me that morning she was having some trouble and to help her out if I got the chance. Anyway, Young Doss was there, and he had his gun. When I left him he wasn't a hundred yards from where Speer was shot."

He remembered something suddenly.

"I forgot to tell you I got the shells."

He reached in his pocket, and stood looking silently at Wade.

"You got 'em, and they're gone?" Wade said coolly.

Ben nodded. The two red shells were not in his pocket. He tried to think when he could last remember they were there.

"I picked them up under that white oak," he said curtly. "I gave them to Loftus. He threw 'em in the ditch. Said they weren't any use any more, you couldn't shoot with 'em. I guess you know they don't go in for any high-falutin' nonsense about murders up here. I went back later and fished them out. And they're gone."

Wade nodded coldly.

"You don't have much luck hanging on to things, do you."

"I don't seem to," Ben said grimly. "I don't get the idea."

A bleak smile flickered in the agent's eyes.

"There seem to be several things about this business you don't get," he said. "One or two of them might be important to you."

He hesitated a moment.

"I'm assuming," he said slowly, "that you're interested in this Currier girl. I don't know what else you're hanging around there for."

Ben stared at him a moment, completely taken aback. Then he grinned. "I'd hate to see you make a mistake," he said. "But go ahead."

Wade nodded coolly.

"You may know what you're up to, down there, if that isn't it, but damned if I do. All right. Let me give you the set-up. The Curriers have had bad luck with women. Old Doss hasn't been out of Currier Hollow for thirty years. This Mincey woman and the girl there are the only women he's spoken to for God knows how long. Her grandfather's been out, off and on, but Old Doss hasn't. Now he's got some notion in his head about that girl. He thought Speer was after her. He still thinks so, and if he'd caught him down there at night he'd have shot him; he says so. More than that: he's half crazy about being turned out of the Hollow by the TVA."

Wade stopped a moment. His cold gray eyes bored into Ben's. "Are you getting this?"

"Go on," Ben said. "I'm listening."

"All right. I got that out of him yesterday. Now this is what's eating the life out of him—and this is where you come in, or I'm mistaken. Old Doss has got the idea that when they're put out, and have to leave the Hollow, where they've looked after the girl all her life, she's going to turn into a Jezebel—like her mother and her grandmother. That's what he thinks. I guess Freud might explain it different. I'm not up on that stuff. But that's what he's got in his head. She's a woman, and all women naturally go bad if they get the chance. So he's going to get her married to Young Doss— and that's why he's mighty dangerous to anybody till he does it. This mean anything to you?"

Ben nodded. "It means a lot to the girl," he said. "I'd give her a hand if I got a chance."

Wade looked at him queerly for an instant.

"All right. There's another point. The Curriers aren't poor. People get it into their heads that all mountaineers are poverty-stricken no-accounts. Nathan Currier had seven thousand dollars in a bank in Knoxville that went under in 1907 in the panic. Since then he's kept his money in his sock. I don't know how much he's got, but it's plenty. And the government is paying him around twenty thousand for his land. That doesn't count what Old Doss makes out of that workshop."

"How much does he make?"

Wade's eyes flickered.

"That's one of the things Speer wanted to know. That's our business. You can forget about it. What you want to remember is we're sitting on a box of dynamite. And none of these people up here are normal right now. They're all giving up their land, getting out of the rut they've been in for a hundred years. And if any fool starts busting loose, there'll be trouble, and lots of it. I'd hate to think of what might happen to that girl over there."

Ben looked silently at him, wondering about the odd expression in his voice. "Do these people think I'm in love with the girl?" he thought. Miss Elly's shrill voice around the bend calling them to breakfast penetrated dimly into the turmoil in his mind.

Wade started on.

"You haven't said much about Young Doss," Ben said casually. "Did he shoot Speer? Or is he a God-fearing man too?"

Wade smiled coldly. "I need a cup of coffee," he said.

22

When Ben came out of the leafy funnel of the hill road above Currier Hollow, he found himself feeling a sense of relief so sharp that it was almost like a shock, so unexpected that he stopped the car and stared at himself for a moment, puzzled and intent, in the windshield mirror. Nothing before had brought home to him so sharply how much he was interested in what went on down in the Hollow below him.

It was the contrast between what he saw in front of him and the undefined but tense picture of danger that he had conjured up back on the road by the Loftus place, talking to Wade. The old business of present fears being less than horrible imaginings, he thought. Shakespeare—or was it the Bible? He'd have to ask Julie. It didn't matter much. The point was the same.

Looking down now from the crest of the ridge, he was so entirely reassured that if it had not been for the extraordinary thing that happened some hours later, the course of many lives might have gone on, unchanged, to unsuspected tragedy.

The Hollow lay below him, almost remote in its complete quiet, calm and lovely with the dew still on the purple iron-weed and the black-eyed Susan. It seemed so peaceful with the smoke wreathing white from the cabin chimneys, so homely and secure and pleasant with the smell of frying ham and boiling coffee, that the quick feeling of insecurity he had had back on the road seemed almost fantastic, like old wives' tales to frighten children when the storm gallops through the banging shutters on a winter's night. Wade's picture of the set-up, his own feeling that something was wrong, inhuman, dangerous, all seemed grotesque and impossible. Even the two old men down there seemed suddenly harmless and natural. They might be strange distorted figures to Speer or Wade —though Wade had said he knew these people. To anybody whose eyes were used to the outside world. But they weren't extraordinary up here. He could name some several, as they said, who were as gaunt and glittering-eyed as Nathan or as emaciated and weird as Doss. You had to know them, that was all.

He joined the detail with a sense of utter security. A derrick was coming this morning to load the great cross-section they had sawed out of the cedar and haul it off to the TVA museum. By eleven o'clock the detail had it propped up on the round, like a giant solid wheel, ten feet from rim to rim, ready to hoist into the big truck. Nathan Currier and Old Doss had been watching them all morning from the cabin porch. It would look like a huge red cheese from there, Ben thought, the clean straight cut facing directly down the hill. He looked down. Old Doss was standing at the near end of the porch, leaning on the rail, exactly as he was when Ben first saw him. Julie had not been out, Young Doss was still missing. Ben remembered that Wade had not answered his question about Young Doss.

At twelve Dave Phinney gave the order. The boys threw down their tools and made a dash for mess kits and water buckets. Ben stood for a moment by the cross-cut section, looking up at it absently, wondering what would happen if he went down to see Julie.

There was no warning. Sounding almost instantaneously came the angry whine of a rifle bullet, the sharp crack of the rifle below him, the dull spat of the bullet into the cedar round two yards from his head. For an instant he stood petrified there. There was a startled shout from the detail. He heard Mike yell, "Hit the ground!" and dived down as a second bullet whined up the hill and smacked into the cedar. There was a third shot and a fourth, and a fifth. They were coming from the same place, and they were going precisely and unerringly into the same mark. Ben rolled a few feet towards the road, raised his head and looked down the hill.

Old Doss Currier was standing on the cabin steps, feet wide apart, his head bent over the long gleaming blue-black barrel of his rifle, pouring shot after shot into the cedar butt, regularly, methodically, loading with lightning rapidity. Ben realized that he was not firing at anybody; the bullets screamed by, spatted one by one into the cedar butt. He looked down into the yard, towards the workshop. Neither Julie nor Nate Currier was in sight. Ben's heart sank. It was the act of a maniac. He's mad, he thought. Old Doss still fired. Eighteen, nineteen, twenty, Ben counted. The rifle was lowered slowly, raised again. There was a last spurt of flame, a final "spat!" into the cedar. Old Doss lowered the rifle and went slowly into the cabin.

Ben got up. Mike Shannon came over from the shouting group by the road.

"Thought the battle of Currier Holler had begun that time," he said, grinning. They went over to the cedar section. Mike shook his head wonderingly. "Jeez, will you look at that!" he said.

They stared up at the round flat disc of new-sawed wood. Twenty rifle bullets had buried themselves in the red surface in a clean-cut pattern, branding the letter "C" into the new wood with deadly accuracy. The old man's last shot had placed a period neatly after it.

Ben stood looking at it a long time, hardly hearing the excited shouts of the CCC boys swarming around. He looked down at the cabin just in time to see Old Doss's loose lean figure cross the dirt yard and go slowly down the road, not to the workshop but around the curve of the hill towards the spring. He waited a little, thinking that now Julie would come. When she did not he strode down the hill, stopped a moment at his car, went through the corn and climbed over the fence by the smoke house.

Nathan Currier closed his jackknife and put it in his pocket. He watched Ben cross the yard with long firm strides, his eyes alive and glowing.

"Where's Julie?" Ben said cheerfully.

Nate Currier leaned back in his chair. A little glint of admiration showed in his deep-sunk eyes.

"I reckon you jes' ain't afear'd a' nothin', Mr. Davidge," he said. "Or you ain't got good sense, one."

Ben grinned. "Where is she?"

Currier called over his shoulder. "Julie!"

Ben looked around. She came out of the far door, from the room where the Currier fire burned constantly, the lines of her slim body drooping wearily. Then a sudden smile lighted her white face, and she gave a little impulsive cry of joy as she saw Ben standing beyond her grandfather. She came across the yard quickly, breathless, lips parted.

"There!" she cried softly, touching Nathan Currier's sleeve. She looked anxiously into Ben's face.

"Uncle Doss said you wouldn't dare come again," she said shyly. "I . . . I knew you'd come, once more anyway."

"Sure," Ben said. Neither of them noticed Nathan Currier get up and go into the cabin.

"Where've you been all morning?" Ben asked. "I've been worried about you. Heard from Doss?"

She shook her head.

"I've been making a quilt. I'm not very good at it, like the other girls, because I don't like to stay inside."

She hesitated a moment.

"Gran says if you still think your mother would let me come see her, maybe I can go."

Ben felt a sudden quickening of the pulse. "That's great!" he said. "I'll wire her tonight. And . . . look here, Julie—I brought you a present. To cheer you up in case you did have to . . . I mean in case you couldn't go."

He took the box he had got from the car out of his pocket and handed it to her. Her fingers trembled as she lifted the cardboard cover. She stared blankly at the white tissue paper.

"You close your eyes," Ben said. He took the silver mirror out of the paper and held it up in front of her.

"Now," he said.

She raised her long lashes and looked breathlessly at her image in the clear glass.

"That . . . that's me?" she whispered.

"That's you, Julie."

She was gazing with shining eyes at her image, her face aglow.

"Oh!" she whispered. "*That* isn't ugly!"

They stood there so wrapped in the extraordinary experience of a woman learning for the first time that she is beautiful that neither of them heard or saw Old Doss come into

103

the yard, until his long gaunt arm reached out and tore the glass out of Ben's hand. His eyes blazed, his face was livid with rage.

Before either of them could move he threw it down on the hard earth and ground his heel savagely into the glass. It smashed into a thousand shining slivers. For a stricken second Julie stared down at it. Then her face paled as Ben took a step forward, white with anger.

"Oh, please go!" she cried. "You've got to go!"

He stood there for an instant. Old Doss wheeled about and strode towards the porch. Ben could see the blue-black barrel of the rifle leaning against the door frame.

Julie's hand rested for an instant on his arm. "Please!" she said. "Please go!"

He nodded. "All right, Julie."

As he walked towards the gate he waited to feel the first bullet strike, wondering how much of a "C" Old Doss would be able to tattoo on his back before he fell face forward in the dirt. But there was no sound except Julie's rapid steps as she ran into the cabin.

23

It was after five when he got back to the Loftus place. Ed Loftus had taken Wade to Bradleyville, Miss Elly said.

"That there white-faced man was here lookin' fer you again las' night," she added, looking in from the kitchen. "Why don't he never come when you're here, I'd like t' know?"

She winked significantly. "I tol' him so, too."

That would be Sisky, Ben thought. "What did you tell him?"

"I told him you was gone up thataway, t' Knoxville, I reckoned, 'cause you don't never wear a hat like a Christian less'n that's where you're a-goin'. That there bobbed wire he run into give him a bad-lookin' hand. My mother was tellin' me oncet when she was a little girl a feller was bit by a mad dawg an' they tied him down in his own bed and jes' smothered him t' death with pillers, because they wasn't nothin' else they could do fer him."

Ben finished washing in the tin basin on the back porch and went inside to change his shirt. The green shades were drawn tight so that no light could fade the red and green Brussels carpet. Ordinarily Ben did not bother to put them up; Miss Elly would have them down again the minute he left. But it was too dark in the pine wardrobe to pick out a tie. He ran them up. The setting sun streamed in, falling on the tiny parlor organ in front of the sealed fireplace, lighting up the worn roses in the carpet. In the middle of the center rose was the blurred outline of a man's boot.

He looked at it for a moment, and lifted up his foot. The bottom of his boot was clean. He had not been near mud all day. He reached down and scattered a little of the mud on the print with his finger. It was quite dry. He got down on his hands and knees, sighting along the carpet. There were faint tracks coming from the front door to the door of the wardrobe. He got up and went carefully along the line. There were traces of dried mud on the imprints. There was another trace at the head of his bed, another in front of the old organ.

He tried the front door. It was unlocked. The door leading into Wade's room was locked. Ben stood thinking a moment, then pulled his Gladstone bag out from under his bed and opened it. He ran through the things in it, snapped open the leather pocket at one end, and stood looking down at it for a moment. His revolver was gone.

He shrugged his shoulders and closed the bag again, wondering why Sisky should bother to steal the revolver. Maybe it was just as well, he thought.

He finished dressing and drove up to the CCC camp. He wanted to see about two things there. The first was simple enough. Captain Dell, in command of the corps, was quite willing to give him a week's leave. The second was information, which Captain Dell volunteered. He had given Raymond Sisky leave that morning to go to Lexington to see a friend. Sisky's face was better but his hand and leg were still bad. He had left the camp shortly after three o'clock.

Captain Dell chuckled a little about the barbed wire and watched Ben's car round the officers' quarters and disappear down the hill. He stood on the steps of his office listening to the boys washing up for mess. It was a little patch of life and laughter in three million acre feet of silence. From the steps he could look out over miles of valleys and ridges with only an occasional plume of white smoke curling up against the green to show that people lived there. "It's a lonely damn spot," Captain Dell thought. He went back into his office. The account for Mrs. Kilgore's cabbage, milk and butter was still to be entered for the day. Funny, their bothering to sell cabbages up there. The boys said they were supposed to have barrels of money stowed away. Captain Dell added up a column of figures and wrote Mrs. Kilgore a check for $23.42 for the month's supplies.

The sun had gone down behind the hills when Ben turned

into the gravel road by the mill at Jones Crossroads. It would be dark before he reached the Hollow. The river road would be quicker if he happened to hit the right fork each time, but it wasn't worth the chance, not with night falling. He switched on his lights as he passed the deserted cabin. By the time he reached the hill up from Murray's Hollow it was very dark. He drove up the hill, straddling the deep corrugations like a beetle straddling the cracks in an attic floor.

He stopped in the woods at the top of the ridge and sat there a moment, drinking in the healing quiet of the night. Somewhere, it seemed very far away, he could hear Edrew Mincey thrumming his new guitar.

The scene early in the morning came back to him. He tried to remember what Mis' Mincey had said about the fuzz she had picked out of the splintered back of the old guitar. Flagging. Mis' Mincey had said it as if it ought to mean something to him. Suddenly one thing that it did mean came to his mind. The fuzz was from the brown cat-tail spears; and that meant that Edrew's guitar was broken down at the workshop. It probably also meant that it was Old Doss that had broken it. What else there was to it, what Mis' Mincey, pale with some fear that he did not understand, was trying to say to him, he couldn't tell. He closed his eyes, listening for the slow plaintive melody whispering through the trees, but it was already gone.

Ben shook his head impatiently. It was not Edrew Mincey who had brought him back to the Hollow; it was the smell of danger in the air, as acrid and disturbing as an electric blasting fuse. Until he had talked to Captain Dell he had had no idea of going back there that night. It was not a wise thing to do, not with Old Doss blazing out "C's" all over the place. But there was the reasonable probability that Raymond Sisky had not gone to Lexington; and he was afraid of what Sisky, prowling around Currier Hollow in the dark, might precipitate. There was no telling what idea Old Doss could get into his head if he saw him, what price Julie might have to pay for it.

He shifted gears and went slowly down the road. Currier Hollow was dark. The shadow of the hill behind the cabin had fallen over it like a heavy pall, the waning moon was still low in the east behind the hills.

He put his foot on the brake, stopped the car in the road just above the gate, and got out. The door crashed loudly in the silence of the night. Everything else was almost supernaturally quiet. An owl flitted through the branches, a chicken clucked and was silent again. His boots grated on the gravel slope down to the gate, the chain clanked noisily as he lifted it off the post and creaked the gate open. He expected Kilgore to rise up from somewhere in the deeper shadows and come to meet him, but there was no sound or movement. The only movement there was the weaving plume of smoke from the far chimney. It was fainter than he had seen it before, as if it were suddenly tired after a hundred years.

He felt in his pocket for his flashlight and took it out, stopped on the top step and rapped on the upright. A sudden unreasoning fear seized him with icy fingers.

"They've gone!" something whispered in his ear. His collar choked him, and he pulled at it with fingers that were not quite steady. Then, as if he had heard it before but was only gradually aware of it, he heard a soft whimper in the deep shadow of the porch. He straightened quickly and flashed on the light.

"Here, boy!" he said quietly. "Kilgore!"

Something stirred farther along, past where the beam of the light ended. His boots, noisy on the porch floor, drowned out the sound he had heard. He went past the first door, listening. Towards the end of the porch he heard a faint tapping. He turned his light towards the far door. Kilgore was lying there, tongue out, eyes rolling. Ben stared motionless, sick, an icy fear at his heart, the sweat suddenly cold on his forehead. The dog was horribly crushed, skull smashed in, back broken, by savage blows. He whimpered again and moved his bony tail.

Ben caught his breath. The blood pounded in his temples in a wave of cold fury. He turned the beam across the dying animal, over the bed inside, towards the fireplace, and went in. A few dying embers kept the mountain tradition alive. Ben steadied himself against the door jamb. The light jerked crazily in his hand. In front of the fire lay Nathan Currier, his grizzled head half buried in a sodden bed of blood-drenched ashes, his clothes ripped half off his gaunt body. Ben took a step closer to him. His eyes were staring and glassy.

Ben swept the light around the empty room and brought it back to the fireplace. At Currier's feet lay the knotted cedar branch he had brought down the hill the morning before. Ben stooped down and picked it up. It was wet with blood. He hesitated a moment, holding it, and then, carefully, as if he were performing a rite sacred to these people, laid it on the dying fire. A splinter of it caught and flared up briefly, like a candle in the wind.

Ben turned his eyes to the door. He did not dare think of Julie. He did not know where to look for her.

Kilgore's broken body twisted convulsively and was still.

Suddenly Ben moved to the end of the bed and stopped, every nerve quickened and alert.

"Julie!" he shouted.

There was a muffled sob and a sudden scraping sound above him. He sprang onto the edge of the bed and pushed desperately at the trap door to the loft.

"Julie!"

He could hear her fingers pulling at the door. Then it opened a little.

"Ben!" she cried. "I can't . . ."

He did not hear the rest of the terrified cry. There was a sudden metallic click behind him. He swung around, standing there on the bed with one hand on the beamed ceiling. Old Doss was in the door ten feet away, his rifle leveled. Young Doss stood just behind him.

24

Ben Davidge stood where he was, silent and perfectly still, looking down into those two faces growing out of the deep shadow, holding off death. The flickering uncertain flame glinted in their hostile staring eyes. It glinted along the blue barrels of the two guns, tense fingers on trigger, leveled at his stomach. One movement of his body and hot fire would spit out of the round black holes, boring into him across the maple bed.

A doomed man's life passes, they say, kaleidoscopic, in quick review before that last long instant stretches on into eternity. Ben's did not. He was aware of the girl in the prison loft, the dead hollow sockets above the high blackened cheekbones of Old Doss's gaunt ghost-ridden face, the dark arrogant face of Young Doss in the shadows beyond him.

The fire licked the cedar knot, caught the dry bark and flared up, lighting the three tense motionless figures. Only their shadows moved, crowding back, grotesque and crooked, against the rude cabin walls.

Ben could not tell if they had seen the grim pitiful figure sprawled on the floor. They gave no sign, waiting, eyes narrowed, mouths hard, silent . . . waiting for him to move. There was no sound in the cabin. Outside, only the lonely night.

Suddenly the yellow flame licked the wet blood on the cedar knot and died with a sickening hiss. The black moving shadows fell back into the darkness, the faces in the door faded.

Ben hardly saw Doss move in beside his father until he had glided into the room, as lithe and noiseless as a mountain cat.

He did not look down or waver as he came to the crushed lifeless figure of his uncle sprawled in the ashes on the hearth. At the foot of the bed where Ben stood balanced, waiting, he stopped, gun raised, dark eyes gleaming.

"Git down, Mister Davidge," he said. "I'm goin' t' kill you."

Ben shrugged, started to move, and stopped. Out of the corner of his eye he saw the gun in the doorway, still leveled into his body, shift a little closer to its aim. He saw Old Doss's mouth contract, his finger tensing, and waited, jaw set, for the hot fire to spurt out. Suddenly he saw the old man jerked back, the gun muzzle raise and swerve sharply. There was a flash and a report, and the clock on the mantel shattered into a hundred pieces as the gun fell from Old Doss's hands, crashing to the floor. Behind him, scarcely visible in the deep shadow of the vine-covered porch, pinioning the lean arms in a grasp of steel, Ben saw the Federal agent.

Wade thrust the old man aside, stepped into the room and kicked the gun under the bed.

"Put that gun down, Currier."

His voice was quiet and cold. Doss Currier stood motionless.

"Put it down," Wade said.

Ben saw the dark slow flush that crept into Doss's face. The gun lowered slowly. Ben put his hands down and jumped to the floor. A dry strand of cedar bark caught fire and flared up as Wade crossed the room. He stopped short by the foot of the bed and stared down at the sprawling body of Nathan Currier. Then his cold eyes searched the white faces of the three men standing there.

He knelt down silently and turned his flashlight on the sharp gnarled features of the dead man. The round disc of light rested for a moment on the crushed battered skull sunk in the ashes on the hearth. It traveled slowly to the cedar knot smoldering wetly, the dry strand of bark curled into a thin gray ash ribbon. He took the tongs leaning against the stone chimney, beat out the little tongues of flame licking the charred dry end, lifted the knot out of its ashes and laid it on the stone hearth. Only a few embers remained of the hundred-year-old fire. Old Doss moved suddenly, shifted his long gaunt body from the dark corner. He moved deliberately across to the fire, took a handful of oak chips from a sack in the corner and tossed them onto the smoldering pile. He stood there a moment until the little flame leaped up, and moved silently back into the shadows lying behind him.

Wade looked at him silently and turned his flash back to the dead man. It rested on Nate Currier's bearded, upthrust chin and moved slowly over the rough homespun shirt. Ben saw for the first time that Currier's belt had been ripped off and that the coarse blue denim trousers were torn at the waist. He looked at the two other men. Both of them were staring fixedly at him. He looked back at Wade. Their eyes met steadily for the first time since the Federal agent had come into the cabin that night.

"What do you know about this, Davidge?" Wade asked quietly.

"He was there when I came."

Ben hesitated. "So was the dog—there by the door."

Wade's light moved and rested on the dead animal lying in a pool of dark blood a few feet from the door. Ben stared at Old Doss. He was looking at the dog, but there was nothing in his face that could be read. Nor in Doss's. Neither distress nor surprise, only the same veiled hostile stare.

Wade turned back silently. He pointed down at the charred cedar knot.

"What about that?"

"I put it on the fire," Ben said.

Wade's cold eyes darted swiftly at him, narrowing.

"He brought hit down yere from up yonder," Doss Currier drawled. He shifted his weight to lean against the foot of the bed in the corner.

Wade glanced at him and back at Ben. "Is that right?"

"Yes."

Wade nodded.

"You're under arrest, Davidge. Go out to my car and wait there till I come."

His voice was like a splinter of cold steel.

Ben nodded without moving. "That's all right with me," he said coolly. "I didn't have anything to do with that."

He nodded towards the inert figure on the hearth.

"But I'm not going to leave Miss Currier here."

Wade hesitated, looking at him. Old Doss moved out from the shadow of the wall.

"I reckon Miss Currier's kin'll be able t' take keer of her, without none a' your help, Mister Davidge," Young Doss said slowly.

Wade looked from him to his father. The old man was gripping the bedpost in his gnarled shaking hands, his eyes burning coals in their deep sockets.

"Where is Miss Currier?" Wade said shortly. He looked from one to the other. Neither of the Curriers spoke. He turned to Ben.

110

"She's up there. Tied to a post."

Wade hesitated again. His eyes darted around to Doss.

"Bring her down," he said curtly.

Doss Currier looked at his father. The muscles in the old man's throat worked violently. His lips moved. Ben had never heard him speak. His voice when it came was like the creaking of a rusty hinge on a door that is never opened. Ben could not understand what he said, but the idea was plain enough. He took a step forward. Wade turned.

"You keep out of this, Davidge," he said.

He turned to Doss Currier.

"How old is the girl?"

Doss hesitated. "Eighteen," he said sullenly.

"Then she's of age. She can do what she wants to. Get her down."

Old Doss moved forward, his lips working, eyes wild, strange inarticulate cries choking in his throat. Doss went towards the bed without looking at him.

"I'll git her down," he said. "Don't fret, Pappy."

Ben moved out of his way back into the shadows against the far wall. He watched Doss step up on the bed as he had done and raise his hands to the trapdoor in the beamed ceiling. He was tall and strongly built, as lithe and straight as a mountain pine. He pushed aside the trap and drew himself up into the opening as easily as he walked on the ground. Ben heard the quick sound of the girl's voice and a low reply, the sharp fall of a buckle on the ground, and Doss was back on the edge of the bed again, hanging by one arm, Julie Currier in the other, held as lightly as a sack of down. Then she was standing on the floor, white-faced, gazing anxiously from Old Doss to the Treasury agent.

The light from the fire was full on her face. Ben, in the shadows against the wall, saw her lips move and saw her turn frantically back to her cousin.

"You've killed him!" she whispered. "Where is he?"

Wade stared at her for a moment. He moved to one side from in front of Nate Currier's body, watching her gimlet-eyed. She turned her head slowly as he moved. The firelight flickered over the mass sprawled on the floor. Julie shrank back, her eyes wide with horror, then moved forward, dazed, one hand stretched out. Suddenly she gave a wild sobbing cry and threw herself on her knees beside her grandfather.

"Gran, Gran!" she cried. "Oh, Gran, Gran!"

She bent her bright head down to the rough homespun shirt and crouched there still, only her fingers pressing against the clutched old hands.

Ben turned his eyes to where Old Doss stood, his gaunt

111

ravaged face held high, his dead hollow eyes fixed somewhere in the dim shadows. In his face there was no sign of grief, only pain, and something else that made him more terrible, Ben thought, than he had ever been before. What it was he could not say, only that it was a light, fanatical and intense, shining under the hooded lids, on the thin toothless mouth, on the narrow chin thrust up above the tense working throat. Ben bit his lips uneasily. He looked back at the girl, and over at Wade, standing stolid but wary against the stone chimney. His cold gaze was fixed intently on Young Doss.

Doss Currier was watching Julie, very much as Wade was watching him. Hard men, Mrs. Kilgore had called them, the Curriers and the Kilgores. Ben felt in his pocket for his pipe. One thing was certain. Julie couldn't stay there. Not with Old Doss staring into nothing like a maniac, and Doss watching her lying there with as little feeling as he would watch a butterfly impaled on a pin.

The slim gray homespun shoulders quivered, Julie raised her head slowly. Her face was white as wax, her eyes great dark tearless pools. She got slowly to her feet. Wade made no move to help her. Ben was too far away. She wouldn't have expected it. He realized that as she stood facing the shadowy room, her back to the fire. She did not speak, but stood looking at Doss, questioning and accusing at the same time. He met her gaze a moment. Then he raised his hand and pointed silently to Ben.

Julie turned her head slowly to where Ben stood. He heard the swift intake of breath as she saw him. Her lips moved.

"I thought they'd killed you," she whispered softly, still gazing at him, dazed, as if she was not sure she could trust her eyes.

"We're aimin' t' kill him," Doss said slowly. "He killed your granpappy."

She looked at him and back at Ben.

"He says he's aimin' t' take you out of yere, Julie."

Ben came into the firelight.

"I didn't kill your grandfather, Julie," he said quietly. "And I do want to take you away from here . . . now he's gone. He wanted you to go."

"I reckon that's what you killed him fer, because you knowed he warn't lettin' her go," said Doss Currier.

His slow contemptuous drawl brought the blood surging to Ben's head. He caught the sharp warning in Wade's quick step forward.

Wade spoke curtly. "It's up to you, Miss Currier."

His flat impersonal voice cut through the taut strained shadows. Ben shrugged his shoulders. Wade was right, of

112

course. He put his hands in his pockets and relaxed against the smoke-blackened logs of the cabin wall.

"If you want to leave here, I'll take you in my car," Wade said. "You're of legal age. Nobody can make you stay here if you don't want to."

His voice became suddenly gentler as he looked at her.

"Your grandfather has been killed. Davidge here is a Federal prisoner pending investigation of what happened here tonight."

Julie looked at him with uncomprehending eyes.

"Is it . . . is it true—that he killed my grandfather?"

Her head dropped forward like a tired child's.

"I didn't say that, Miss Currier. He's under arrest till we find out who did it."

Wade hesitated a moment.

"How long have you been up there?"

"Since supper."

She spoke in a low voice without raising her head.

"Did your grandfather know it?"

"I don't know."

"You can hear what's going on down here, when you're up there, can't you?"

She nodded.

"Who did you hear down here with your grandfather?"

She stood motionless, silent a moment, then shook her head.

"I heard Gran come in. I didn't hear anyone else. Except Kilgore. He growled. Then he cried, like someone had kicked him. I heard Gran call him and go out on the porch yonder. He was talking to somebody a long time. I couldn't make out who it was or what they said, but Gran kept telling Kilgore to hush. Kilgore's the dog."

Wade nodded. Ben looked at him suddenly. He could not tell if the idea had occurred to Wade that had occurred to him that moment.

"I tried to listen, because Gran spoke my name, but I couldn't hear what they said."

She went on in the slow musical cadence of the mountains.

"They were out on the porch, and then I heard Gran come in, alone. I . . . I thought he'd leave me come down. I waited a long time. Then Kilgore growled again and Gran said something. I thought he'd thrown a log on the fire, and then I thought he'd kicked at Kilgore and stumbled, because Kilgore yelped like he was hurt. But then I heard him go out again, off the porch, and only Kilgore stayed crying."

She moistened her lips.

"It wasn't Gran that went off the porch," she whispered

113

desperately. "He's . . . he's been here all the time . . . hasn't he?"

Wade nodded. Julie's eyes moved slowly from Doss to her great-uncle, standing gaunt and erect between her and the door. She did not speak, gazing from them to the Federal agent. She did not look at Ben.

"How long was that before you heard Mr. Davidge?"

She shook her head.

"Not very long. Not more than a little while. I don't know how long."

"How did you know Mr. Davidge was here?"

"I heard him call Gran. I knew his step on the porch."

"Do you know your cousin's step on the porch?"

She nodded.

"Whose step was it you heard before?"

Julie stood for a moment, the firelight weaving strange uneasy shadows over her white face. The room was silent as a grave under the willows.

"I . . . I don't know," she said quietly. "I don't remember hearing it before."

Wade's swift appraising glance rested for a moment on her face. She looked straight ahead of her, her pointed chin out, her lips closed.

Wade nodded.

"Are you going with me, Miss Currier, or staying?"

Ben could see the rise and fall of her breast under the close-fitting gray bodice. The white muscles of her throat moved convulsively. She went back against the fireplace and stood a moment. Suddenly she bent down, picked up a handful of oak chips, and put them slowly on the fire.

"I'm staying here . . . with my people," she said quietly. Her eyes were bent over the hearth.

For a moment no one moved, watching the flames flare up. Wade stepped back between Old Doss and the door and looked at Ben.

"Wait in the car for me, Mr. Davidge," he said crisply.

Ben nodded. He strode out without looking at the girl kneeling on the hearth, in front of the fire, where four generations of Currier women had knelt.

Julie's lips trembled as she listened to his quick step crossing the porch, going down the steps, striking sharply on the dry hard surface of the courtyard. The rattle of the rusty chain as it fell back into place over the fence post came to her, crushing out the last struggling hope aching inside her.

"He's gone," her heart whispered. "He's gone."

Each anguished beat echoed his steps through the silent

114

Hollow. She groped blindly to her feet. Her body drooped hopelessly back against the rude stone chimney, her mind swirling faint and sick with misery greater than she had ever known.

"You can go if you want to, Miss Currier."

Wade's flat voice cut quietly through the shadows. For an instant a wild panic showed in her eyes, then died again as she remembered the rattle of the chain on the gate post. He was gone. Her grandfather was gone. Her life was here. She shook her head and tried to speak. No sound came from her aching throat.

"She ain't never wanted to go," Doss Currier said. "Hit was that feller put hit in her head."

Julie heard him speak without moving. Nothing mattered.

"You think he killed Nathan Currier?" Wade said. His voice came to Julie as if it were a mile off down the Hollow.

"There warn't nobody else yere," Doss said. He looked at his father. "He warn't goin' t' let Julie go no place. I reckon that's why he done hit."

Wade nodded. His eyes rested on Nathan Currier's torn belt.

"Did he carry money on him?"

"I reckon Mister Davidge could tell you how much."

Doss Currier's lips curled.

"I reckon hit ought t' be round twenty-five thousand dollars."

Something behind Wade's cold fishy eyes flickered out like a lizard's tongue and was still again. He turned his torch slowly around the room, letting the white beam fall on the primitive stool by the fire, the pine table, the mahogany cupboard in the corner. Beside it, between the cupboard and the fireplace, the torch beam rested on a rusted iron safe. The door was partly open. In the center of the safe was a tin lard bucket. There was nothing else.

"I reckon he cleaned that out too," Doss said. "There ain't nothin' but that old pail left, so fer's I kin see."

"What's in it?"

Doss shrugged.

"Chinkapin money. If hit ain't been carried off too."

Wade stepped across to the safe and took out the bucket. It was almost full of small silver. A few pennies showed brown and discolored on the top. He put it back.

"We ain't never had much use fer small change up this-away," Doss drawled.

He spat out of the small paneless window into the dark leaves that pressed against the cabin. A shadow that might have been from the fire passed over Julie's white face. She passed her hand over her forehead and drew it down over the nimbus of smooth gold hair. Outside in the bushes on the hill that rose up obliquely at the back of the cabin, the leaves framed in the tiny window moved, vaguely disturbed, as if some small animal was passing through. Julie's ears, attuned to the night sounds, caught it. She straightened her body and moved towards the door, her head erect, face calm. Old Doss moved uncertainly towards her and stopped. She took a step forward past him, then stopped abruptly, looking down at the crushed body of the dog.

For a long time she did not move. Then she turned slowly back to where Doss Currier stood watching her.

"You shouldn't have said Mr. Davidge killed Gran," she said in a lost far-off voice. "Because he wouldn't have done that to Kilgore. You . . . you could have known that."

She hesitated a moment.

"And it wasn't right to make believe he took anything out of Gran's safe. Because there wasn't ever anything in it, except the little money in the pail."

She turned again and looked down at Kilgore. Then she went out along the porch to the other room where her bed stood in the corner. She stood there motionless in the dark, listening, and crept across the room to the door and onto the stoop. She stood there a long time, listening to the lonely familiar sounds of the night, her head resting against the rough logs, gazing up into the deep starry sky. From somewhere lost in the hills came Edrew Mincey's faint plaintive notes, seeping into the Hollow like the dying wind. Julie gazed up into the stars. Her face was wet with tears, her heart ached so that she could hardly bear the pain.

She was still there when Wade left the Hollow. She heard his car start and saw the long yellow beams light the car ahead of him. The cars disappeared up the hill. She heard a step in the room behind her and waited without turning around. The heavy boots treading on the wood floor stopped, then came on. Julie closed her eyes. Doss was coming closer to her. She could smell the strong odor of his work clothes, feel his breath on her face. She opened her eyes. He was standing close to her, looking down at her.

Her eyes met his without shrinking, and they stood there in the night. After a long moment he spoke quietly, looking almost humbly at her.

"I reckon I could bury Kilgore most any place you'd want him, Julie," he said. "I don't reckon they'd keer if Kilgore stays in the Holler."

Quick tears stung her eyelids. Her grandfather couldn't

116

stay. She hadn't thought of that. He was an exile even in death.

"Down by the branch," she whispered. "Put him down there."

25

Ben cleared the top of the ridge and stopped his car. Behind him the Federal agent's lights shone like two round yellow eyes on his darkened windshield. Wade drew up beside him and leaned over.

"Go on to Loftus's place," he said. "I'll follow."

"I thought I saw somebody in the bushes over there."

Ben pointed to the right of the road. Wade switched his long lights on and peered out along the broad white beam. A startled rabbit hopped across the road and disappeared.

"You're getting jittery," Wade said curtly. "Not likely to be anybody up here, except that half-wit, and I heard him down by the river road."

He stepped on the accelerator, drowning out the sound of a night owl flitting nervously overhead, blinded by the sudden light.

"Go on. I'll follow you."

Ben put his car into gear. As a matter of fact it was not likely that Nathan Currier's murderer would be up there. It was far more likely that he was still down there in Currier Hollow—in Currier's cabin. He looked over at Wade and shook his head. If he knew what was going on behind the agent's fish-gray eyes and hard jaw it would be easier. It didn't seem believable that Wade could think he would crush in Nate Currier's skull and then hang around, waiting to get a load of buckshot in his stomach. Ben shrugged his shoulders, shifted to second and went down the narrow road.

It was not until he had got down to the bottom and turned along the road in the next hollow that he stopped and looked back up the hill. Everything was dark. There was no sign of Wade's headlights. Ben scowled, puzzled. Then he got it. There was somebody up there, and Wade knew it; but Ben Davidge was not to be in on it.

He filled his pipe absently, thinking hard. Since he had let the chain fall back over the gate post, closing him out of Julie Currier's life, he had struggled to keep her white anguished face out of his mind. She was staying there; it was her own choice. She had told him, in effect, to mind his own business and leave hers alone. It was plain enough in that room in the cabin. Wade had made it even plainer when he came out.

Ben lit his pipe. Nothing could be plainer than that he was out of it. It was all over, everything was dandy. Julie and Doss would marry and get along as well as most people that got married in the hills, or anywhere else for that matter. His hands were washed of it, and by her own act. If she hadn't guts enough to get out when she had a chance . . . And Wade could go to blazes too. Ben shrugged unhappily, tried to grin, slipped the car into second and went along the dirt road.

Then suddenly the monstrous idea came to him. He wasn't out of it at all. Far from it—he was actually under arrest, suspected of having committed murder. You couldn't wash your hands of that so simply.

He whistled softly and drove on. At Loftus's place he turned off the paved road and stopped under the pear tree at the corner of the porch. Nothing had changed. For a moment he could scarcely believe that back in the hills, in Currier Hollow, everything had changed. Loftus's old car was in its usual place. The house was dark. A chicken flew down from the geranium tub and scrambled across the porch. Ben went around the house and sat down on the steps. Prince's tail thumped in the darkness behind him.

It was fifteen minutes later when Wade's car stopped in the yard. A moment later Wade came around the house. He sat down on the steps.

"Who was it?" Ben asked.

He could see Wade's head shake in the half-dark.

"Nobody important," Wade said shortly. He hesitated a moment. "That Hollow seems to have an attraction for people, considering how out of the way it is," he added.

Ben puffed his pipe. Wade took a leather cigar case out of his pocket and sat holding it in his hands.

"Well," he said, "what happened there tonight?"

Ben looked around at him.

"A man and a dog got killed," he said coolly. "They got their heads bashed in. I thought you'd noticed it, or I'd have pointed it out to you."

Wade bit off the end of a diminutive cigar and spat it out.

"And somebody tried to burn the cedar knot they were clubbed with," he said.

Ben nodded.

"That was me," he said. "I guess I did it without thinking. The fire was going out. It . . . it's never been out before. Foolish, wasn't it."

"Damn foolish," Wade said. "If you didn't kill them. You're going to offer temporary mental aberration?"

"No. I'm not going to offer anything. Nathan Currier was

118

lying there dead when I got there. The dog died a minute later."

"Nathan Currier," Wade said slowly, "left the workshop at eight o'clock. Old Doss waited there for Doss until a quarter of nine. Doss was late. The old man went up to the cabin then and met Doss coming down the hill. They saw your car and went in—and found you just climbing up to the loft where the girl was. They covered you, and they'd have shot you dead if I hadn't come in. Old Doss told me that, and I guess you know it as well as I do."

"Haven't a doubt of it," Ben said.

"Good thing I was hanging around. Don't bother to thank me for saving your life."

Ben flushed at the dry irony.

"What the hell good is that, if you think I murdered the old man?" he demanded hotly.

"Wait a minute," Wade said coolly. "I guess you don't see that if you came up for trial tomorrow, a jury wouldn't think twice about you. You're known to have been hanging around Currier Hollow. You've been warned away by both the old Curriers and Young Doss, who aims to marry his cousin. Both the old fellows want it that way, and until you barged in there wasn't any doubt it would go that way. All right. You come along. You fall in love with Julie. You try to get her to run away. You even suggest to her grandfather that he let her go visit your mother. He's fooled by your slick city ways and decides maybe she can go. Then he thinks it over and sees it's all wrong. So he tells you she can't go, and he locks the girl up so she can't run away with you at night. He knows you're coming, and he goes to the house to meet you. He tells you she can't go. You pick up a cedar knot which you'd carefully brought down to the cabin yourself. You club him to death. The dog attacks you and you serve him the same way."

Wade stopped, waiting for him to speak. Ben waited.

"Then there's something else too. I understand you know that Nathan Currier was in Knoxville yesterday."

Ben nodded.

"You know what he went for?"

"About his land, I guess."

"Do you happen to know what they were giving him for it?"

"I heard twenty thousand. They've got a lot of land back there."

The red tip of Wade's cigar glowed brightly a moment.

"Nathan Currier," he said dryly, "had the money in his belt. Tonight. When he was killed. It's gone now."

Ben took his pipe out of his mouth. Wade cast a sidelong glance at him in the dark.

"What did you do with it, Davidge?"

Ben sat for an instant. It was even more than Julie, then. He took a deep steadying breath.

"Listen," he said. Then suddenly it all seemed preposterous, unbelievable. There was hardly any use in saying anything.

"Why didn't you search me?" he said quietly.

Wade shook his head.

"I saw you didn't have it on you," he said coldly. "You can't put that much money in your vest pocket. You could have done something with it, I suppose. What was it?"

"I'll have to have notice of that question, Mr. Wade. I'm not good at thinking things up offhand."

"I'm *giving* you notice."

There was a curious quality of tired patience in his voice. Ben looked at him sharply.

"I'm giving you notice. A lot of people are waiting for the answer."

Wade was silent for a moment. "I'm also giving you notice and fair warning to keep away from the Curriers."

"I thought I was under arrest."

"You are. But there isn't any lockup to put you in. If you tried to get away we'd get you. The Federal government has a long arm nowadays. But if you took it into your head to go back to that girl, the Federal government and nothing else is going to save you from the buzzards. I'm just telling you."

Ben nodded. "I'm not likely to be going back."

"Glad to hear it."

Wade grunted sardonically and tossed the stub of his cigar out towards the branch.

"Hope you'll feel the same way about it tomorrow."

Ben looked towards him curiously. "Do you think I don't know when I've been given the air?"

Wade grunted again.

"I think you're just the sort of young fool that gets it into his head that a certain mountain girl is 'different,' and sets about trying to do something about it without thinking what he's likely to get into. You're worrying too much about what you're getting her out of."

Wade lighted a second cigar.

"She's got to get out anyway," Ben said. "The TVA and the dam are fixing that. I think she's . . . she ought not to have to marry Doss—when she doesn't want to."

"Are you planning to marry her?" Wade asked quietly.

"Good God, no."

"That's what I thought. Going to be hard to explain to a jury up this way, isn't it?"

Ben looked at him in the tiny light of the cigar cast up on his lean face.

"Nathan Currier understood all that," he said. "He didn't think I was trying to . . . get away with anything."

"Nathan Currier's dead," Wade said coolly. "The people that make up juries in these parts are going to believe Old Doss and Young Doss. They say Nathan Currier had changed his mind about letting the girl go. They say the Curriers have always had trouble with their women because of men like you coming in from the outside. No jury'd believe you for a minute. They know about women. Especially Currier women. They know about men. If a young fellow is interested in a girl as pretty as Julie Currier, he either wants to marry her or he doesn't. And you don't. You'd never get them to see it any other way. Looks bad, doesn't it?"

Ben was silent a moment.

"What do you think?" he asked.

"I think you're in love with the girl, whether you know it or not."

Ben stared at him.

"Do you think I killed her grandfather—and robbed him?"

Wade hesitated.

"I think you've got a good chance of being the guy that pays for it," he said slowly. "Whether you did it or not. I think we're going to have a hell of a time keeping the Curriers from killing you, if you don't use your head."

"I didn't ask you that. I asked you if you thought I killed him."

"I might . . . if it hadn't been for the dog," Wade said coldly. "I don't know. I don't think you'd kill the dog."

"Thanks," Ben said. "What about the twenty thousand dollars?"

Wade got up. "I'll put it this way," he said curtly. "You didn't have it on you."

"Thanks again. One more thing. Am I supposed to have killed Speer too?"

"You still being funny?" Wade said. His voice had no tinge of friendliness in it. "I don't know whether you killed him or not. You had the empty cartridges and you lost them. You're one of the few people around here that would be likely to know you can fingerprint a shotgun cartridge by the way the firing pin strikes just as well as you can fingerprint a revolver bullet."

"I didn't happen to know it," Ben said. "What about my

motive? Did Speer have twenty thousand sewed up in his belt?"

Wade looked down at him.

"Son," he said, "when you're as old as a lot of us you'll find out that when there's a woman involved, people aren't going to go far hunting motives. Speer was supposed to have been interested in the girl too."

"You know he wasn't."

"I *think* he wasn't. I don't pick the juries in these parts. And I'm going to bed. Good night."

Ben sat motionless on the steps, his mind going back slowly over the strange ground he had covered since meeting Speer, looking over the barrier at the Norris Dam. That was the first time the people of Currier Hollow had taken on any definite meaning for him. And he now found himself in a fair way of being hanged for the murder of one of them.

It was funny, the way he had got mixed up in it. It was on account of the tree, chiefly. If it hadn't been for his going up there to tell them he was cutting the tree down, there would never have been the business of the dog, and Julie hauling him off. Or his going back and finding Sisky. There would never have been the letter Speer gave him. There might still have been murder—Speer and old Nate Currier—but it wouldn't have been tangled up with the girl.

Ben shook his head, filled his pipe, lighted it, and got up. The maddest thing was the idea Wade seemed to have, that he was in love with the girl. It was absurd on the face of it, the sort of an idea you would expect people like Wade and Loftus and Mis' Mincey to have. Yet he was worried about her, back there alone in the mountains. And, in some way, it wasn't only that. If it was only her white anguished face as he had seen it last that kept slipping in and out of his mind, it wouldn't matter; but it kept shifting back and forth into her calm lovely face under the two smooth gold wings of her hair, and two long deep-fringed gray eyes would be there, lighting up suddenly the way they did with new wonder, or joy, or quick impish humor. That was why the white drawn little face was more poignant than it should have been.

He thrust his hands deep in his pockets and paced up and down in front of the porch. Suddenly he stopped and stood leaning against the crab apple tree by the kitchen stoop. A frail light had begun to dawn in the back of his mind. Was someone quietly playing him for a sucker, using Julie Currier for bait—and had he, like a sap, fallen for it hook, line and sinker? He stood there a moment, went back to the porch and sat down.

"It's time you pulled yourself together, old son," he said soberly. "Before you turn into a first-class corpse."

For the first time he realized the truth of what Wade had said. If Doss Currier shot him now, it would be instantly taken for granted, in the simplest possible way, by both jury and judge, that Doss had not only saved the girl he intended to marry, but also had, according to the old law of an eye for an eye, avenged the murder of Nathan Currier. That would explain why Doss had not met his father at the shop —if his father had ever been at the shop. If he hadn't, it explained how both of them appeared the moment they did. It also explained why Doss had not shot him already—as he would have done if all the things they said about him up in the hills were true.

Then another idea came to him. He glanced at the dark oblong of the door leading into Wade's room and got up. A board in the porch creaked as he went across to the agent's door. He rapped softly, not to wake Loftus or Miss Elly, then louder. He grinned suddenly. Wade was a swell detective, if that didn't wake him. He tried the door. It was unlocked. He opened it, looked into the pitch-dark inside, and listened. There was no sound.

"Wade," he said quietly. "It's Davidge."

His voice sounded eerie in the quiet of the night. He went inside and closed the door.

"Wade," he said again.

There was no sound. He took out a box of matches and struck one. It flared an instant, half blinding him, and went out. He struck another and held it over his head. The double bed was empty. The quilts were still thrust neatly up under the coarse linen bolster. Wade had not even sat on the edge of the bed. Ben dropped the blackened match stump and lighted another.

The door leading onto the front porch was closed. He went over to it and opened it. Wade's car was in the yard. Ben looked around and listened. He could not see or hear him.

It was queer, he thought. He went back into the room and closed the door. He did not light another match, remembering where the door in back was. Halfway across the room he stopped. The door behind him had opened softly. He looked back quickly. The wiry form of the agent was in the faint oblong of light.

"Want something, Mr. Davidge?" he asked quietly. His voice was cold, ironic, questioning.

Ben flushed in the dark.

"I wanted to tell you something. I thought you'd be in bed."

"Let's have it."

Ben started to speak and stopped. It occurred to him abruptly that he had no proof that Doss had killed Nathan Currier. Furthermore, the idea that they were using him as a fall guy was certainly not likely to appear as obvious to Wade as it did to him.

"It doesn't matter," he said. "I guess I was having a brainstorm."

"Have 'em in your own room after this, will you?" Wade said. "You'd better go to bed. The farm hands'll be getting out to milk in a few minutes. They don't understand people who stay up nights, in these parts."

He opened the door to the tiny vestibule between his room and Ben's. Ben heard him turn the key in the lock. Wade went to his suitcase, unlocked it and put two empty cartridges, badly burned and faintly pink where any color showed, with one bright red cartridge burned at the end, into a concealed compartment in the bottom of his collar box.

26

Ben sat down to breakfast next morning aware of the dark pointed looks of Miss Elly and the averted eyes of the three farm hands at the foot of the long table. Wade sat on Ed Loftus's right, his gray cold eyes bent on the plate of ham and string beans in front of him.

"They say you was there when hit happened, Mr. Davidge," Loftus remarked. He reached for the corn bread. "Is hit a fact?"

"No. I got there after it happened."

"I reckon some folks'll be wonderin' what you was doin' there at all."

Loftus shook his head soberly.

"They ain't so fond a' havin' people hangin' round Currier Holler."

Ben flushed, and caught the warning flicker in Wade's eyes. He shrugged his shoulders and went on with his breakfast.

"I reckon Yancey Turner'll be comin' along any time now."

Loftus examined the big silver watch he carried chained across the front of his blue overalls. He pushed his chair back and scratched his head under his black felt hat.

"They tell me hit ain't goin' to be no use in Jess Kilgore's holdin' out agin the gover-ment. All they got to do is condemn th' land, an' take hit fer anythin' they want t' give fer hit."

He spat in the empty fireplace. Ben glanced up. Wade was stirring his coffee with no apparent interest in Loftus's comments on the local scene.

"They tell me you was along t' see Jess las' night, Mr. Wade. You ain't got th' idea Jess is mixed up in killin' Nate Currier? 'Cause if you have, you're plumb crazy."

Loftus spat again and wiped his mouth with the back of his hand.

"If Jess had a' killed 'em, he'd a' killed th' whole kit an' caboodle. He wouldn't 'a stopped with Old Nate."

He looked at Wade quizzically and winked at his sister, standing tight-lipped and beady-eyed at her place at the table.

"I reckon Mr. Wade ain't one a' them that's goin' t' die talkin'—air you, Mr. Wade?"

An amused smile flickered behind Wade's eyes and vanished.

"Doesn't pay to tell all you know, Mr. Loftus."

"That's what I tell Elly there, but shucks, what's th' use? Might as well save my breath."

Miss Elly's eyes snapped.

"There's Yancey Turner comin' down th' road," she said sharply. "An' he ain't goin' t' git a mouthful t' eat in this house."

Loftus grinned.

"Now, now, Elly.—Yancey, he used t' court Elly when she was younger'n she is now, an' a heap better lookin'."

He ambled slowly out onto the porch.

"Howdy, Yancey."

He shook hands with a bright little man with bulging eyes and a pug nose that made him look like an old and unamiable Pekingese. The Attorney-General walked with a limp, and all in all, Ben thought from a hasty glance, was not much more prepossessing at present than Miss Elly. Ben finished his breakfast, listening with only half an ear to their talk.

When he had finished he went out onto the porch with Wade. The talk stopped abruptly. The Attorney-General looked at him, bug-eyed, with open curiosity.

"This yere's Mr. Wade, General," Loftus said genially. "An' this young feller's Mr. Davidge."

General Turner nodded, and spat calmly over the rail into the yard.

"You're the gentleman who was at the Curriers' last night?" he asked.

Ben nodded.

"I'll be wanting to have a talk with you."

"He's staying here," Wade said shortly.

125

General Turner nodded and spat again. "It's safer," he said laconically. "That's one thing. Well, we'd better get along. I'll leave my car here. Yours looks more comfortable."

Ben watched the three of them squeezing into Wade's small car, and glanced at the Attorney-General's bright new sedan.

"Yancey Turner'd skin a flea fer hits taller," Miss Elly said. They watched them turn out into the road and set off towards Currier Hollow. Miss Elly turned to Ben.

"Hunt yerself a seat, Mr. Davidge."

Ben looked at her. It was the first time he had heard a gentle note in Miss Elly Loftus's high incessantly nagging voice.

"Thanks," he said.

"You ain't used to folks' ways up thisaway," she said, nodding her head wisely. "An' they ain't used t' yourn. Fact is, they think you're plumb crazy."

Ben managed a grin.

"I guess maybe I am," he said.

Miss Elly picked up a handful of peas. Ben listened to the rhythmic drop of the small green pellets against the bottom of the tin basin. He knew when the bottom was covered without looking at the little woman rocking back and forth. It was very hot. The warm sweet odor of ripe pears and the bees in the honeysuckle, the smell of the barns and all the sounds and odors of the farm carried him back to Currier Hollow—to Julie Currier's front porch. He chewed at the end of his pipe.

Everything brought her back into his mind, in some way— the chickens and the ducks in the yard, the pink roses climbing over the tree stumps beyond the smoke house, the great blue morning glories that covered the cow shed, the doves on the wires along the road. He sat on the top step, head in his hands in the sun. Miss Elly watched him with her shrewd beady eyes, shaking her head. After a while she got up and went inside. Ben ran his hands through his crisp sun-bleached hair and grinned helplessly at himself. He must be a mess if Miss Elly could sit half an hour without chattering.

He got up and went around to the front of the house, and sat down again. Julie Currier came with him. So did the aching feeling in the pit of his stomach. Her white face and great dark eyes turned up to him in front of the ever-burning fire; looked up to him from the pink geranium in the tub beside him. And then suddenly Ben Davidge realized that Wade was right, of course. There wasn't any use trying to fool himself any longer. He loved her. It wasn't anything impersonal, like trying to help the girl—and apparently everybody but himself had seen it for days. He *was* in love with her. And

126

nothing else mattered. Nothing but the slow soft cadence of her voice and the quick sweet smile on her mouth and in her eyes.

Ben jumped off the porch and wrenched open the door of his car.

Miss Elly's querulous voice sounded behind him. He turned sharply. She had come around the corner of the porch and was standing there looking at him, wiping her hands on her faded checked apron.

"Mr. Davidge," she said. She stopped by the geranium tub and picked out a handful of weeds. "I reckon Edrew'll be goin' over t' Currier Holler, if you should happen t' have anythin' you wanted to say t' Yancey Turner. Edrew, he cain't read, so's I reckon hit'd be safe."

She tossed the weeds out into the road.

"If you was goin' thataway, there's a mess a' beans I've been aimin' t' send Mis' Mincey all week."

Ben looked at her for an instant. He grinned happily.

"Thanks," he said. "That's a good idea."

"You wouldn't mind carryin' 'em in a pail? Sure nuff?"

Miss Elly went back around the house. Ben stared after her for a moment. Then he went into his room.

Miss Elly put the pail of beans on the porch and nodded her head with satisfaction. Miss Elly went to the movies every Saturday in Bradleyville, and knew how things were done.

Ben sat down at the table, pushed back the lavender crocheted cover and took the top off his pen. He wrote "Dear Julie" in a firm quick hand and stopped. It wasn't as easy to write what he had to say as Miss Elly thought. "I'm sorry about last night," he wrote, and crossed that out. He took another piece of paper and began again. An hour later the floor was covered with crumpled white balls of paper and one sheet was left in the box in front of him.

Ben groaned. "Dear Julie," he wrote again. "I must see you."

Her face, calm and lovely, swam between him and the paper.

"I love you, Julie. I never knew it till now."

He groaned again and crumpled it up. The empty box stared him in the face. He smoothed it out.

"Will you meet me on the ridge, after the detail's gone? I've got to see you, Julie."

It wasn't what he wanted to say, but it would have to do.

Mis' Mincey was sitting in her chair in front of the tiny whitewashed shop, rocking back and forth. Behind her, lying

127

sprawled on the bench against the wall, was the queer-turned boy, his long delicate fingers wandering listlessly over the bright strings of the new guitar. His thin blue-veined lids were closed over the staring china eyes. He did not open them when Ben spoke to his mother, but his fingers stopped moving and rested motionless on the strings.

Mis' Mincey spat at the base of the gas pump. Her face was drawn, and her old brown claws trembled as she wiped her toothless mouth.

"Howdy, Mister."

"Hello, Mis' Mincey."

"Hit shore was too bad 'bout old Nate Currier. I knowed hit was comin'. Th' cards knowed hit."

Ben looked at her intently, wondering.

"Do the cards know who did it, Mis' Mincey?"

Mis' Mincey's hand dove into the mousy folds of her green-black skirt and whipped out the greasy pack. Edrew stirred. Ben looked over at him. He was staring vacant-eyed at the cards his mother laid on the dirt floor in front of her.

"They say you never done hit, Mister," she croaked solemnly. "But there's trouble—a heap of hit—comin' your way, Mister."

She flicked the queen of diamonds next to the jack of spades and shook her head, staring at it, mumbling. She dealt off the king of clubs, put it down beside the queen, and rocked back and forth, making queer inarticulate sounds. Edrew slipped off the bench and knelt beside her, moving his body up and down in a nervous frenzy.

Ben waited, but she said nothing. He took his message out of his pocket. It wasn't safe, perhaps, but it was his only chance. Mis' Mincey looked up. A crafty smile spread over her wrinkled old face.

"If Edrew goes to Currier Hollow, I'd like Julie to get this," Ben said.

Mis' Mincey nodded quickly. She took the envelope, folded it in two and handed it to Edrew. Then she pointed to the queen of diamonds, and nodded, smiling. She picked up the jack of spades, the king of spades and the king of clubs, and threw them down, face up, apart from the queen, making strange sounds as she stroked the boy's thin shoulders.

Edrew stared vacantly at the cards on the ground, nodding his head up and down. His gaze rested for an instant on the three black cards. Then he slipped the folded envelope under the strings into his guitar and before Ben could speak to him he was gone, hopping like a wild thing down the road.

128

Mis' Mincey picked up the cards and put them back in her skirt. She rocked back and forth silently.

Ben looked down at her for a moment. "Have you decided what you're going to do, Mis' Mincey, when you have to leave here?"

She sat staring down the road a long time.

"There ain't so many places fer us," she said slowly. "I got half an acre here. They're givin' me three hunderd dollars fer th' store. That's three hunderd twenty-five dollars. But Ed Loftus, he holds a mortgage fer four hunderd, an' I ain't goin' t' make no tobacco this year."

She spat at the pump and wiped her mouth.

"I don't know what we're goin' t' do."

"Loftus won't foreclose. I mean they've got plenty without your four hundred."

Mis' Mincey shook her head.

"Hit'll be all right if Edrew don't plague him," she said. "They tell me ol' Mis' Lucy Kilgore, that's Jess's aunt, she says she ain't leavin' her place 'thout they kill her fust. I reckon hit ain't easy, when you've had everythin' like th' Kilgores had, t' be without, in a strange place."

"The Kilgores won't be bad off. They'll get a good price for their land."

Mis' Mincey nodded.

"Mos' folks don't know Ed an' Miss Elly hold the mortgage on their place too. Hit was et up lawin' with Nate Currier 'bout mineral rights."

Mis' Mincey spat again. "There's always been hard feelin' between 'em."

Ben nodded. His mind was far over the hills with the crippled boy. He scarcely heard what Mis' Mincey was saying.

He went slowly back along the road to Loftus's place. The Curriers weren't the only people in the hills facing exile, he was thinking. They were all going, all tearing up their roots deep in the mountain soil and going out into a strange changed world. People weren't normal under such circumstances. Speer and Wade had both said so. He shook his head over what Mis' Mincey had told him. But even if it was true, the simple if horrible solution of the murders in the Hollow seemed too pat altogether.

He felt for his pipe and put it between his teeth. A voice spoke from the roadside.

"Hi, Mr. Davidge!"

He looked up. Mike Shannon was sitting on the whitewashed concrete culvert beside the road. He jumped down and came towards Ben, his battered irregular face beaming.

129

"Hello, Mike."

They shook hands like old friends meeting unexpectedly after a dozen years.

"Why aren't you out with the gang?"

Mike grinned.

"I am out with it. They got us workin' up the hill over here."

He pointed up the road.

"Account of the murder. Jeez, what a country."

His squint eyes peered into Ben's, abruptly sober.

"The Fed and Old General Popeye was up at the camp. That's why I came down. They're puttin' the screws on that white-livered berry Sisky."

Ben scowled.

"Thought he had leave. Friends in Lexington."

"Hell, Mr. Davidge, that guy ain't got no friends, and if he has they don't live in Kentucky."

Ben pulled himself up on the culvert and lighted his pipe. "Go on, Mike."

"He turns up this morning about three, says he was hitch-hiking to Lexington and couldn't get a ride. Looked more like he'd been playin' Brer Rabbit in the blackberry bushes. He was all scratched up an' scared pea-green."

"Where'd he been?"

"Thumbin' his way to Lexington. Anyhow, Captain Dell sends him out with the detail and along comes this fellow Wade an' General Popeye an' drags him off the job."

Mike grinned.

"I wasn't exactly listenin' to what they was sayin', but I couldn't avoid hearin' it, not after I got close enough up behind 'em. You see what I mean?"

"I see."

It was the closest Ben had been able to come to laughing for some time.

"Go on, you old so-and-so."

Mike's face was troubled again.

"It ain't so funny from there on. This fellow Sisky wasn't thumbin' his way to Lexington. He went to Currier Hollow and hung around there on the ridge, havin' a look-see just for the hell of it. Old Popeye says, 'An' what were you doing there, young man?' "

Mike's imitation of Yancey Turner's high nasal falsetto was very passable.

"Sisky says it had come to his notice that certain people —meanin' you, Mr. Davidge—had been hangin' around there after the detail left, an' he wanted to get the low-down."

"What did he see?"

"He saw you."

"Yes?"

"Yeah!"

Ben nodded. "Wade knew I was there. He saw me too."

"Well, he told Wade you'd given old Currier a lift from the Crossroads to the Hollow in the morning, and when the detail truck passed, you was sittin' by the side of the road quarrelin' with him."

Ben thought about that. "He did?"

"Yeah. Wade calls a couple of the kids and asks 'em, an' they says Yeah, you was sittin' in your car an' the old man looked like he was cryin'. Wade asks Dave Phinney about the cedar knot you took down to the cabin."

Ben nodded. It all seemed to be working out very smoothly, from Wade's point of view.

"But Old Popeye he don't like Sisky, you can see that right off. Sisky says he wasn't off the ridge, and Wade pulls out a piece of blue thread and says he found it on a nail in the gate and how does Sisky figure that out, because there's a tear in his town pants he was wearin' to Lexington."

"So he was in the cabin."

"Yeah. And Popeye says, 'Where's the money?' and Sisky goes green again and licks his lips an' says he ain't got no idea."

"What did Wade say?"

"He didn't say nothin'. He just watched Popeye and Sisky. Then he says, 'Where'd you see Mr. Davidge?' and Sisky licks his lips again and says he saw you bendin' over the corpse. Looked to him like you was friskin' him. That guy hates your guts, Mr. Davidge."

Mike said it with a reluctant admiration, whether for Sisky or himself Ben could not tell.

"I'd like to have a little talk with Mr. Sisky," he said.

"I'd like to be along, Mr. Davidge."

Ben shook his head regretfully. "Where is he? Is he up with the detail now?"

"He's in the lockup. Popeye took him off."

Mike emptied a few brown shreds from a small white bag into a thin yellow paper and rolled himself a cigarette adroitly with one hand.

"I'd hate to think what would 'a happened it he hadn't. Nine to one ain't a fair fight, no matter how you take it. The kids didn't like him tryin' to pin the murder on you."

Mike looked up at the sky.

"Well, time I was gettin' back. You let me know if you need any help, Mr. Davidge."

"Thanks, Mike."

" 'S all right, Mr. Davidge. You might wham the guy on the conk, but you wouldn't break up no hound—that's the way the gang figures it. Account of the girl, I guess."

"Thanks."

Ben watched him silently as he went off up the road. There was something more disturbing to him in Mike's report than the fact that Sisky had seen him at the cabin. The detail was no longer in the Hollow. Therefore Julie was alone there with Old Doss and his son. He had counted on the detail, and on Wade's being there until the afternoon. They would be watching her.

He thought of the note he had sent. What would happen to her if they had got hold of it?

He jumped down off the culvert and ran along the road to the Loftus place, opened the door of his car parked by the porch in the yard, put his foot on the running board, and stopped.

Wade's cold voice came from the window of his room.

"Mr. Davidge . . . you're under arrest. You're not to leave this house."

27

Edrew Mincey slipped off the paved road into the tangled honeysuckle a hundred yards above the culvert. With a quick wild gesture he flung his shining new guitar under his arm and dived into the narrow tunnel that zigzagged, like a ricochetting bullet, through the knotted undergrowth to the river's edge. He slipped in and out like a small four-footed thing until he came to a leafy screen above the river bed, shallow with white boulders sticking out, except in the deep narrow channel where the water raced. He peered through the leaves up and down the bank, then quickly he darted to the oak stump above the rocks and pulled out a narrow plank. He carried it down balanced on his shoulder, stepping lightly with his tough bare feet across the dry stones to the channel, rested one end in a groove hollowed out of the rock and let the plank fall, deftly, so that its far end wedged securely between two projecting rocks across the silent swirling water.

For an instant he raised his head, staring vacantly back into the woods, up and down along the leafy banks of the river. Then he slipped quickly across the plank, bending under his light weight until it barely cleared the swiftly-moving surface. He pulled it up behind him and dragged it to the hiding place behind the buckeye on the bank, and quickly, scarcely moving a branch, he dived into the woods again, slipping in and out across the low ridge towards Currier Hollow. He moved swiftly and tirelessly, stopping when he came to the river road just long enough to peer up and down and see that no one was there. Then he slipped across it into the leaves again.

On the ridge over the Hollow he looked down with staring china-blue eyes at the vine-covered cabin lying snug and peaceful below him, weaving its age-old frail blue feather of smoke. No one was in the courtyard. Edrew's fingers wandered over the bright strings of the guitar, picking out a melancholy dirge for the dead men in the Hollow. The sun rose high in the blue heaven. Edrew sat there, only his fingers moving, very softly, to make them think he was far away in the hills. It was a trick he had learned by himself, listening under the stars. His eyes rested steadily on the cabin, waiting.

The sun was directly overhead when Old Doss Currier came out on the back stoop and emptied a pail of water over the rail. Edrew's thin fingers caressed the strings. Old Doss did not look up. He went down the steps and crossed the dry uneven yard to the gate. Edrew watched him go slowly up to the road and start down to the workshop through the yellow corn.

When he had got out of sight Edrew slipped down through the undergrowth to the road, went quickly down to the yard, and climbed over the gate, his guitar slung over his shoulder. He crept up to the porch, noiseless as a weasel, and stopped, peering into the kitchen.

Julie was sitting by the table, her hands folded in front of her, her face white above the black dress her mother had worn when her father died. Her eyes moved slowly around to the crippled boy. He hopped along the porch to the room where Nathan Currier had lain, peered in, and hopped quickly back across the doorsill to Julie. She watched him without shrinking back as she had always done instinctively from his grotesque vacant eyes and loose hanging lips. There was no horror greater than what she had already known, and another that she must look forward to.

Edrew turned the guitar over, shook it and ran his long thin fingers through the hole. Julie watched him draw out the folded envelope, grinning, and put it on the table in front of her, peering anxiously into her face. She stared at him and at the envelope. He hopped up and down excitedly, tapping it, and Julie took it with troubled hands and turned it over. It was the first letter she had ever got. Her fingers trembled as she tore open the flap, and she stared wide-eyed at the writing.

133

"Dear Julie—I must see you. I love you, Julie. I never knew it till now. Will you meet me on the ridge, after the detail's gone? I've got to see you, Julie."

Julie's head bent closer to the white paper, her eyes searching through the unfamiliar words. Her hand stole to her face, across her eyes, as if she thought she was dreaming. She turned the page over and back again, gazing at it, unbelieving. Edrew watched her, his eyes glued to her face. Gradually the blood came into her white face, staining it with crimson. Her lips formed the words as she read them again and again, painfully, not absolutely sure, because she was not used to reading any but printed words. How long she must have pored over them, her cheeks burning, her eyes shining like stars, she did not know. It was Edrew who dragged her back from her trance state, plucking at her sleeve, hopping up and down, tapping the letter, pointing frantically back towards his mother's cabin.

Julie started up and ran to the fireplace where her grandfather had kept his pen and ink behind the clock. She stood on tiptoe and brought down the bottle. It was empty. A few dried purplish-brown crystals in the bottom were all that was left. Her hand trembled as she put it back behind the clock.

Edrew watched her, his blue eyes vaguely troubled, trying to understand. She came close to him and touched his arm gently.

"Listen, Edrew. Tell him 'Yes.'"

She pointed to the letter and nodded her head, smiling. Edrew's face lighted. He grinned, struck the guitar with soft complacent fingers, and hopped out of the door as noiselessly as he had come.

Julie's hands trembled as she sat at the table gazing at the letter. She bent her head shyly to touch the cool paper with her burning cheek, and closed her eyes, her whole being quivering, lost in a strange new ecstasy. She did not hear the gate close, or hear Doss cross the courtyard, or hear him at all until he had picked up the dipper in the bucket and the water he did not drink splashed on the ground. She started up in terror and closed her hands over Ben's letter, crumpling it in a small white wad.

Doss stood in the door, stopping abruptly. One look at her face before the rosy flush faded in her cheeks was enough . . . and her eyes still held their deep starry glow. He frowned, puzzled, his lips tightening. Julie started towards the stove. It would be like burning a part of herself, but it was safest. Then she drew back. Doss's eyes were on her, following her, dark with suspicion. She moved slowly, trying to keep from seeming to hurry, through the door to the kitchen stoop, stepped across the threshold. She picked up the bucket of corn for the chickens, and put it down quickly. It wasn't time to feed them. Doss would know that. She went to the top step, out of view of the door, and raised her hand, struggling with the high-buttoned bodice to thrust the letter down her neck. When she turned back Doss was standing in the door, his dark arrogant eyes ripping through the stiff black cloth.

"Give me that, Julie," he said quietly.

She shook her head, breathless with terror.

"Give hit to me, Julie."

"No. I won't, Doss . . . I won't."

She tried to keep her voice from trembling the way her knees trembled.

"Give hit to me, Julie, or I'll take hit."

Doss's voice was cold, his dark face wore a strange terrifying smile. Instinctively Julie shrank back, clutching at her breast. Doss moved a step closer.

"Give hit to me, Julie."

Julie caught her breath in a low tearing sob. She couldn't run. There was no chance of getting away.

She turned her back and fumbled awkwardly with shaking fingers for the bit of paper. Doss jerked it roughly out of her hand and unwadded it with his lean hard hands. He looked at Julie, standing defiantly in front of him now, two crimson spots blazing in her cheeks, her chin up. Their eyes met, hers afire with fury and contempt, his smoldering black under hooded lids, and held a long time before his dropped to the paper in his hands.

Julie watched his eyes move slowly across the page as hers had done, not quite believing, as hers had not believed, what they saw. She saw his lips tighten, his eyes blaze with anger. His strong iron fingers closed suddenly. He stepped over the threshold and lifted the stove lid. She saw the quick flame flare up, and turned her head, tears stinging her lashes, her lips trembling.

"Come in, Julie."

For a moment she stood defiantly. She tried to speak, but the words were hardly a whisper. Her feet in their heavy copper-toed shoes moved reluctantly across the doorsill. Doss was standing by the table. He had a sheet of paper, yellowed with age around the edges, and a stub of lead pencil. He pointed to the chair.

"Set down, Julie, and write."

"What do you want me to write, Doss?" she asked softly. In some queer way that she could not fathom, she was not afraid of him any more. She was no longer so completely

135

and terribly alone. What they could do to her now did not matter—and all because of a few words written on a piece of paper. Not even the paper existed now, but that didn't matter either. The words sang themselves in Julie's brain and glowed in her heart.

She sat down. Doss Currier leaned on the table across from her, his eyes fastened on hers.

"Write him you ain't comin' to the ridge—that you ain't seein' him no more," he said slowly.

She shook her head steadfastly.

"No, I won't, Doss."

Her voice seemed small and far away, as if it weren't in her own throat but out away somewhere in the hills.

"Because you tried to make me think he killed Gran. But I know he never did. You killed Gran, Doss. Because he was letting me go away. And you stole the money. You know I'm not going to marry you, and Gran said the money belonged to me. You know that's the truth, Doss, and you're trying to lay it on him when he didn't do it."

His hooded eyes burned into her upturned little face growing like a snowdrop out of the high black collar. Something in them flickered dangerously. His voice was scarcely audible between his clenched teeth.

He bent close to her.

"Julie—you write what I say. If you don't, I'll blow his brains out . . . when he comes to the ridge this evenin'. You hear me, Julie? I'll blow his brains out."

His face was within a foot of hers, his breath hot against her face, his voice hardly louder than a whisper.

"I'm a man of my word, ain't I, Julie?"

She nodded, staring fascinated into his eyes.

"Write what I said."

He stood up, the dark proud eyes still fixed on hers. She took the stump of pencil in her icy fingers and put it to the paper. Not to see him again . . . she couldn't do it. But Doss was a man of his word. He would kill him. She looked up.

"Doss," she said. "I'll write it to him, the way you said. But I won't marry you, Doss—not ever."

Her voice was still far away, but it came closer as she looked him directly in the face.

"I'd rather die first, Doss."

A sound in the door made them turn sharply, and Julie's breath strangled in her throat. Old Doss stood there, looking silently at her, his dead colorless eyes pinioning her to the chair.

"Write what I said, Julie."

136

Her hand shook as she made the letters, big round letters, like a child copying from a blackboard.

"Dear Ben—I can't see you any more. You must go away and not come here again."

She wanted to put in other words, but she did not dare, not with Doss watching her and Old Doss never taking his eyes away. She wrote her name at the bottom of the page. Doss folded it and put it in his pocket. Julie watched him move across the room. She stood up quickly.

"Doss!" she cried.

She ran in front of him, thrusting her body between him and the wall where he had stood his gun when he followed her out on the porch.

"You're not going to take your gun!"

She faced him, eyes blazing, chin thrust up defiantly. For an instant she felt his lean fingers buried in her shoulder with a grip of steel. She stiffened her body, trying desperately to hold her ground. Then the fingers relaxed. Doss stepped back.

"I reckon you're right, Julie," he said quietly. "I ain't got no call to carry my gun along."

He went out into the sunlight. Old Doss came inside the room and sat down at the table. His eyes never left her. Even when she went out to feed the chickens he came to the door, watching her, always watching.

28

Wade and General Popeye left the Loftus place at two o'clock. Ed Loftus, his black hat on the back of his thick thatch of graying hair, went out to the road with them and watched them until they disappeared at the turn in the road where the bank jutted sharply out. He ambled back to the porch, meditatively chewing a blade of hog grass. Ben watched him, wondering if he would stay around. Wade had made it clear that in his absence Ben was the "deppity's" charge.

Loftus sat down on the porch and spat between his knees. He glanced up at Ben after a moment.

"I reckon if I was t' go down to th' sweet peraty patch fer a couple a' hours, you'd be all right, wouldn't you now, Mr. Davidge? You wouldn't be runnin' off t' Currier Holler, now? 'Cause I wouldn't have no way a' knowin' hit, an' Elly she wouldn't tell me. There jes' ain't nobody I kin depend on round here, nohow."

Ben's face brightened. This was better. He grinned cheerfully.

Loftus shook his head and spat again.

"Well, there ain't nothin' I kin do," he drawled easily. "Reckon I'll just have t' take a chance on you bein' here when I git back. Hit ain't healthy over to Curriers', jes' now, an' you ain't likely t' be such a damn fool nohow."

Ben watched him amble round the end of the porch, heard him call out, "Aw, Elly," heard Miss Elly's shrill voice answering. After that it was quiet, except for Loftus's old buggy rattling down through the branch to the narrow wagon road leading to the Loftus fields beyond the hill.

He looked at his watch. Loftus had given him two hours. It was a little after two. Julie wouldn't expect him until four. The detail wasn't there, but that was the time they would have knocked off for the day. He wouldn't be able to get back—not in two hours. But it didn't matter. He might not come back at all. Loftus knew that as well as he did. Wade would be sore as hell. That didn't matter either, and to Loftus less than to Ben, probably, Loftus having been born with less respect for constituted authority. It was part of the independence of people living away from society, under laws almost entirely of their own making and their own enforcing.

Ben went into his room and stood there a moment, thinking. It occurred to him seriously that perhaps he really would not come back. In that case there was his mother and his father—and Julie. He sat down and scribbled a few lines to Wade, folded the paper and wrote Wade's name on it. He could give it to Miss Elly to give him when he got back.

But Miss Elly was down at the smoke house. He could see her haranguing the dull-witted girl who helped her with the work. Ben went across the room and opened his door into the little hall. Wade's door was unlocked. He went in, put his note on the table and hurried out to his car.

As he was turning out into the road Miss Elly came running out around the porch. She waved at him and shouted breathlessly.

"If you have th' time while you're in Knoxville, Mister Davidge, git me a box a' them headache powders!"

Ben waved back with a happy grin. Knoxville was just in the opposite direction, and no one knew it better than Miss Elly.

Half an hour later he was struggling in second up the steep narrow road, straddling the deep center gully. He rounded the sharp bend to the top of the ridge and drove along to where the road narrowed to shoot down again into Currier Hollow. He stopped the car. It was here that he had heard someone in the underbrush the night before. He remembered, almost startled, that it was only the night before. In a relatively few hours his whole world had changed. Its center had shifted from the elegant Georgian house in Chestnut Hill, its core even when he had left it, to a small bright head down in the lonely hollow.

Ben humped down on his spine behind the wheel and stared with unseeing eyes into the undergrowth. He looked at the clock on the dash. It was a little after three. She wouldn't come for an hour yet—if she came at all. His heart sank; all the things that could happen to her trooped through his mind. He leaned down to the clock to see if it was still running, and wound it up. Then he looked at his wrist watch and got out of the car, pacing up and down.

Suddenly he heard a sound down the hill, and turned quickly, his pulse hammering in his throat. He stood there staring. Someone was coming up from the Hollow, but it was not Julie. It was Doss Currier. He was coming steadily up along the road. Ben stood, tense and waiting, jaw tightened.

Currier came on towards him, and stopped a yard away. The dark smoldering eyes met the frosty blue eyes levelly. Ben noticed for the first time that Doss did not have his gun, and smiled grimly. This time it was man to man. Neither of them spoke. After a moment Currier's hand went to his pocket. He took out the folded yellow-edged paper and handed it to Ben.

Their two glances met steadily again. Ben took the paper and unfolded it. He read the short message, something poignantly tender striking him suddenly, in the round absurd little letters staring up at him from the faded paper. He folded it and put it in his shirt pocket. Then he looked up at Doss silently.

A slow dull flush shadowed Doss Currier's lean sun-blackened face. His lips tightened.

"You wouldn't let her come?" Ben said.

"No, Mister Davidge. An' we ain't goin' t' let her come."

The two of them stood facing each other squarely, the silence between them a living sentient thing, speaking for them until at last Ben tore it away.

"You don't honestly think I killed Nathan Currier, do you?" he asked, his voice deadly cool.

"I ain't sure, Mister Davidge. That's why you ain't dead."

Doss answered in the slow sing-song cadence of the hills.

"I warn't sure last night, or I'd 'a shot you down like a yeller dawg."

"Then *you* didn't kill him—or you'd have shot me just the same."

"You ain't as big a fool as I'd thought, Mister Davidge."

"You and your father could have rigged up a story that would have got by with a jury at Bradleyville in a big way."

Doss shook his head slowly.

"We ain't aimin' to rig up no story," he drawled. "Thar's thirty thousand dollars missin', Mister Davidge—maybe more. Me an' Paw reckon if you'd got your hands on that, you'd 'a lit out fer town. You wouldn't 'a hung 'round, tryin' t' git at Julie."

His eyes held Ben's, dark and hard and intent.

"Who was it, then?"

"That's what I'm askin' you, Mister Davidge. You war there before we war."

Ben shook his head. It seemed incredible. There they were, the two of them, on top of a lonely ridge, ready to kill each other because of a girl a quarter of a mile away—yet it sounded as if they were talking sense. Ben did not understand it.

"Look here," he said suddenly. "If we leave Julie out of this . . ."

Doss Currier shook his head.

"We cain't leave Julie out," he drawled. "Julie's worth more'n money to us."

"She's worth more than money to me," Ben said. "That's why I want to leave her out for a minute. I want to know about this other business. Your uncle and last night."

A shade of something he could not name went over the dark arrogant face in front of him.

"I mean this. If you didn't kill your uncle, and I didn't— that leaves the people round here who knew he had that money on him. Who are they?"

"There's you, Mister Davidge."

"You and your father."

Doss nodded coldly. "That's about all."

Ben shook his head.

"No. Everybody in the valley knew it. There's a man named Sisky in the CCC camp. The Kilgores—"

A sharp spasm of hatred flashed along Doss Currier's face.

"The mail carrier—what's his name? Edrew Mincey, Loftus. Is that all?"

Doss Currier spat to one side.

"Wade," he said.

Ben nodded. "That doesn't make sense."

"Thar ain't nothin' t' keep a feller from hankerin' after a pile a' money. Thirty thousand dollars is a heap a' money."

Currier shrugged his shoulders.

"That ain't what I come up here to tell you, Mister Davidge. I come up here to tell you to leave Julie be. Julie belongs to me. I don't want t' have t' kill you, an' I'm a-goin' to do hit if you come up thisaway again. I told you that once. I ain't a-goin' t' tell you again."

The dark eyes and the blue eyes met squarely.

"Listen, Currier. Julie doesn't belong to you. She belongs to me. I'm going to have her—or else she's going to tell me herself she wants you instead, and not with you holding a gun over her. She's afraid of you, and you know it, and her grandfather knew it. I'm going to marry her, Currier, and take her out of here. You're not going to keep on treating her as if she was a slave."

For a moment the two men stood staring into each other's faces, a primitive hatred burning between them that Ben had never thought he was capable of. Doss Currier relaxed.

"Try an' git her, Mister Davidge," he drawled.

Suddenly the smile left his lips. The dark pupils of his eyes contracted sharply. He stared past Ben at the mouth of the road leading down the hill. Ben turned quickly. A car was coming up. They stood there waiting, watching the road. Why, Ben did not know, when he thought about it later, except that Doss Currier's sudden tense watchfulness transferred itself to him. It was like the sudden hoisting of a new danger signal on an already stormy sea.

There was a sound of gears shifting and a straining motor. A black coupé rounded the bend onto the ridge. It was Wade. He stopped his car beyond Ben's and got out. Ben saw him take his revolver out of its holster under his left arm and look at it before he put it in his pocket.

Wade came up and looked coldly from one of them to the other.

"You're under arrest, Davidge," he said icily. "I've told you that often enough."

He looked at Currier, a sharp question in his eyes.

"I had a private matter to settle with Mr. Currier," Ben said coolly.

Wade's eyes glinted.

"Yes?" he said. "I wish to God you could get it into your head that you'll settle no private affairs when you're in my custody. I don't want to handcuff you, but by God I will if I have to. Get in your car and go back to Loftus's. I'll see you later."

He turned to the other man.

"And let me tell you this, Currier. You're not getting away with anything around here. I know your whole set-up, and I know what's worrying you. And there's not going to be any shooting over that girl. If you shoot anybody, you'll hang.

141

Get that. You'll hang higher than a kite. Now you get back down the hill, and you tell your father what I've said."

Wade turned on his heel and went back to his car. He waited until Ben had started his, got in and slammed the door.

Through the leaves the white face and staring eyes of the crippled boy peered vacantly after him. Then Edrew Mincey hopped silently through the undergrowth to his seat on the hill overlooking the Hollow. He was there when Doss Currier came striding down the hill and crossed the courtyard into the silent cabin.

29

Ben got out of his car. The Federal agent drove in beside him.

"Get in here, Davidge," he said. He opened his door. When Ben got in he backed into the road and headed off without a word.

"Taking me to the county jail?"

"No."

Wade pulled off the road under a wall of solid overhanging rock and turned off his engine. He shifted sideways in his seat and fixed Ben with cold gray eyes.

"Look here," he said curtly. "I haven't got the time to follow you around the country saving your hide. I've done it for the last time. After this you can go and get shot for all I give a damn."

He stopped as suddenly as he had begun, staring angrily at Ben. Then he shook his head and gave Ben a sour smile.

"I'm trying to keep you from getting killed, Davidge, and I'm getting damn little help or thanks. Maybe I ought to thank you for leaving me the note."

He took his case out and bit the end off a tiny black cigar.

"Now let's get this thing straight. I've got the idea now that you're O.K. I wasn't sure about you—not with your putting that cedar club on the fire and all the rest of it—until I checked on you."

He patted his inside coat pocket.

"I've got all the stuff on you right here. That's one of the first things you learn in my business. That set-up with Speer didn't look so hot. Well, I've got you labeled now, so I'm going to let you in on enough of this business so you'll keep out of it."

He lighted his cigar and threw the match out the window.

"I told you the Curriers weren't moonshiners. They aren't. I told you they weren't doing anything actionable. That's straight too. This is what it's all about. There's a big-time crook in Philadelphia that's distilling more corn liquor right now than he ever thought of before repeal. That's Mr. Pete Hromanik. You've probably never even heard of him. He's a big man, Pete is. He's got a plant that's probably bigger than any two old Prohibition plants, and he's working full time. I guess you may have heard that one-half the liquor that's drunk nowadays—two years after repeal—is bootleg liquor that's never paid a damn penny of tax. Well, the Alcohol Tax Unit wants to know where that plant is. So far we haven't got an idea. All we know is that when we raided one of his barns in Yonkers, we found ten fifty-gallon barrels and the liquor in 'em wasn't three weeks old."

Wade puffed deeply on his cigar.

"I guess you know this liquor's sold over the bar for a nickel a shot in the houses in the lower end of any big town, and most of it comes out of nice respectable labeled bottles. That's why there's a fine of $2,000 for anybody who doesn't break his empty whisky bottles. You know that?"

"Never heard of it."

Wade nodded seriously.

"There's a fellow in New York has a bottle-crushing business. He collects from restaurants and saloons every morning. Anyway, the point is that these crook distillers have got to get bottles—and they've got to get barrels. And they can't get the barrels in the open, because we check on 'em. And that's where the Curriers come in. That's where Speer came in."

Ben filled his pipe, listening. It was beginning to make sense.

"Speer's been hunting down Pete Hromanik's plant for two years. He had one clue that kept turning up. Those fifty-gallon barrels we found, and some others we turned up, that we knew were Pete's, had a 'C' burned in the head. They were white oak, hand-made, old-fashioned barrels. Kind you don't often see these days. Well, there was an idea in that. Those kegs were being made out in the country somewhere, where there was a lot of white oak and an old-fashioned cooper. Speer kept at it, and he traced 'em to Tennessee. He spent three months going in and out of these hills, and one day he happened to come up here with a fellow that works for the TVA, and on Currier's gate post damned if he didn't spot that 'C' burned in the wood. You've seen it there, if you've ever looked."

143

Ben nodded. Julie's fingers, shyly marking the outline of that "C" as he looked down at her smooth head gleaming in the sun, leaped into his mind.

"I guess you saw it on the bottom of a tree too, didn't you?"

"Hell, I saw it *put* on the bottom of a tree, about three feet from my head."

Wade's eyes almost twinkled.

"Well, that's what brought Speer into this. I guess that's what's in that letter he left for you."

"You didn't know it, before you came?"

Wade shook his head.

"I've seen the 'C' on the kegs. I knew Speer was in the Alcohol Tax Unit. When I went down to the Hollow I saw that 'C' on the gate, and it was clear enough. Loftus had told me Speer was out nights. I guessed he wasn't 'courtin' ' the girl, as they all seemed to think. I knew him pretty well."

Wade was silent a moment.

"He wanted to get the people who came for the kegs?"

The agent shook his head, threw his cigar away and took out another.

"No. It isn't that easy. Most people don't realize that hunting down crooks is a damn painstaking, grubbing, long-winded business. If it was just figuring out who did things, we could walk up to a thousand people tomorrow and take 'em in, and we'd be right every damn time. But we've got to have evidence, so even a jury can see it. No use pulling a man in if you can't convict him. So Speer would have sat there, getting ticks and chiggers in his pants, for six months, just to get the license number of the truck that came in after those barrels. If he got a break, perhaps he could recognize the driver. Perhaps he could follow him. But it usually wouldn't work out that easy. He'd get the license number, and sooner or later some service station man would pick up that truck, and it'd take us to Pete Hromaník's plant. That's the way we've got to work. It wouldn't do any good to take in the truck driver. It's not illegal to haul a load of handmade fifty-gallon kegs with a 'C' burned on the heads. But if he'd traced it to Pete's plant, he'd have made the biggest strike in the history of revenuing."

Ben took his pipe out of his mouth.

"Look here. Mike Shannon—he's one of the CCC drivers —saw truck tracks down in the field, in the road going to the workshop. He spotted them again the morning we found Speer. The road's damp down there."

Wade nodded. "I saw 'em. I checked up with the camp trucks. That's one of the things I've been going on."

"What about that truck driver killing Speer?"

144

Wade shook his head.

"He'd have used a revolver, a sawed-off shot-gun or a sub-machine gun."

Ben thought a minute. "But the same person didn't necessarily kill both Speer and old Nathan."

Wade's bleak eyes were fixed in front of him. "Not necessarily."

"Speer was shot, Currier was clubbed to death. There's a difference."

"Not so much as you'd think," Wade said slowly. "Speer was shot in the back. Currier's head was beaten in—from behind. The dog was kicked before his head was crushed. His hind leg was in splinters."

He hesitated.

"It looks like the same fellow to me. Taking other things into consideration. A coward, strong as an ox, and pretty damn shrewd too."

Neither of them spoke for a moment. Ben knocked out his pipe.

"It couldn't have been Edrew Mincey?"

"The half-wit?"

Ben nodded.

"Why?"

"One of the Curriers smashed his old guitar. There was cat-tail fuzz—calking, Mis' Mincey called it—in the wood."

Ben grinned suddenly.

"She thought calking would mean something to me. It didn't, not till you mentioned the barrels. I've got a vague idea about some connection."

"Flagging, they call it," Wade said. "They soak the fuzz and plaster it around the head."

He glanced at Ben.

"Is that what happened to the old guitar?"

Ben nodded.

"His mother's poor as the devil. Her place is mortgaged for more than she'll get from the government."

"A lot of 'em are. That's the bad part of the TVA. But hell, it's the same all over the country. Well, I don't know about the boy."

"He's not strong enough, I guess."

"Don't you believe it. That boy's like steel and whipcord. He couldn't get around like he does if he wasn't."

Ben glanced at him a little troubled, sorry he had said anything about the boy. Wade nodded.

"Don't let it worry you. We'd have got him anyway, if it was him. Anyway, what you've said about the mortgage applies to lots of people. Kilgore's place is mortgaged. And then if you're as proud as these people—and God knows they are —I guess you don't much like having a mongrel dog named after you. I'm interested in Kilgore."

Wade was silent for a moment.

"General Turner's got it all sewed up," he said sardonically. "He's got this fellow Sisky inside. Turner doesn't like his looks or his accent."

He drew a deep breath and let it out wearily. Ben realized that if Wade had been watching the Hollow as Speer had done he had not been getting much sleep.

"Well, we'll see," Wade said. "The crowd Speer was after have been scared off. I'm really not in it now, except to find out who killed Speer. Currier's not Federal jurisdiction. However, I think they're the same."

"I hope you get the thirty thousand."

"Thirty thousand?"

"Doss said that's what the old fellow carried in his belt."

"He told me he didn't know."

Wade shook his head. "But that doesn't count, not up in these parts."

"He thinks you might have taken it."

Wade gave him a long masked glance and looked away.

"He does?"

"He told me so."

"He thinks you're out of it?"

"Just by the exercise of logic and horse sense," Ben said. "He figured if I'd got the thirty thousand I'd have 'lit out.' Not waited to see Julie. Old Doss evidently agrees with him. So I guess I wasn't in any danger this afternoon. I wasn't sure about it when I left. That's why I left you the note."

Wade looked at him queerly.

"It's a damn good thing you did," he said quietly. "Miss Elly told me you'd gone to Knoxville."

Ben grinned.

"Maybe you'll find out some day that you had a damn close shave, up there on the ridge," Wade said. "Don't you get cocky just because you came back alive that time. If you hadn't left me that note . . ."

He broke off suddenly, and shook his head. Ben looked at him. He was deadly serious.

"Listen, Davidge," he said. "I'm telling you. Keep on this side of the river. That girl will be all right."

Ben shook his head.

"That's not good enough," he said quietly. "I'm going to get her out of there—if she wants to come—if it's the last thing I do."

Wade looked at him silently for a moment. "It won't do

146

anybody much good if you get her out and you stay in—six feet under," he said coldly.

"I won't stay in."

"You don't know how near you've been—twice."

The same tone of cold seriousness was in his voice. Ben turned in the seat to face him.

"Look here," he said. "Have you . . . do you know who you're looking for?"

A light flickered in the agent's bleak eyes.

"I've got an idea—thanks to you."

"To me?"

Wade nodded. "That's why I'm telling you, son. Don't go back to Currier Hollow. Stay *this* side of the river."

Ben shook his head.

"I guess you don't understand."

Wade smiled suddenly—warmly, for him. He turned and put his hand on Ben's shoulder.

"I understand, son. If you could keep your shirt on, I'd tell you you're being a damn fool. These things are all right, up here in the hills, where you're out of touch with your own background. It'll be different, taking that girl out of hers into yours."

Ben flushed. Wade shrugged his shoulders.

"That's none of my business. But it is my business to warn you that if you butt in again over there, you're likely to get that girl hurt. As long as you keep out she's safe. It's a matter of *waiting*."

Ben shook his head.

"All right. I guess nobody ever learned how to wait until they were a heap older than you. There's one thing I want, though, or I'll put you under arrest again. That's your word that when you decide to go over there, you'll tell me, so I can come along."

"O.K.," Ben said.

Wade looked at him with a sour smile. "I owe you a lot," he said. "I'd hate to see you killed."

30

General Turner and the Loftuses, with a couple of the neighbors from up the bend, were sitting on the back porch after supper. The low babble of their talk was punctuated with Ed Loftus's deep chuckle, Miss Elly's cackle, General Popeye's high nervous whinny. Ben paced up and down the yard between the geranium tubs on the front porch, chewing at the stem of his cold pipe. Wade had stepped out, down to the Kilgores', Loftus had said when Ben asked for him. It seemed to Ben that it was just a stall to keep him from going over to the Hollow.

Only one thing kept him from going—Wade's last warning to him. It kept running through his head, beating down his own desire. Julie was safe as long as he let her alone. He knew it was true—but every instinct he had urged him to her. He sat down on the steps and reached for his tobacco pouch. It was empty. He tried to tell himself that that was what had made him jumpy. But he knew it wasn't.

Out in the road a farm wagon loaded with rush chairs, cupboards with ornamental tin doors, beds and cooking utensils creaked by. A frail worn-out woman with a baby at her breast sat in the seat by the driver, a lank bearded man with his hat on the back of his head. Three ragged children huddled asleep on a streaked yellow mattress on the top of the pile. Ben stared at them. There, but for the grace of God, went Julie Currier—and Doss. He jerked his lean body upright and tried not to think of them.

The creaking wagon pulled off to one side of the road in the shelter of the jutting rocks at the bend. Ben could see them getting out. A child cried. They were camping for the night. It was a part of the tragic exodus of families through the hill roads—with nothing but a crying child to mark the numb silent pain of exile. The woman's bent weary figure was going down to the branch with an iron kettle in her hand, the children tagging anxiously behind her. The man sat by the roadside, whittling a stick, the dog at his feet savaging a tick on his flank.

Ben suddenly looked down past the little camp and got to his feet. He went slowly out to the road. In the bushes along the road past the whittling man a small twisted figure was hopping in and out. Ben stared down at it, a sense of something unusual growing in him. Edrew seldom came that way —his mother's cabin was behind him—or in the open road. For a moment Ben thought he might have been coming to inspect the little camp, but as he came up to it he cut off the road and disappeared in the trees. Ben turned back towards the porch. Suddenly he heard a low vibrant chord—miles away, he would have thought it. He turned sharply. No one was in the road. Then the leaves moved, across from him, up on the bank, and a shiver ran through them to the bottom. Edrew's twisted figure slipped out, his guitar pressed close to his side. He darted a swift vacant glance up and down the road and hopped across, light and quick as a hawk.

148

His breath was coming in short sharp gasps. He closed his thin fingers as strong as steel ribbons on Ben's arm and tugged urgently at him, pointing with his other hand down the road. Ben stared down at him, trying to read the meaning in the vacant mindless face. Edrew's fingers relaxed, took up his guitar; then as if remembering again he seized Ben's arm, pulling him towards the road. He let go and hopped a few steps along the side, stopped and looked back, like a dog urging his master on.

Ben's heart missed a beat. He pointed to his car. The crippled boy's face relaxed to a grin. He had forgotten again. Then his face contorted suddenly, and he hopped along, looking back at Ben.

Ben took a deep breath of relief. If Edrew wanted him to go that way, it wasn't Julie. Probably his mother who wanted him. He nodded and came out into the road.

Edrew hopped along, disappeared behind the undergrowth, looking back as he went in so that Ben could follow along the open road. He did not appear again until they had passed the camp where the woman was bending over the fire. Suddenly Edrew came out again, far ahead of him in the road. Ben quickened his pace. He could see the whitewashed cabin ahead of him, quiet and peaceful in the falling dusk. Suddenly Edrew darted across the road and dived into the brush, waiting there for Ben to follow.

In that instant began a nightmare journey that seared Ben's brain, through the tangled honeysuckle, in and out between rocks and bramble-hung bushes, tearing his face, his hands, his shirt. Snakes slithered past his booted feet, cobwebs blinded him. The afflicted boy hopped ahead like a firefly, disappearing and appearing again, urging him on with every device he knew. The blood trickled down Ben's torn cheek into his mouth with a sharp salt taste. He wiped it off with his sleeve and plunged on. He knew now that he was going to Currier Hollow, by Edrew's private road. He closed his mind to keep from asking why, following grim-jawed, hoping, cold with despair. Suddenly he smelled the river, and they burst out on the bank.

Edrew was hopping across the dry protruding boulders in the shallow edges of the stream. Beyond him Ben could see the narrow single plank bridging the swift racing torrent of the channel. He followed up to it. Edrew's ninety pounds bounded lightly across it. It swayed under him to the water's edge. A hundred and eighty pounds on it was out of the question. He hesitated an instant, looking down at a heavy sycamore log, flattened on one side, lying at his feet. It would

149

have held him. But there was no time to lose. He let himself down into the current and struck out upstream with steady powerful strokes.

The boy across the frail bridge watched him with staring china-blue eyes, bobbing up and down excitedly, as he neared the bank, swept down by the swift stream. Ben's feet struck the sandy bottom, he pulled himself up and struggled out of the channel. Edrew was gone. Suddenly his head flashed up in the trees on the bank and was gone again. Ben labored up the bank and followed, through the trees, across the river road up the ridge, through brambles, ducking down into the narrow tunnel made by the half-witted boy. They doubled across the road again. The boy stopped, clutched at Ben's arm, slipped quietly along, as silent as a night owl flitting through the branches. Ben's heavy boots crashed and tore through the broken twigs and dried leaves. Suddenly Edrew stopped again. Ben came up beside him. Edrew was peering vacantly down through the leaves. Beyond him Ben could see the smoke rising like a frail gray plume from the cabin in Currier Hollow. Edrew grinned suddenly and sat down, picking delightedly at the bright strings of the guitar.

Ben stared at him, puzzled and a little angry. A wild goose chase through brambles and rivers just to gaze down at the cabin in Currier Hollow was a little too much, even from an idiot. Edrew looked vacantly around. Suddenly he made a quick bird-like movement to one side and picked up a stick. Something fell from his pocket and struck Ben's boot lightly. He leaned over in the fading light, and saw a narrow folded oblong of curious yellow paper. He looked sharply at Edrew. The boy had dropped the stick and was picking again softly at the guitar. Ben picked up the piece of paper and unfolded it. It was a hundred-dollar gold note. Edrew Mincey looked at it blankly, only his long fingers living as they moved lightly over the strings. There was no meaning in his face that Ben could interpret as he looked at the yellow note.

His fingers on the guitar strings wavered and died as he looked up at Ben. Edrew had remembered again. He moved his twisted body so that he could point down directly at the cabin; and then, as Ben still stood there, looking at him, he suddenly clutched his own throat with his long frail hands, letting the guitar hang by its cord. He dug the two hands into his throat until his eyes bulged, his tongue protruded, his white face was purplish.

Ben turned and ran down the hill to the road, and down the incline to the cabin gate. The gate stood open. The branded "C" in the post seemed to stand out like fire as he dashed through and up to the porch. The kitchen was empty.

150

The table was turned over. A granite skillet of half-cooked food was lying on Julie's spotless floor. Ben ran along the porch to the room where Nathan Currier had been killed. No one was there. Ben jumped on the bed and drew himself up to the empty loft trapdoor. A tin platter with dried corn bread and a piece of bacon was on the stool beside an earthen jug of yellow milk; but no one was there.

He ran back to the porch and stood staring down the Hollow. Far down, across the cornfield, he saw a wreath of smoke rising from Old Doss's workshop. He cleared the steps with a stride and tore across the yard to the road. His boots pounded on the narrow road through the corn, past the road leading up to the fallen cedar, past the tracks of the truck tires Mike had pointed out that first day, along the rough road to the shop.

There was no light in the log building. No sound came from it; only the white plume of smoke rose from the rude chimney. Above the sky was clear and star-studded, the hills rose, clear dark walls hemming in the unbroken loveliness of the Hollow. Ben's feet pounding madly on the ground made the only sound in the night. He ran, faster than he had ever run in all his life, towards the dark oblong that was the shop door. As he came on, the darkness there diminished, crossed by faint waves of light from the fire inside. There was still no sound but his own pounding feet.

All his senses were bent towards the dark building. Almost there he stopped running and crept along quietly up to the porch, to the door, and peered into the workroom. In the corner, the firelight playing on her terror-distorted face, Julie crouched, hands thrust out before her as if to keep off some terrible fate. Ben's blood froze with horror.

31

In front of him was the room he had come to see the night the cold muzzle of a shotgun pressed into his spine had warned him off. He hadn't seen it then, nor did he see it now: the fire burning in the crisit, the windlass with the cable drawn tightly around the ends of a half-finished barrel, the oddly shaped knives, the champfers, inshaves, spokeshaves, hoopshaves, the truss hoops of hickory and birch, hanging around the dark walls. All he saw was Julie, faint with terror, her gray eyes fixed in an agony of horror on the old man in front of her, her lips white as death, her body crouched back against the rough wall.

In the silence of the dark room fragrant with old odors of charred oak and hickory, Old Doss's gaunt colorless form towered like a ghastly specter. His dead eyes glowed, his gnarled hands were clutched tightly round a long iron. The end of it, curved to form the letter C, glowed white-hot in the dark shadows, a living symbol, primitive and awful. He raised his arm, brought the frost-hot iron down, pressed it for the fraction of an instant against the white clean staves in the windlass. There was a sudden movement of smoke and the sharp smell of new damp wood burning, and in the still white glow of the iron Ben saw the small charred letter that Speer had traced from the seaboard to that remote hollow in the Tennessee hills.

The old man's skeleton-like body moved slowly forward. A sound, rough and unused, came from his lips. He was speaking. Ben had never heard words that he had spoken before.

"Ye're a Currier. Ye're goin' t' stay a Currier."

It was hardly more than a breathed hoarse whisper in the silence of the Hollow. Time seemed to stop for Ben, standing there, each fraction of an instant prolonging itself into an eternity of horror. He stared for a moment, paralyzed, at the two, the fear-crazed old man, goaded by the terror of a new exile, warped and twisted by seventy bitter lonely years, creeping towards the white-faced girl, her eyes glued to the white-hot brand.

Ben's brain reeled dizzily and caught itself, steadied icy cold. Controlled as a tight-rope walker poised above a packed plane of seething humanity, he put his foot over the threshold until he touched the hard earth floor. Julie must not see him, mustn't waver in that horrible fascination. He crept forward a step. Still between them, the small brown "C" burning into his brain, was the half-made keg on the windlass. He had to pass it, not to stumble over the hoops littered on the dark floor, not to take his eyes off the old man, creeping like a tattered buzzard towards the girl in the corner. Three yards, cluttered with old staves and tools, with the windlass and the schnitzel bank, between him and Old Doss. He slipped past the windlass.

"Ye ain't goin' t' git off. Ye're a Currier."

It sounded in the stifling room with the concentrated malignancy of hell.

"Currier's mark . . . they'll know ye're a Currier."

Ben could not make out all of it. He took a step closer. Julie opened her mouth. Only a strangled sob broke through her lips. Then Ben dived forward with a tremendous shout, caught the old man around the waist and closed his

152

right hand on the sinewy wrist holding the iron. The scream of an animal in pain came from Currier's mouth. He struggled forward like a madman to reach the girl, then wrenched his body to the side and his arm loose and struck out with the iron. Ben felt it strike his leg and smelled the burning leather, felt the sharp pain. His feet firm on the ground, he heaved the old man into the bench, forced him back over it, caught at his hand again.

"Run, Julie!" he shouted.

Currier screamed again and brought the iron down. Ben caught his wrist in his left hand, and the two stood there, straining every muscle, the old man with a power in his gaunt frame that was inconceivable. The hot sweat rolled down Ben's face. He felt the sharp stabbing pain in his leg. The room was silent again except for the hot blood pounding in his temples. Currier's left hand closed on his throat. Ben let go with his right, dug his head into the old man's chest to break the grip and caught the hand holding the iron with both hands. He put everything he had into one great heave. Currier's unbalanced body hurtled over his shoulders and onto the floor; the iron, wrenched out of his hand, clattered on the floor.

Ben turned to dive for it and stopped. Julie stood by it, Old Doss's shotgun in her small steady hands, her face a mask through which nothing showed that Ben had ever seen there before.

"Stand back," she said.

Old Doss struggled to his feet and took a step towards her. Ben saw her face quiver with a sudden spasm of pain. He knew that the old man would still come towards her, and that she couldn't shoot him. His head reeled with the pain of his burned calf. He moved closer to Julie, in between the two of them. Back to the door, he saw the sudden light in Old Doss's face and heard Julie's gasp. A shot cracked out in the night. Old Doss's face was sharply distorted with pain. He still stood there, his eyes fixed on something behind Ben, by the door. Ben turned as the old man, unaware of anything else, pushed by him, shaking like a willow, and knelt down on the floor beside his son. Young Doss's face writhed as he lay there, and his hand clutched feebly at his side.

Ben stared down in dumb amazement. His eyes moved slowly to Julie. She was standing there, eyes wide, lips parted, the gun still in her hands. Ben saw her look at it bewildered. She raised her hand and passed it in a slow and dazed gesture over her eyes. Then she swayed a little. Ben caught her with one hand and took the gun.

"Did I do that?" she whispered.

153

He let her body down gently on the head of an upturned keg and steadied her against him. Suddenly he whirled around. Behind him where the iron had fallen against a pile of dried flagging, brisk flames sprang up. In an instant the whole side of the room was alive with fire. Ben seized Julie in his arms and sprang to the door, the gun pressing hard between their bodies. The red light flared. Ben forgot the streaking pain in his leg as he strode off the porch. All his being was focused on the small precious burden in his aching arms, and the gray eyes looking up into his.

"I did it because he was going to hurt you," she whispered.

She closed her eyes as Ben's lips touched her cold cheek. He put her down on the ground under the soft silken rustle of the tall corn, the gun beside her.

Behind him the yellow flames flickered joyfully up over the roof. In the bright glare he caught a glimpse of the crippled boy, standing up the road, watching with wide empty eyes, weaving his fingers over something in his hands as if it were the guitar that was hanging silent on his shoulder.

Ben dashed across the yard strewn with stripped cat-tails to the red angry door of the shop. Inside Old Doss, weak and broken, was dragging helplessly at his son, mumbling incoherently, the tears furrowing his yellow cheeks.

"Get out!" Ben shouted. He pushed him towards the door, bent over and lifted Doss. The blood, warm and viscid, wet his hands. The fire roared behind him like a furnace. The flames played across the dried oak chips to the truss hoops, making bright circlets of flame that licked his boots. He staggered out over the low threshold into the cool clear night.

Outside he laid Doss Currier on the ground, pressed his handkerchief over the jagged wound in his side, and held his pocket flask to his lips. Currier turned his head away from it. A sardonic gleam came to his eyes.

"Hit'll be all right," he said. "Whar's Julie?"

Ben looked around. Between them and the burning building Old Doss stood silhouetted like a giant scarecrow, his tattered coat moving grotesquely in the evening breeze. Doss tried to raise himself on his elbow.

"She's all right," Ben said. "Take it easy."

"Whar's Julie?"

Ben pointed to the corn. Julie was standing there, gazing into the fire. The flame playing across her face made a nimbus of gold of her hair. Doss lay down. He touched Ben's knee with his hand. A spasm of pain contracted his thin mouth.

154

"If I don't git no better, take keer of Julie, Mister Davidge," he whispered. "Paw'll kill her if you don't." ·

Ben nodded. He went over to the old man. "I'll carry him up to the cabin," he said. "Will you go on ahead and get some water hot?"

Old Doss stared silently at him for an instant, and nodded slowly. Then his head raised and he stood there listening. Someone was running rapidly along the road from the cabin. Ben peered up the road, blinded by the light from the fire. He could not make out who it was. Not Edrew, for he had been there in the firelight, staring into the flames. The pounding steps came on and a dark figure appeared, running towards them powerfully. Ben took a deep breath of relief. It was Wade. He stopped at the end of the corn, blinded at first by the fire, blinking from one to the other of them. Old Doss, Ben standing by him, bedraggled, dirt-stained, his clothes burned and torn, Doss Currier wounded on the ground. Then he came slowly up to Ben, and stared silently at him for a moment.

"May I be everlastingly God damned," he said.

"Currier's hurt," Ben said. "We've got to get him up to the cabin."

They turned at a sudden movement in the corn. Julie came slowly across the yard, and went to the old man standing there without a glance at Ben.

"I didn't mean to do it, Old Doss," she said. "I'll stay with you now, and take care of him, like you want. You don't need to fret. I'll do for you, as long as there's breath in my body. I won't try to go away any more."

Ben saw her shoulders quiver under the coarse black homespun. She went slowly over to Doss.

"I won't give you any more trouble, Doss. I didn't mean to do it."

He looked at her queerly.

"That's all right, Julie. Hit ain't nothin' t' speak about."

She turned her head quickly. Ben saw her catch her lip in her firm white teeth. The tears gleamed along her lashes and streaked down her cheeks.

Wade stood watching them, a puzzled scowl on his face.

"You shot him?" he demanded.

She nodded. "I didn't mean to do it."

"Where's the gun?"

She went back to the corn slowly and brought it to him. Wade looked at it, and broke it with a quick twist of his hands.

He looked back at her, still more bewildered.

"Hell!" he said. "This gun hasn't been fired. You haven't shot anybody."

Ben looked at him. Then he turned and shot a quick glance to the tree by the branch where Edrew Mincey had been sitting. No one was there. Ben listened. There was no sound of his guitar in the still night.

Julie looked up at the Treasury agent, her lips parted, her breath coming in quick little sobs. She turned to her cousin.

"Oh, Doss!" she whispered. "I'm glad it wasn't me. I'm glad it wasn't!"

32

Ben took the basin of blood-stained water to the kitchen stoop and threw it into the bushes, rinsed it out with cold water from the bucket on the bench, brought it back and filled it with clean hot water from the kettle on the stove. He put it on the chair by the bed and went out. Wade and Old Doss were better at that sort of thing than he was . . . and Julie had gone out onto the porch.

She was standing on the steps, looking down the Hollow at the burning shop. She did not turn when he stood beside her, too choked with the sense of her to speak. He felt for her hand, blindly but surely, and held it, cold and forlorn, in his own.

"I love you, Julie . . . so much!"

It was a broken whisper, stifled against the cool fragrance of her hair.

For a moment her hand clung to his. Then she raised her face, breathless.

"I love you, too," she murmured. His lips touched hers softly for an instant. Then she drew away.

"But I can't go with you, Ben. I see it all much better now."

He turned her sharply to face him, staring at her.

"Julie . . . after tonight? Listen . . ."

Her slow smile was softened with the age-old wisdom of the women of the hills. She shook her head sadly.

"No. It was because I was so headstrong that it happened, Ben. It wouldn't have, but I said I'd never marry Doss, not after he took your letter. I said I'd die first. That's why it happened. Old Doss doesn't mean any harm."

It was incomprehensible. Having seen what he had in those few nightmare moments standing in the workshop door, Ben was speechless for a moment. He shook his head helplessly. Then he said, "Julie—you didn't mean what you said in your letter, the one Doss brought. Did you?"

She shook her head slowly.

"I didn't, then, because Doss made me write it, or he'd have killed you. I . . . I didn't want him to kill you."

She turned her head away and closed her eyes.

Ben drew her to him and held her, yielding like a tired child, against his damp dirt-stained shirt, until she drew back again, looking up into his eyes.

"But I mean it now," she said softly.

His hands gripped her slim little shoulders, holding her tightly. "No," he said. "No, Julie."

She nodded.

"It's right, that way. They know. You'll get tired of me. I'm an ignorant mountain girl. You're educated. You know other girls, girls your own kind. When you get back where they are you'll see how . . . how ignorant I am. I've never been out of the Hollow. I've . . . I've never even been to school—or to a movie."

He tilted her chin up, and smiled deep into her clear tear-washed eyes.

"I love you, Julie. I don't care if you've never been to a movie. You can go to one every day the rest of your life if you want to."

She drew away, bewildered and a little hurt.

"None of that matters, Julie. I love you, and that's all that counts—if you love me."

"It's all now, Ben. But it wouldn't be all after a while. They say it's like my grandmother. She went away with a man from outside. She had to come back . . . to the Kilgores'. That's why we . . . we hate the Kilgores."

He laughed a little shakily. "Oh, Lord, Julie, it's not the same! Because I love you, and you're going to marry me."

He caught her roughly to him and buried his aching lips in her soft smooth throat, crushing her in his arms.

The sweeping headlights of a car across the Hollow and the sound of an engine brought him to his senses. He felt her body stiffen quickly, and turned towards the gate. Two men were coming down the gravel incline. She put her hand softly on his arm.

"I don't care what happens now," she whispered. "But I can't leave Doss. He'll need me more, now. Good-by, Ben."

He heard her feet in the coarse shoes running quickly along the porch.

The gate chain fell back over the post.

"Hullo, there! Anybody home?"

Ed Loftus's voice rang through the empty courtyard. He peered up at Ben.

"Evenin', Mr. Davidge. Looks mighty like you all been havin' a fire down yonder."

Ben nodded. "Hello, Mr. Loftus. Looks like it. Good evening, sir."

"Evening, Mr. Davidge." General Turner's high falsetto identified his short fidgety steps coming across the hard dirt yard with Loftus's firm heavy stride.

They came up onto the porch. Loftus hesitated a moment by Ben, looking down at the smoldering ruins below in the Hollow.

"Ain't been no trouble, has there, Mr. Davidge?"

Ben's leg ached like fire, his head pounded.

"Nothing to speak of."

"Where's everybody?"

"Inside. Doss got shot. I don't think it's very bad."

Ed Loftus chuckled a little.

"I never knowed you toted a gun, Mr. Davidge."

The Attorney General stared at Ben nervously. It was plain that he did not really care about mountain shooting.

"I declare, Ed! I reckon we'd better look into this."

Mr. Loftus winked prodigiously at Ben.

"I reckon you better be mighty careful round yere, Yancey. Don't look very healthy to me."

General Turner looked hastily about with agitation. "Now, I've always been mighty friendly with you boys up here, Ed. You know that, Ed, don't you?"

"Shore do, Yancey."

Loftus spat over the side of the steps.

"Ain't nary a thing goin' t' hurt you, Yancey, less'n hit's by accident. You better stay by me closer'n a brother."

He winked at Ben again. They went on into the cabin. The smell of carbolic acid suddenly made Ben dizzy. He sat down by the stove, looking at the strangest collection of human beings that he could have imagined. Doss Currier lay on the maple spool bed, his dark eyes glowing, enormous in his bloodless face. Old Doss, a ragged colorless skeleton with the faded sparse wisps of whiskers falling from his chin, the faded yellow hair sticking out of the rents in his hat, the frayed sleeves falling on his thin hairy arms well above the wrists. They looked, the two of them, with the lamplight falling on them from the mantel, like two timeless beings into whose world the wiry hard-faced Federal agent and the little pop-eyed Attorney General in his wrinkled Palm Beach suit and Panama hat had wandered by mistake. Only Ed Loftus, standing at the foot of the bed where he could spit into the

158

woodbox, had any kinship with them. Yet he had it equally with Turner and Wade, as if he stood somewhere on middle ground between the timeless hills and the new world outside, as if he alone could touch them both.

Looking at them Ben felt a queer tightening in his throat. If that was true, what of himself, and Julie? Was the gulf between them, of convention and custom, something they could never bridge? But she had to go out, she couldn't stay here in the lonely world she had always lived in. Her world, the sticks and stones and the trailing fragrant vines of it, would be sunk by the great dam, buried under eighty feet of water. She had to go into a new life.

Ben looked intently at the lean dark face, drawn with pain and loss of blood, lying against the coarse homespun pillowcase. Would she be better off with Doss than with him? He shook his head unconsciously. If you picked a wild orchid, it was no harder on it to be taken to a lovely place, like his mother's home, than to take it to the barren place that Doss Currier would make for her, himself a stranger in the world outside.

He rubbed his hand hard across his forehead, trying to clear his brain of the trailing vestiges of horror that clung to it like gray moss ribbons to a live oak. Only gradually he heard the talk going on around the bed. It was Yancey Turner's nasal whinny that brought him back to it.

"Jess Kilgore says you were down there after supper askin' him some mighty plain questions," he was saying.

Ben saw the sudden dangerous flicker in Wade's eyes.

Ed Loftus grinned.

"Bet you didn't git a heap a' plain answers, did you, Mr. Wade?" He spat into the woodbox and wiped his mouth.

They all laughed heartily. Even Old Doss's face lighted, and he rubbed his dry hands together. Ben had a curious sense of all of them ganging up on the Federal, enjoying his discomfiture, even though it was their deadliest enemy who had discomfited him.

Wade smiled bleakly.

"I got something pretty interesting," he said laconically. The lamplight shone on his spare sharp face as he looked from one to the other of them. He reached in his vest pocket, took out his billfold and a metal spectacle case. He put on a pair of horn-rimmed spectacles, opened the billfold, and holding it down in the light took out a folded piece of paper. He unfolded it and held it flat on the palm of his hand where the dim light shone full on it.

It was an old yellow gold certificate. Ben felt hastily in his own pocket. Edrew's note was still there. He looked back at the circle of faces under the lamp. They were all fixed with varying expressions, gazing at the paper bill in Wade's hand. Old Doss's hands on the spool headboard shook violently. Doss Currier's face flushed. Ed Loftus put on his own spectacles, reached out for the note, examined it a long time silently and spat into the woodbox. He handed it to the Attorney General.

"This yere's a gold note," he said.

The General nodded nervously. He looked apprehensively around the room.

"It's not legal to have these, nowadays," he said.

"I don't reckon Nate never heared much about that sort a' thing," Loftus said. "Probably never heared about hit nohow."

Wade turned to Old Doss. "I suppose that was your brother's?"

Doss answered. "The numbers air in th' book. I reckon hit's hisn, all right."

"Whar'd you git this, Mr. Wade?"

Wade smiled.

"Edrew Mincey," he said coolly. "I guess he knows where the whole lot is, if we could get him to talk."

There was a little silence.

"Edrew's right fond a' Julie," Loftus said. "I reckon he'd tell her, if we was to find him."

Yancey Turner nodded. "He'll have 'em scattered all over the creation if we don't get him quick."

A spasm of pain crossed Doss's face as he tried to raise himself up.

"You ain't goin' t' take Julie no place huntin' money t'night," he said. "I reckon there ain't no dead rush."

"Hit's her money, ain't it, now, Doss?" Loftus said amiably. "Old Nate he always talked like he was aimin' t' leave hit all t' Julie."

He winked at Ben. "I reckon Yancey could take a look at his will an' see how hit is, couldn't you, Yancey?"

Wade put the bill back in his pocket.

"Currier's right," he said shortly. "There's no rush. I'm going home. Come on, Davidge. You look all in. Where's your car?"

"I didn't bring it."

"Then come along with me."

Ben hesitated. He did not want to go. But there was nothing he could say or do about Julie in front of all these people. He followed Wade out onto the porch and looked around. Julie was not in sight.

At the bottom of the steps he stopped.

"Look here. We can't go and leave Julie."

"Shut up," Wade said coolly. "Come on down here."

They went across the yard and up the incline. In the road Wade stopped.

"What happened?"

Ben told him about the scene in the workshop, still smoking faintly across the field. He pulled out the bill he had taken from Edrew. Wade took it, looked at it in the faint light and put it in his billfold.

"Now I'll tell you something," he said quietly. "I've got a job to do, and with any kind of a break I'm going to do it tonight, if that fool Turner hasn't gummed the works. The girl's *safe*—safer than she'll ever be again, probably. Old Doss is burned out, for tonight anyway. Nothin's going to happen, with Loftus and Turner there."

Ben swore under his breath. "They won't be there all night."

"I'd like to have a bet that Turner won't. He's shaking in his boots. He won't go back across these hills, not when he knows all the money is loose somewhere around here."

"Is it?"

"It is," Wade said coldly. "I've been following this half-wit. I've had a talk with his mother. I've got a pretty good idea where that money's cached. Not the exact place, but near enough to catch some bird with his pants down when he comes to get it. I tell you I've been doing my job."

"You think he'll come tonight for it?"

"You let me worry about that. Now come on and shut up. The girl's all right. Hello, what's the matter with you?"

Ben swayed and leaned against a tree. His leg streaked and stabbed with fire, his head was splitting.

"It's all right," he said. "I got the old-fashioned cooper's brand in my leg instead of my back. It's O.K."

"By God, it's got to be. Here. Let me have a look."

Wade bent down and took out his flash. He whistled a little as he saw the rent seared flesh. He took out a handkerchief, tore off a piece, folded the handkerchief and tied it roughly over the burn. The cool linen felt like ice on the stabbing surface. Ben's head swam.

"It's clean," Wade said. "Best I can do now. You'll be all right. Here. Have a drag at this."

Ben felt the Treasury agent's hand gripping his shoulder, shaking him violently. He swallowed the brandy from Wade's flask.

"Come on, man! Buck up. We've got work."

His head cleared a little. "I'm all right."

"Come on," Wade said.

161

33

Ben moved after him dizzily, his leg shooting spurts of fiery pain through him, stumbling and walking on, looking back at the cabin with aching longing.

"Get in," Wade said. He opened the door of his car and pushed him in, slid under the wheel and drove off. Not up the hill but back along the river road. He came to a cleared path made by the CCC around the base of the hill, parked the car behind a clump of alders and got out. Ben followed. They went back to the road and started off retracing their way.

Wade looked back at the car. "I don't want anything to happen to that," he said. "I guess it's out of sight."

They went along the road, feeling their way through the deep ruts, sticking to the roadside where they could. It seemed miles to Ben before Wade touched his arm.

"Quiet now," he said. "Here we are. Slip in here."

Ben saw the tiny building in front of him in the blackness. He put out his hand and felt the boards. Then his fingers touched a familiar object. It was a gourd cup.

"This the spring house?" he whispered.

"Yes. Get behind it. Take this."

Wade pushed a small cold object into his hand.

"It's yours, by the way. And I've checked up on the registration."

Ben could hear him chuckle a little in the dark.

"Where'd you get it?"

Ben asked it without surprise or interest.

"Never mind. I got it. I've got one, and a torch. If he comes, you go out that side when I give the signal. I'll go out here. We'll cut him off. Remember he'll shoot to kill. We can't use the flash. Too much of a target. He doesn't miss."

"Who is it?"

"Wait and see."

"How do you know who it is?"

"I may be wrong. Wait."

"You're sure he'll come tonight?"

"He may have been here already. I don't think so."

Ben was silent a moment.

"It's pretty well narrowed down."

"Why so?"

"Doss is wounded. He can't get around. Sisky's in the jug."

"Sisky's not in the jug. He's out."

"How do you know?"

"I *let* him out. This afternoon at four o'clock."

"Where is he?"

"He *said* he was going back to New York."

"I see," Ben said. He was quite sure he did not.

It was very dark under the spreading limbs of the great sycamore. That would have to come down, he thought vaguely. The detail would get to it the first of next week. But it would be later now. Julie would be gone before they cut it. He shook his head. Everything he saw or thought led him back to her. Her face with its pointed uptilted little chin, and the two long wide-set gray eyes, so clear and lovely when the pale oval of her face was calm, so gay and dancing when she laughed suddenly, transforming the smooth bright hair from a nimbus to shining wings of gold. He bent his head forward on his hands, rubbed his fingers through his hair, breathed deeply. The pain in his leg was almost intolerable.

"You still think the same fellow killed the two of them," he asked after a long silent interval.

"Yes."

Wade's voice was barely audible, but Ben noticed that he did not whisper. A whisper carried in the night.

"Did he have a motive, by any chance?"

"Two of 'em."

"How do you know it's the same person?"

Wade was silent for a minute.

"I've got enough evidence to convict him ten times over," he said curtly. "Except with a mountain jury, maybe. I've got a used cartridge from damn near every shotgun in the valley. The two cartridges you fished out of the ditch were fired by one gun round here and no other. The firing pin's off center. That's why they were stolen out of your pocket."

"Who stole them?"

"The fellow that stole your gun."

"That's a help."

"Figure it out—and shut up."

"O.K."

Only the pain in his leg kept Ben from going to sleep in his tracks. He shook himself and tried to force his mind back along the daily routine of the last weeks to see who had had access to his pockets and his gun. It was no use. His brain reeled dizzily.

"Jess Kilgore wouldn't have any reason to kill Speer," he said.

Wade was silent.

"Or the dog."

Wade chuckled quietly.

163

"If you had a mongrel cur named after you by an old enemy, would you like it?"

"That doesn't account for Speer. You don't think Kilgore was helping them . . . Hell, they're enemies!"

Wade grunted.

"That's what they all say. Maybe they say it too damn much."

He caught Ben sharply by the arm. "Listen."

Ben leaned forward, his gun in the palm of his hand, hardly breathing, straining every nerve to listen and to forget the burning ache in his leg.

"He's on his way," Wade murmured. "Get ready!"

Ben closed his eyes, listening. Gradually he heard a sound, soft on the damp roadbed, creeping closer, stealthy as a cat. His heart pounded in his ears. He knew only one man who moved like that. Or two: he remembered the silent tread of the queer-turned boy padding through the woods up the ridge. The footsteps stopped and he heard the soft rustle of leaves. Suddenly he had a sharp instinctive sense of someone very near him in the dark. He focused his whole being on that one sensation, trying to find the silent creeping figure he knew now was concealed there in the blackness, creeping closer to his loot.

From somewhere far away as the sky he heard the doleful moan of the guitar. There was a quick angry snarl from the man in front of them in the dark. Wade moved his body silently. He gripped Ben's arm with his left hand and leaned far out to the right. Suddenly across the narrow road the white beam of his torch sprang out, and Wade ducked back behind the spring house, leaving it lying on the ground, just as the quick angry blast of flame from in front of them shattered it to bits. Wade fired twice and tore around the house.

"Put 'em up!" he yelled.

Ben sprang to the other side and rushed out blindly. He collided obliquely with a powerful figure and closed his hand on a rough garment. As his foot slipped on the wet moss-covered stones the man tore his coat out of Ben's hands and leaped over him. Ben could hear him running down the narrow road, Wade after him.

"Stop or I'll shoot!" Wade shouted. He ran on. Ben pulled himself up and ran after them, pounding along the road. Wade fired again. There was a blast of fire from in front. Ben ran on. For a moment he could hear only his own steps and those in front of him up the road. Then he heard Wade again. He was running lightly along the grassy edge of the road. Ben leaped over across the road to the other side and followed. It was easier running except that the branches cut his face. He tried to ward them off with his arm.

Wade stopped suddenly. There was no sound ahead.

"He's gone to cover," he said curtly. "Stay there."

Ben could hear him creeping along, barely moving, crouched down. Somewhere along that dark tunnel of leaves lurked a desperate man, gun raised, ready to shoot when he knew his aim was true. Ben went along silently on the grass. As his foot struck a stone by the roadside he remembered something he had once read. He picked up the stone, stepped out into the middle of the road and threw it out into the undergrowth ahead of them. Not thirty feet from where it struck a blast of flame spat out. Wade's revolver barked twice, sharp and savage. A man's voice swore.

"Give up!" Wade shouted.

The only answer was heavy feet pounding on in front of them. Ben knew the man was loading as he ran before another flame spat out up the dark tunnel and hot bits of lead winged his shoulder. He leaped to the side of the road again. How far they had come he had no idea. All he knew was that they were tearing along the river road, and that somewhere further along was the Kilgore place.

Suddenly he saw the figure of the man ahead of them, dark, bent almost double, dash out of the tree-lined road into the open and swerve sharply. Wade fired again. The man was lost in the undergrowth. Wade caught Ben's arm.

"Wait. He'll get us both if we go in there. This way." He curved off the road to the right through an opening between the trees and crept along a dark passage hollowed through the tangled honeysuckle. Ben followed, wondering if he would be able to keep on, vaguely aware that he had been in this place before.

"This is one of Edrew's trails," Wade said quietly as they stole along. "I found it that day I saw you talking to him at the Kilgores'."

They went on. Ben stopped when Wade stopped, listened dizzily when Wade listened. There was nothing else to do but go on, tortuously slow, through the narrow channel. How long they went he couldn't tell. Suddenly the dense undergrowth cleared and they were standing on the dry bank of the river. Wade sprang along the boulders showing white and dry in the light of the myriad stars above them. They rounded the bend, scrambling along the bank.

A hundred yards above them Ben saw the dark figure of a man creeping out of the woods. Ben stared. It was the bent twisted figure of Edrew Mincey. He was hopping quickly from boulder to boulder. Ben steadied himself for an instant and stared, fascinated, at him. Edrew stopped at the edge of the channel and bent down, and Ben could see the splash as he shoved some heavy object into the water. Then he sprang on his frail little bridge across the swirling stream and hopped lightly to the other side.

Ben started quickly down towards the channel. Wade, who had been staring silently at the crippled boy, caught his arm and dragged him into the shadow of the overhanging trees.

"We've got him," he whispered.

At the same instant another figure came out stealthily from the woods. He crept, crouching down, along over the boulders, and stopped, hesitating, weaving right and left. Wade leaped forward. Ben stumbled after him. The man standing by the channel, turning back and forth among the dry rocks on the shallow margin, heard the agent, turned, lifted his gun and fired. Wade crouched behind a boulder and fired from the side. The man stood dead-still a fraction of an instant by the stream, then he dashed across the single plank bridge. Ben followed Wade along. Then they both stopped suddenly and stared down; for half-way along the plank that carried Edrew Mincey's weight they saw Nathan Currier's murderer fling up his hands as the swaying board cracked and go plunging down into the dark water.

They ran down to the channel, over the boulders and around them, into the shallow water. The man was already swept down by the swift racing current, and Ben saw with a thrill of horror that he could not swim. Two hands raised for an instant above the water, the man was thrashing violently, spasmodically. Then he disappeared and the water swirled on, dark and silent and swift. Wade tore off his coat and dived. Ben, standing dizzily on the edge, saw him strike out with swift strokes. The thrashing body came to the surface again, struggling, feebler now, carried relentlessly along. Ben stumbled along the bank, falling over the stones, running where he could. He could see Wade, swimming strongly, gaining; then the hands ahead of him came out again in a last despairing useless clutch, and the dark body sank. Then Ben could no longer see Wade. He ran along, his head swimming, staggering down, falling, making himself go on.

It was two hundred yards below that he rounded the bend and saw Wade, standing in a shallow, struggling with a dark inert mass, dragging it towards the shore. Ben made his way slowly out to him and caught the limp drowned figure. The thick thatch of iron-gray hair was plastered wetly against the swarthy head, and Ed Loftus's eyes were forever closed.

166

34

They stood an instant looking silently down at the body lying on the shore. From far off in the woods Ben heard the eerie joyful melody of Edrew Mincey's guitar. He tried to understand.

"It was Loftus kicked in his guitar," he said suddenly.

Wade nodded. "That was a mistake," he said. "We might not have caught him otherwise. Not this way. You saw the half-wit shove his bridge over?"

Ben remembered the flattened log that he had thought of using that afternoon.

"All right," Wade said briskly. "We'll have to carry him to the Kilgores'. It's closest. I'm not leaving this side till I get that money."

The cabin was dark as they came up the road with their heavy sagging burden. Ben realized later that as far as he was concerned, the journey was a dim half-remembered struggle to keep his end up, and the last two hundred yards, after he heard the Kilgore dogs, was utterly blank. He had no memory of getting the dead man up the stairs, or of his knees buckling, pitching him forward in an unconscious heap on the floor; no memory of his struggling to get up later, or of Jess Kilgore's strong hands holding him while Mrs. Kilgore packed his burned leg with tea-leaf poultice and picked the shot from his shoulder. Through his feverish brain ran the nightmare scene of Old Doss and Julie, and he struggled to get up, calling to Julie to run. In the dim light of the coal oil lamp the patient eyes of the mountain woman and her husband met. The son that Old Doss had killed had struggled, Julie's mother's name on his lips. The tears ran down Mrs. Kilgore's broad kindly face. She soothed his head with her toil-roughened hands until he slept at last.

The gray light was seeping up in the east when Wade tiptoed out of the quiet room. In the kitchen Mrs. Kilgore moved solidly from the stove to the table, bringing him hot coffee and corn cakes dripping with butter. She sat down at the spotless scrubbed pine table, her hands folded in her lap, watching him eat.

"Hit's hard to think Ed done Nathan Currier thataway," she said slowly. "Most times butter wouldn't melt in his mouth. But he was a hard man. Them that knowed him knowed that."

Wade nodded, chewing thoughtfully. At last he pushed

back his chair and got up. It was almost light. He took his hat.

"I'll be back, Mrs. Kilgore," he said.

She watched him go down the steps and set off towards the narrow ridge that divided their land from the vast tract that centered in Currier Hollow. Then she turned back to the kitchen to prepare the water to wash the dead. It was a neighbor's task. Mrs. Kilgore's hands had performed it countless times. It was part of the folkways that the waters of the Tennessee would wash away for them, as they would wash away the barrier between Kilgores' place and Currier Hollow.

Wade stood an instant looking down at the shattered remains of his flashlight, and shook his head. The man was a good shot. He could easily have lost a leg then. Then he went out past the big tree and bent down to the road, following the broad prints of Loftus's boots in the damp road. It was just as Wade had thought. Loftus had come from the cabin, running lightly on his toes, and he had stopped just at the base of the sycamore. Wade went up to it and circled round the gray white-spotted trunk until he saw up above his head a hole that had been hollowed out. A squirrel could have done it, or a branch could have been broken off long ago and the trunk rotted away there.

He looked around for something to stand on—Edrew could have scaled up there like a fly, Loftus could reach up. He pulled a small moss-covered log across the road, leaned it up against the big trunk, and climbed up. He reached his hand inside. A flicker of satisfaction lighted his eyes as he drew out a sweat-blackened leather belt. Inside it, sewed to the lining, were twenty one-thousand-dollar bills, bright new and crisp. Wade put his hand back and reached down and around in the hole. He brought out a little sack of coins. In five minutes he stood at the bottom of the tree with the money belt, fourteen one-hundred-dollar gold certificates and the sack. He opened the sack and looked in; the coins were gold. Wade nodded with satisfaction, and unfolded the dirty crumpled paper, wadded at the bottom of the hole, that he had brought out last. He knew before he had unfolded it that it was the letter Speer had left for Ben.

It was written in ink, the letters blurred by the damp.

"Davidge," it said. "In case I don't show up, get in touch with Wm. R. Wade, United States Treasury, Alcohol Tax Unit. Tell him I've traced the white oak hand-made kegs with the burned 'C' to Currier Hollow. They're trucked out by a truck carrying the Tennessee license 64321 T/X. They carry

Ohio truck license A 6305 T/X, Pennsylvania T 301A4. Ed Loftus is the go-between, and if criminal conspiracy charges can be pressed he's the man to go after. This is strictly confidential.—T. S. Speer."

Wade nodded to himself, folded the letter carefully, and put it in his pocket. Speer was dead but he had done his job. Step by step the painstaking war against crime carried on by the Federal government would take its course.

He looked at the money belt in his hands and jingled the little bag. Then he set out up the road to the cabin in Currier Hollow. The sun was already showing over the ridge as he crossed the yard.

Julie Currier came out on the kitchen stoop and picked up the clean bright milk pail. She stood there looking down the Hollow at the charred remnants of the workshop, still smoking, and brushed her hand across her forehead. All that remained of the night before was the hot aching memory of Ben's voice as he crushed her to him, and his mouth pressed into her hair. She moved in a trance, knowing she must forget it all and go on in her old way of life, wanting to keep it real and glowing before she locked it in her heart, nothing but a memory.

She went down the steps and slowly across to the cowshed. After a while she came out carrying the steaming pail and went back to the cabin.

She made the fire, moving quietly so as not to wake Doss or the old man sitting beside him, his head resting on his arms on the foot of the bed. She did not look at the bed until she had put the coffee on to boil and poured the corn meal into the wood bowl to make the batter for their bread. A movement on the bed made her look up. Doss was lying there, his head moving slowly on the pillow, his dark hollow eyes following her. Their eyes met and held a long instant before she spoke.

"How're you feeling, Doss?"

Doss smiled.

The old man at the foot of the bed stirred and opened his eyes. He looked from Doss to Julie and got up with a dazed uncertain air. He seemed gradually to remember as he stood there, because he came up to the head of the bed and put his gnarled old hand on his son's head. Then he went out. They heard him going about the chores, chopping wood and feeding the stock.

"Julie."

Doss lifted his strong lean frame on his elbow. Julie looked up.

169

"You're purty, Julie."

Her eyes dropped again. Doss flushed, fumbling for words.

"Julie, I knowed hit warn't you shootin' at me, last night. Hit was Edrew. I reckon he got your granpappy's gun. Hit ain't there on the rack."

She looked up at the mantel. Only two guns were there, Doss's and his father's.

"Julie. I don't want you should marry me."

He spoke after a silence in which the smooth wooden spoon clapped softly on the side of the bowl to the tick-tock of her mother's clock on the mantel.

"I know you love this other feller. I ain't as low-down as you think, Julie."

He stumbled for the words, unaccustomed to speaking what he had in his heart.

"I reckon I love you, Julie honey. That's why I ain't wantin' t' see you droopin' this way. You kin marry that feller, Julie."

Sudden scalding tears filled her eyes and melted the tight sick pain in her throat. She turned away quickly and ran out onto the porch. Doss watched her, pale and troubled, and closed his eyes. He opened them again when she came in and took up her spoon. He watched her put the batter in the pan and put it in the oven. She got down the ham from the hook in the corner and cut off four dark red slices. When it was in the skillet and on the stove she went to the table.

"I'll marry you if you want me, Doss," she said at last. "I told him that last night. I told him I meant what I said in the letter. He won't come back any more, Doss. It's all like it never happened, now."

She wrapped up the ham and hung it up again.

"I reckon I don't want to talk about it any more, Doss."

Old Doss finished his breakfast and stopped with his chair pushed half-way back, listening.

"I reckon hit's Yancey Turner gittin' up, Pa," Doss said.

"He's left," Julie said. "He left as soon as it was light. He's mad at Ed Loftus for going off without him last night."

Doss turned his head and stared at her as she went out.

"It's Mr. Wade!" she said.

Wade came up on the porch. "Good morning," he said. "How's your cousin?"

Julie nodded. She clenched her hands in the folds of her full black skirt to keep from asking the question that pleaded in her eyes. The Federal agent stepped past her into the cabin.

"Howdy," he said. He put the money belt and the bag

down on the table and counted out the yellow-backed bills.

"There's the money. Loftus stole it. He killed Speer and Nathan Currier, and he's dead."

He turned to Doss.

"Last night he said something about this money belonging to Miss Currier. Is that right?"

"Hit's all Julie's, every penny of hit," Doss said.

Wade nodded.

"Then she can do pretty much as she pleases, without asking anybody's leave, can't she?"

Doss nodded.

"If that ain't enough, thar's more still," he said slowly. "Thar ain't nothin' we-uns got that Julie cain't have."

Wade scratched his head and gazed blankly from one to the other of them. He had planned to say something about young Davidge. But it didn't seem possible, some way. Just as it didn't seem necessary to say anything now about the barrels. The shop was burned and the go-between was dead. Contacts in the future would have to be made from the other end, and as Speer had done his job that was in the bag.

"Well, so long," he said. He started out.

Doss propped himself up on his elbow.

"Whar's Mister Davidge?" he drawled.

"Davidge? He's down at the Kilgores'. He got pretty badly messed up last night. He'll be going home in a day or so."

He waited a minute, but no one spoke.

"So long," he said.

It was late the next day that Wade returned from Knoxville and drove out to the Kilgores'. Mrs. Kilgore was sitting on the porch with her apron full of beans, her fingers shelling them methodically, her eyes fixed off over the sunny fields. She greeted him with a friendly smile on her gentle face.

"How's Mr. Davidge?"

"He's gittin' along, if he'd jes' stop frettin' himself. He's in thar."

Ben was sitting up in bed, his head propped against the pillows.

"Hello," he said.

"You don't look very chipper, young fellow."

"I'll be all right, as soon as this damn leg heals a bit. Thought you'd gone."

Wade nodded. "I'm on my way. Just thought I'd come in and see how you're making out. I brought you some tobacco."

Ben grinned.

"I needed it. Thanks."

"Also I thought you'd like to know that the letter Speer

171

left for you was in the sycamore tree, with Currier's money. The money's the girl's, by the way. Let me see. Doss's getting along all right, too."

Wade looked sideways at him for an instant and went on.

"It's interesting about Loftus. He's out in the world, with that place of his on the highway. I guess Pete's men probably contacted him direct, or some newspaper guy or TVA man pointed Loftus out to him. I'll find that out some day. Loftus knew about the Curriers, of course, so it was easy. I guess he got as much as they did out of the deal. They've been making kegs and selling 'em for five or six years now, Miss Elly tells me."

"Did she know about it?"

Wade nodded. "She knew that part of it, anyway."

Ben puffed deeply at his pipe.

"How'd you get on to Loftus?"

"Largely from what you told me, in the first place. The letter Speer gave you started it, of course. He was the likely fellow to have stolen it. Then I had a pretty good idea what was in it. The fact that the envelope was in his pocket when you found him showed it had been put there. If Speer had taken it back, he'd have destroyed it."

Wade's eyes flickered with amusement.

"Then it was easy. There's one thing about dealing with people like Loftus. They're damn shrewd, but they don't know all the tricks, and what they don't know they don't believe in. Like fingerprints, for instance. The envelope in Speer's pocket was lousy with Mr. Loftus's prints. So was the letter in the tree. So was Speer's car."

Ben looked at him, puzzled.

"How'd you get 'em tested?"

"Federal Bureau of Investigation. They have laboratories all over the country. There's one in Knoxville. They gave me the dope as fast as I needed it. The cartridges, for instance. They've got your prints on 'em, but they came from Loftus's gun. Not from any gun on the Currier place."

He lit a black cigar and examined the end of it meditatively. Suddenly he chuckled a little.

"It was Loftus ran you out of the workshop that night," he said. "One killing was enough, really. He didn't want to make it too hot down here. You remember he didn't speak to you? And you remember I told you you'd had another damn close shave? That was the day you went up to the ridge and met Doss there. Loftus knew if Doss killed you, they'd just pass the two murders off to you and that'd be the end of it. You were sort of on the spot there, for a while, if you'd only

172

known it. Well, if you sent a note to Doss's girl, and you were shot over there somewhere, of course everybody'd think Doss did it. So Loftus counted on that."

"But he wasn't this side of the river that day."

Wade nodded.

"He gave you two hours to yourself while he was in the sweet potato patch. Miss Elly was to help out by saying you'd gone to Knoxville—she thought it was a nice innocent romance. They didn't count on you playing square and leaving that note for me. That's how I caught on to Loftus's bridge across the river. I went down to the patch to see him. He wasn't there, but I could see him going down to the river. I came back and drove around. I'll tell you I broke all records for these parts that day. I didn't expect to see you alive when I got to you.

"Well, it happened that Edrew Mincey hated Loftus, for two reasons. He made life miserable for his mother about the mortgage, and he busted in the old guitar. And when you got him a new one you were made for life as far as Edrew was concerned. Now, the day I came, you said Nathan Currier was in Knoxville, and Doss was up by your car when you left, and yet you'd seen two men coming up from the shop. You didn't see a car or a truck. Sisky was on the ground too, and he didn't see a truck. Therefore either you didn't see a second man, or it was somebody pretty closely connected with the barrel business. That eliminated—without the fingerprints and Edrew and all the rest of it—everybody but Kilgore and Loftus, supposing Kilgore's feud was a smoke screen. And Loftus was the fellow who was on the outside and was the shrewdest. I was sure it was him from the beginning. Then he knew Currier had gone to Knoxville. He knew he carried his money with him. Currier wasn't in the barrel business at all—he was a farmer. He never sat in on any of their meetings or had anything to do with them. So, Loftus wanted that money—and the Curriers were pulling out. He arranged a meeting with Doss and Old Doss, and the coast was clear. He killed Nathan and the dog. He was afraid of dogs, Miss Elly tells me. Most mountaineers I ever ran across were."

Wade pushed back his chair and got up. "Well, that's that. I'm going back to Knoxville. Anything I can do for you, Davidge?"

Ben sat up.

"Yes. You can take me with you. And stop by Currier Hollow a minute."

"You're not fit to move."

"I'm O.K."

173

Wade looked at him curiously a moment.

"Haven't you got sense enough yet to stay away from there? That place is dynamite."

Ben put his feet on the floor and reached for his breeches —washed and mended by Mrs. Kilgore. Wade smiled a little and helped him dress. He stretched his arm gingerly.

"Lucky I didn't get it in the stomach instead."

"That's where you'll get it now," Wade said. "The Curriers don't miss."

Ben grinned. "They'll be all right."

Julie Currier sat on the vine-covered porch looking listlessly down the Hollow. She had known he wouldn't come again, and she told herself that it was right. But every time a pebble had been dislodged in the road she had looked out, hoping it would be Ben, almost seeing him when he wasn't there, so vividly he moved in the silent rooms of her heart. When the mail carrier's car went by she had seen him too, in spite of the fact that she knew he would never come again.

She sat there now trying not to think of him, to still the longing that brought tears to her eyes suddenly, even when she was not thinking of him. She could see across the Hollow Doss and Old Doss down there, looking about in the charred embers of the shop. It was all so changed. The shop was burned, her grandfather was gone, Kilgore gone, Ben was gone. Currier Hollow too, the cabin, the smoke house, the spring house—they would be gone in a few months. All her life gone, buried away from her.

She closed her eyes, a bright tear crowding under the long fringed lashes. She heard a car somewhere, and then steps; but this time she did not open her eyes. She had looked too many times to bear again the stabbing pain that came of not seeing him. She couldn't even be sure any longer that she had actually heard steps in the road, she had deceived herself so many times.

But someone was coming. She heard the chain fall back on the gate post, and bent over her workbasket to hide the blinding tears while she wiped them away. Then she looked up with a brave attempt at a smile; and the blood surged to her cheeks, burning them the way frost burned her fingers in the winter.

She closed her eyes again. "Ben," she whispered.

"Julie!"

She couldn't have heard it if he hadn't spoken. She opened her eyes, stretching out her arms. He was on his knees on the steps, his arms around her, his face buried in her lap.

"Julie, Julie!" he whispered.

174

She bent her head down and rested her lips on his head.

"I wanted you to come . . . so much," she breathed.

"You'll go with me, Julie . . . now?"

She nodded slowly.

"I'll go, Ben . . . now."

Marie Davidge slipped her mink cape off her elegant brown satin shoulders and smiled at the women seated around the luncheon table at the Acorn Club.

"I thought you'd all love it," she said sweetly.

"But, darling!" cried the henna-haired faultlessly gowned woman on her left, "how *awful* for you!"

The lean horse-faced woman at the end of the table spoke.

"I think it's simply ghastly, the way young people treat their parents these days. In my time no child would have dreamed of running off and getting married without his parents' consent. My dear, I should think you'd be simply livid!"

Marie Davidge smiled.

"On the contrary, we're simply charmed!"

She glanced from one to the other of the concerned worldly faces around her, and put down her cocktail.

"You've no notion how charmed we are. Imagine having a daughter-in-law who's never seen a moving picture, or a train, or heard a radio. My dear, we're enchanted."

She glanced around again and raised her perfectly arched, delicately penciled brows.

"My cousin in Knoxville wires that she's perfectly beautiful, and quite well off too. No, we're both amused and pleased. You know, we've had a notion that Ben was rather odd. It turns out he was just awfully particular—and we adore it!"

Marie Davidge smiled again.

"Isn't it lovely? Just imagine anyone never having been to a movie. And my cousin says she wears clothes marvelously."